A Conflict of Time

June Summers

Cover Design by Lee Helton

Full Moon Publishing, LLC
Glade Spring, VA
Fullmoonpublishingllc.com

ISBN: 1946232122
ISBN-13: 978-1946232120

DEDICATION

Dedicated to Wendy, my shining star in heaven.

CONTENTS

ACKNOWLEDGMENTS

To BJ, my niece, friend, and assistant, whose tireless help was greatly appreciated. To Joyce, my avid reader, correcting my many mistakes.

CHAPTER ONE
Unchartered Territory

"Sometimes you're not worth shit!" Ma bellowed from the kitchen doorway holding a pot of water in her hands. It was a Saturday, and she had just gotten home from working at Carneys Superstore and was fixing hot dogs and macaroni and cheese for our dinner. I was still in my boxers and tee shirt comfortably slouched on the couch in the living room watching a *Fast and Furious* rerun on TV. I had been in that very spot all day, doing nothing but loafing, eating junk food, and waiting for Ma to cook dinner.

"I asked you last night to have dinner started by the time I got home. I work six days a week to keep this roof over our heads, and you can't get off your ass and boil some water. Is that too much to ask? Talbott, we're not going to make it if you don't start helping out around here. I can't do it by myself."

She was right. I was a loser. Ever since Dad died a year after my graduation, I had simply given up. He was killed in a drive-by shooting right outside our Pine Hills house. One evening, he

1

walked out the door to buy a six pack of beer when this black Honda pulled up. Ma and I were in the living room watching TV with only the screen door closed when we heard somebody yell really loud, "Hey, Honkey!" Then we heard three, quick gunshots. We ran outside as fast as we could. The upper part of Dad's body was slumped over the seat of his pickup truck with the driver side door wide open. His legs dangled on the driveway, and the blood from the bullet holes in his back was splattered all over the truck door and the cement drive. Ma was hysterical. I wasn't much better. I got the license plate number as the black Honda pulled away. However, it turned out the car was stolen, so the police never caught the bastards who shot him. Ma and I were questioned endlessly, but we didn't know anybody who'd target Dad. Nobody could've hated him enough to kill him. The police determined it was merely a random act of violence. A random act of violence? Sure, it wasn't their Dad who was murdered.

And that was that. Our entire lives changed forever in a split second with a so-called "random act". Ma took it really hard. I guess I did too. For weeks Ma just sat on the couch, staring out the window, barely eating, barely drinking. Then when she started to function again, she sold the house, and we moved into a two bedroom apartment in Nawinah. We needed to get out of Pine Hills. Every time either one of us walked out the door and saw the pickup in the driveway, the memory of that gruesome scene of Dad's body draped over the front seat was simply too much to endure. She sold the house and the truck.

Ma is a department manager at Carneys, but in no way does she make the big bucks. It's just Carneys, an ordinary superstore that sells anything you want—cheap. I know she does all she can for the two of us. She works really hard, so I don't know why I don't help her out more. I don't have any incentive to do much of anything. I know; I'm a jerk. I don't deny it.

It didn't start out that way. I graduated from Evans High School a couple of years ago. I even went to Valencia College for a year, majoring in history. I'm a big history buff. I love to learn about the past. I like to study and analyze facts and timelines and then try to interpret their outcome. I think history actually gives us a better understanding of current culture and trends. And I'm good at remembering things too, like dates and numbers. I don't exactly have a photographic mind, but most of the time, once I learn something, I don't forget it.

After Dad was murdered, everything changed. I dropped out of college, having no desire at that time to get a stupid degree. Plus the expense of a college education was getting too much for Ma. I was supposed to help her with the bills, but I wasn't doing so well in that department.

Once I got my shit together, I planned to go back to school. Ma said Dad had some insurance to help with the college, but she kept asking me what I thought I could do with learning about time so long ago. "It's over and done with," she'd say. She thought I should go to a technical school to be an electrician or plumber, but I told her I couldn't work in those professions. I could barely change a lightbulb or fix a leaky faucet. Ma didn't believe me, but I did plan to go back. Someday.

After dropping out of college, I went from job to job. I worked at a fast food restaurant for a while, but I got fired for eating on my shift. After the restaurant, I worked nights at a furniture warehouse as a janitor, but I fell asleep on one of the king size beds and got fired from there too. Then I worked at a quick auto oil changing business, but I didn't know anything about cars. So I got fired. Dad had been a mechanic at a car dealership nearby. Of course, I never bothered to listen when he tried to teach me the fundamentals of car repair and maintenance. I just wasn't interested. Then Ma got me a job stocking shelves at Carneys, but same scenario, I got fired from there too. They said I was too slow.

I was a pretty big guy. I weighed about three hundred fifteen, and I'm over six feet tall. I knew I weighed too much for a twenty-two year old. I'd been a star fullback on Evans High varsity football team, a pretty popular dude back then. But that was high school, not real life. My real name is Talbott. Who names a kid Talbott? My mom. I guess it was my great grandfather's name on Ma's side. Ma gets mad when I tell her it's a shitty name. So everybody calls me Tank—except Ma. Thank God!

I finally got a job at Fantasy Empire, one of the local theme parks, on the nightshift custodial staff. I worked late hours cleaning up after the park closed. I was beginning to get used to the odd hours and adapting to the shitty work. If I got fired from that job, Ma would kill me. I really did have to start helping her out at home and stop being an asshole.

So after I ate the hot dogs and macaroni and cheese that Ma cooked for dinner, I took a shower and put on my maintenance uniform. I apologized to Ma while she was loading the dishwasher. "I'm sorry, Ma. I'm really going to try to do better from now on."

She wasn't angry at me anymore; she never stays mad for long. I gave her a kiss on the cheek. "I love you, you know."

She rolled her eyes and shook her head. "Love ya too, Talbott, but I'll believe it when I see your ass stay at a job for more than a couple of months."

In the apartment complex parking lot, I got in my used pickup truck, Stacey, that Ma and Dad had given me for graduation. I called her Stacey after this girl I had a crush on in the seventh grade, a gorgeous, popular cheerleader who never even knew I existed. I was a fat nobody invisible to the female gender even in high school when I was a football player. Who'd want to be seen with a fat slob like me?

My job at Fantasy Empire was to go throughout the grounds and empty all the trash cans into a big dumpster. I pushed it around, preparing for the next day's opening. Sometimes the cans were really gross and messy with food leftovers, smelly napkins, and obnoxious unidentifiable garbage in them. I then sprayed the trash barrels and wiped them dry, replacing the plastic bags with clean ones. When my dumpster was full, I pushed it through the wide cast member doors to a truck dumpster on the back lot of the park. I attached my dumpster to the truck dumpster, pulling the lever so it mechanically emptied into the truck. When I completed my shift for the night, I squirted out my push dumpster and parked it next to the others on the back lot. Before driving home after my shift, I took a shower, changed into my jeans and tee shirt, and dropped my uniform off at the cast laundry, picking up a clean one for the next day's shift.

On the night that changed my life forever, I drove the back roads home after my shift ended about one in the morning. The steady, light rain unexpectedly started to pour down like I was driving through a car wash. I had the windshield wipers on full blast, but I still had difficulty seeing where I was driving on the slick pavement. The road curved and wound through the deserted, unpopulated area between Nawinah and Fantasy Empire. Slacker that I was, I had not gotten around to replacing Stacey's bald tires. As I tried to steer her around this giant curve called Demon's Bend, I lost control. She swerved and skidded off the road at forty miles an hour through small brush and tall weeds. Since my seatbelt had been broken for several months, I hadn't bothered fastening it when I left work. My body jerked and joggled with every movement of the truck as it vaulted and bumped until it ended up crashing directly into a huge oak tree. My head was hurdled into the front windshield with such force I blacked out.

I'm not sure how much time passed before I finally regained consciousness. I was dazed and confused, and every bone in my body ached like hell. My head felt like it was about to explode off my neck. As I reached up to my forehead, I felt a deep, open gash with blood dripping into my eye and down my cheek, blurring my vision as I tried to focus. My arms were bloody and scratched from the oak tree branches which had torpedoed through Stacey's side window and shattered the glass. I tried to move, but my body refused to obey my brain. I sat for several minutes resting my head on the broken headrest while I regained my senses and strength enough to attempt exiting the truck. With piercing pain throughout my body, I finally was able to open the driver side door and extract myself from the truck, grabbing tightly to the door handle before slipping to the ground.

Still upright, but disoriented and holding onto Stacey's door for support, I looked around the area to see where I had ended up and what kind of a situation I had gotten myself into. Stacey was a mess. Her front end was completely squashed and embedded into the oak tree, which also had a huge chunk taken out of its trunk. Both smoke and steam spewed from under Stacey's broken hood and plumed into the pouring night air. She would probably have to be totaled. Great! I only had liability insurance on her, and I definitely couldn't afford to get her fixed. Nor did I have any money to buy another decent and reliable vehicle. Even if I did, the insurance company would probably raise my rates after this accident. Ma would have a fit. They were already high because of my age.

I retrieved my cellphone from my pocket to call my mom. Just my luck! It was smashed and refused to turn on. I threw it onto Stacey's front seat.

Okay. What could I do? I was several yards from the road, and at such a late hour, I doubted if any vehicles would be traveling on it anyhow. Hell, I used this road because of the light traffic and the absence of stop lights and tourists. Definitely, I would've been better off taking the main roads that night. Look at the jam I was in because of my stupid decision.

So what were my options? The rain had somewhat slowed down to a heavy drizzle. Testing my equilibrium, I limped toward the road, hoping at least one car would be driving by so early in the morning. As I was dragging my body onward with pain shooting through my head, my back, and my arm, I also felt a sharp throbbing in my leg. Looking down, I noticed my pants were ripped, and blood was oozing from an open gash on my thigh. I was a complete mess. I needed to get help as soon as possible.

As I suspected, when I got to the road, no cars were in sight in either direction. Standing near the pavement, I waited for about fifteen or twenty minutes, hoping someone would come along. The rain started to come down heavier again, saturating through my clothes. I felt both light headed and nauseous. I needed to find someplace to call my mom. Looking into the distance toward Nawinah, I saw a lit sign on a building up ahead about two hundred yards. I decided to attempt walking to the building. I hoped as late as it was someone would still be there. Maybe somebody could loan me their cellphone to call Ma. Maybe I could use their bathroom to clean up a little.

As I trudged through the puddles and slippery, uneven grass

along the roadway, getting closer to the building, I saw it was a small restaurant or bar. Strange, I hadn't remembered seeing it on this road on my other trips back and forth to work. Going to work, I was always busy listening to my iTunes, singing along in my magnificent baritone voice. Then coming home at one or two o'clock in the morning, I never did any sightseeing. I was simply anxious to get home and into bed.

As I got closer to the building, the shabby sign above the door read "Corky's Bar & Grill." Four or five cars were in the rutted, black top parking lot. I figured the place must still be open. I grabbed the doorknob and opened the door.

The lighting inside was dim, and I had to adjust my eyes after the bright sign above the doorway. A few patrons were sitting at a stained, wooden bar drinking beer. Other guys sat at small, round tables scattered about the room, quietly talking to one another. Behind the bar, a gray haired, bearded man probably about Ma's age was washing glasses in a small sink. He had on a black tee shirt with a white apron around his waist. A pretty girl with long, black hair was serving the patrons at the bar. She was dressed in jeans and a black tee shirt with "Corky's" inscribed across her ample chest. I walked up to the girl to ask if I could use the restroom. When she saw me and the shape I was in, she put her hands quickly over her mouth. "Oh, my God! What happened to you?"

I briefly told her my truck had skidded off the road and hit a tree. "Can I use your restroom and your phone?"

"Sure, sure. The phone is in the hallway next to the restrooms. God! You look awful! Are you sure you're okay? Do you want me to call an ambulance or something?"

"No, no. I'll be fine. I just need to clean up a bit and call my mom to pick me up."

"Uh… okay…," she hesitantly said as she stared at me limping toward the hall to the restroom.

I went down the short hallway where she had pointed. As I was entering the restroom, I noticed a black pay phone attached to the wall nearby. A thick telephone book was on a chain and resting in a small shelf under the phone. I hadn't seen one of those phones since I was a kid.

In the restroom, I moistened some paper towels with cold water and tried to wash off as much of the blood and debris from my face, arms, and legs as possible. I tried removing the tiny slivers of glass stuck in my arm. The water stung like hell as I dabbed at the wounds. Each time I touched the huge gash on my forehead, I flinched and got dizzy. Grabbing onto the sink for support, I looked at my reflection in the mirror. "Shit, I probably need stitches in this cut."

I finished up as best I could and threw the bloody towels in the wastebasket. While I was drying my hands, I thought I heard some commotion out in the bar area. It had been quiet when I had first entered the place. No one had been talking loudly, just drinking and hanging out. I figured some rowdy patrons must've arrived to liven up the joint. After all, if you're out drinking, you might as well party.

I threw the last paper towel into the trash atop the blood soaked ones and turned off the light. My hand was on the bathroom doorknob ready to open the door when I heard a loud gunshot. I almost shit my pants! What was going on? I opened the door a slight crack. Looking out I saw two men dressed in dark clothing and holding semi-automatic rifles. They were yelling at the guy and girl behind the bar. With a heavy accent, the big guy said something like, "You knew this was coming. What do you expect when you neglect to take care of your obligations?"

With his voice trembling, the guy behind the bar said, "No, no, please. Don't shoot. Let me talk to him. Tell him I want to talk. It's just a misunderstanding. That's all."

But the two guys with the guns immediately opened fire. No more talking, just shooting. I think they shot everyone in the room. I heard blast after blast. I heard shrieks and agonizing screams. Then there was complete silence. My entire body was shaking. What had I gotten myself into? What should I do? If I went out to the bar, they'd shoot me too. I kept hoping and praying they wouldn't come back and look in the restroom. Without making a sound, I closed the door all the way and stood flat against the wall directly behind it. I was breathing so hard I thought for sure they could hear me out in the bar area.

Suddenly, I heard footsteps outside the door. I held my breath. The footsteps faded slightly. I let out my breath. Then they got louder again. I stopped breathing. I heard the jiggle of the doorknob. Oh God! They're coming in! The door swung open and the light switch was turned on. Without breathing I tried to fade into the wall.

After a few seconds, the door closed, but the light stayed on. As I heard the footsteps diminish, I began to breathe again.

I didn't know what to do. I didn't want that light on, but if the guy came back and saw it turned off, he'd know somebody was in there. So I just stood melting into the wall behind the door. My body was stiff and sore from the truck accident and also from holding my muscles tensed for so long in the same position. My frazzled nerves didn't help either.

I don't know how much time passed as I stayed glued to the wall. Maybe a half hour. Maybe longer. I slowly forced my aching, stiff body away from the wall and turned the doorknob. Opening the door just a slight crack, I looked into the bar area.

Dead silence. No movement. I smelled gun powder and blood—and death. Inch by inch, I opened the door enough to get myself through the opening. I tiptoed as silently and slowly as possible out of the restroom. I first saw the bodies of the two men who had been seated at the table nearest the hallway. The upper parts of their bloody bodies were lying across the table, arms hanging limply at their sides. One man's head had landed directly on top of the other man's head in a weird, affectionate position.

Before entering the barroom area, I peeked around the corner to make sure the gunmen were gone. When I saw no moving figures, I walked more hastily into the room. It was a massacre!

Everyone in the room was dead, their bodies landing in unnatural positions on the floor and on the tables. Glasses and beer bottles lay broken or completely spilled of their contents as the liquid mixed with the blood streaming from the open wounds on the victims. What a horrific scene! I didn't know what to do. I was like a chicken running back and forth as I kept repeating, "Oh no! Oh, my God! Oh no!"

As I stood transfixed and staring at the massacre before me, I thought I heard a soft moan coming from behind the bar. Now alert, I spun my ear in that direction and listened carefully. Yes! I did hear something. I rushed over to the bar door and lifted it up. The pretty barmaid lay on the floor in a pool of blood, clutching her chest and moaning so softly I could barely hear her. "Please help me."

I hurried to her side, kneeling and clutching her hand. "Okay! I'm going to call an ambulance. Hang on. Where's your phone?"

I expected her to tell me where her cellphone was located, but instead, she muttered, "On the wall…. On the wall…. Hurry…."

Confused, I ran to the pay phone I had seen earlier near the bathroom. I picked up the receiver. Surprisingly, there was a dial tone. How much did these things cost? I never used one before. I reached in my pocket, hoping to find some change. Luckily, I had several dimes and nickels which hadn't spilled out onto Stacey's front seat when we crashed. I started dumping the coins in the slot, one right after another, and dialed 911.

"911, what is your emergency?"

"There's been a shooting at, uh," *What was the name of this place? Oh yeah, Corky's.* "Uh, Corky's Bar. Several people are dead."

"What is the address, sir?"

"Uh, I don't know. It's on Nawinah Cortland Road somewhere north of Fantasy Empire and south of Nawinah. Hurry, please. One woman is still alive. I don't know about anybody else, but I think everybody else is dead."

"Sir, help is on the way. Stay on the line with me. Can you tell me what happened?"

I briefly told her about the two guys who came in and shot up the place.

"Are the gunmen still on the premises?"

"Hell, I sure hope not! I think they left about a half hour ago. That's when I came out of the restroom and found everybody dead except the woman behind the bar. I was afraid to come out sooner. I didn't want to get shot too."

"Is the woman still breathing?"

"Yes, but she's bleeding badly from her chest. I think she might be shot somewhere else too because she's covered in blood. What should I do?"

"The paramedics will be there shortly. Don't move her. They'll know what to do. Try to keep her comfortable. Can you stop the bleeding?"

"Well, I can't do that and stay on the phone too. It's a pay phone, and it's not near the woman."

"As long as she is still breathing, it's best if you don't move her. Try to apply pressure to her wounds. The paramedics will help her when they arrive. Can you see from your location how many have been shot?"

"I can't see all the tables, but when I came into the building, uh, let me think, two people were behind the bar, a man and the young woman who's still alive. I think maybe two or three customers were sitting at the bar. Then, uh, three tables maybe had a couple of guys each sitting at them. So maybe nine or ten guys were shot dead. The girl who's behind the bar is in bad shape."

"Do you know who shot them?"

"I saw them, but, no, I don't know who they were."

"Be sure to describe to the police what you saw and what you heard."

"Okay. I'm going over to help the woman now. Are they almost here? That woman is crying and moaning. Can't they hurry?"

I left the phone dangling from its cord and ran over to the woman. I grabbed a couple of towels from under the sink and applied pressure to the wound in her chest. With my other hand, I applied pressure to the wound on her side.

Then I heard the sirens. Thank God!

The rush of activity began as the first set of paramedics burst through the doorway. I stood up from behind the bar. "Over here! Hurry!"

They rushed to her, carrying a ton of equipment. Two other

paramedics came through the door with a stretcher. The first two paramedics worked on the woman, attaching an IV to her, injecting her with something, checking and covering her wounds, and putting an oxygen mask on her. Within minutes from when they had entered the bar, they lifted her onto the stretcher and wheeled her out to the waiting ambulance.

I had moved back to the hallway and picked up the dangling phone. "Ma'am are you still there?"

"Yes, sir. It sounds like the paramedics have arrived. You can hang up now."

At the same time, more paramedics, firemen, and several policemen burst through the door. The room was filled with commotion and bustling activity. I stood leaning against the wall at the edge of the hallway, mesmerized while watching the macabre scene of these professionals going about what was routine to them. They checked each of the bodies to confirm they needed no medical treatment. A photographer took numerous pictures of each victim with a flash camera. With white chalk, the police traced around every body. Finally, stretchers were brought into the bar, and each corpse was lifted onto a stretcher, covered with black plastic, securely fastened, and pushed outside to be loaded into other ambulances. The crew worked thoroughly, but calmly in a professional manner while I looked on amazed, but still trembling.

I thought whoever was in charge had forgotten I was standing there, watching and staring at all the activity. Eventually, while the bodies were being removed, a burly police detective with wild, gray hair needing trimmed and dressed in a scruffy, blue suit approached me. "Are you the man who called 911?"

"Yes sir."

"What is your name and address?" He took out a pen and small spiral tablet.

"It's Tank Telek. I live in Nawinah at 15002 Marsten Boulevard, Apartment 205.

"Did you see what happened here?"

"Yes, sir. Well, I saw some of it." I explained about how I was about to come out of the bathroom when I heard the gun shots.

"What were you doing at the bar, Mr. Telek? Had you been drinking?"

"No sir. I just had an accident before I came into Corky's. My truck hit a tree. That's why I'm all bloody and scratched. Well, actually some of the blood is from the woman too. When I applied pressure to her gunshot wounds, I got her blood on me also. But originally, I came in here to wash up from my accident and use somebody's phone to call my mother to pick me up."

He looked at me strangely. "Hmm, I see."

Then he started questioning me again. "Where was this accident of yours? Were there any other people or vehicles involved?"

"No, sir. Just me. It was raining pretty hard, and my truck skidded off the road and hit an oak tree several yards south toward Fantasy Empire."

He continued jotting down notes on what I said as I answered his questions. Then he asked, "So you were in the bathroom when the shootings occurred?"

"Yes, sir. That's correct."

"When did you come out of the bathroom, Mr. Telek?"

"Well, I waited to make sure the gunmen were gone. I didn't want to get shot too. I stayed behind the door about a half hour or so. I kept listening to hear if there was any more noise. So, yeah, it was about a half hour after I heard the shots."

He wrote again in his note pad. "Did you recognize the shooters?"

"No, I never saw them before."

"Could you describe them?"

I tried visualizing the killers in my mind. "They were dressed in dark clothes. One guy was fairly tall and muscular. The other was shorter and heavier, not fat, but stockier. Both had hair stubble on their faces."

"If you saw them again, could you identify them?"

"I don't know. I think so. Maybe."

"Did you hear them say anything?"

"When I opened the bathroom door to see what was going on, I heard the tall guy say something like 'that's what you get when you don't do what your told.' Something like that."

The detective stared at me a few seconds before again writing in his notepad. "Do you remember his exact words?"

"No. I was really nervous when I saw them holding the guns. I guess I should've paid more attention."

"Who was he talking to?"

"I think he was talking to the two people behind the bar. He was facing them."

"Did they say anything to the shooter?"

"Yeah, the guy behind the bar asked him not to shoot and said he wanted to talk to somebody."

"Did he say who he wanted to talk to?"

"Uh, no, but I got the impression the gunman knew who he was talking about. Then both the gunmen just shot him dead without another word, and the girl too. That's when I ducked back in the bathroom and stayed as quiet as I could behind the door. I heard more gun shots, but I didn't see who they were shooting."

"Did either of them notice you were in the bathroom?"

"I don't think so. One of them opened the bathroom door and turned on the light, but I was hiding behind the door. He didn't come all the way inside, just looked from the doorway. I don't think he saw me, or I'm sure he would've killed me too."

"Do you know what kind of guns they were using?"

"They both had semi-automatic rifles."

"Is there anything else you can tell me?"

"No. That's all I know." I hesitated. "Oh wait! The tall guy had a Russian accent."

"Russian accent? How do you know it was Russian?"

"My dad's family is Russian. I speak it also. When my grandfather spoke in English, his accent was like that man's accent."

The detective kept staring at me. I was getting a little uncomfortable. He was giving me the impression that he didn't completely believe me. "Like I said, I've never been in this place before. I just wanted to use somebody's phone to call my mom so she could pick me up. That's all."

The officer stood there for a couple of minutes, not talking. I asked him, "Do you think I can call my mom now?"

"I'll tell you what, Mr. Telek. How about if you come down to the police station and give your statement to the captain?"

"Well, what about my mom? She'll be wondering where I am?"

"You can call her from the station."

"Uh, okay. What about my truck? I didn't lock it when I left. I got stuff in it."

"I'll have an officer check it out and have it towed. He'll bring your belongings to you at the station. We'll let you know what towing company picks it up."

"Uh, okay." I was a bit confused. I couldn't figure out what was going on. Why did they need me at the police station? I told them all I knew. I was tired and weak. My head was throbbing from the gash on my forehead. I really wanted to get home and go to bed.

CHAPTER TWO
Guilty Until Proven Innocent

I stood around for about another half hour. Then they took me to the police station in the back seat of a cruiser. The detective who questioned me sat in the front passenger seat while a younger detective drove. The back seat was low, hard and cold, no padding or upholstery at all, just the metal seat. I might as well have been sitting on the floor. A heavy wire mesh separated me from the detectives. I felt like a criminal as I stiffly sat with my bones aching and my head pounding. Sharp pains bombarded every part of me when they drove over each bump in the road. It may have been my imagination, but it sure as hell seemed like they were purposely driving over the roughest pavement they could find. The stagnant air inside the vehicle smelled like stale cigarettes and body odor. This intrusion to my olfactory glands didn't help me combat my nausea at all.

At the police station, the two detectives led me to a small room furnished with a metal table and a few metal chairs. The young detective gently pushed me into the room. "Take a seat.

We'll be back in a couple of minutes."

After they left, I observed my surroundings. A large mirror was on the wall in front of me, probably one of those two-way mirrors you see in the movies and TV detective shows. Probably a bunch of guys were looking at me through the mirror at that very moment. I had told them everything I could remember. I didn't know what else I could say.

I tried to get comfortable in the chair, but the seat was hard and too small for my wide ass. Maybe I was just too tired and sore for any kind of seat. I waited, and I waited. I don't know how much time passed. I started to doze, my head nodding every time I caught my eyes closing. It seemed like hours went by. I had to piss, and I ached all over. Where the hell were these guys?

Finally, just when I got out of my seat to open the door, it flew open and two different detectives entered the room, pulling up the metal chairs across from me and scraping the legs against the cement floor. They straddled the chairs and glared at me. The older one asked, "Okay, buddy, sit back down. Tell us your name and address."

How many times did they have to ask me the same questions over and over again? I had answered these at Corky's Bar. "Tank Telek, and I live at 15002 Marsten Boulevard, Apartment 205 in Nawinah."

"Tank? Is that your real name, buddy?"

"No, it's Talbott. Everybody calls me Tank, though."

"Do you live alone?"

"No, I live with my mother."

"What is your mother's name?"

"Cheryl Telek."

"Okay, Talbott, can you repeat to me what you remember about what happened at Corky's?"

"The name is Tank, sir." Here I go again. I told him basically the same thing I had told the detective back at Corky's. Both detectives continued to glare at me the entire time as I repeated the incident. They didn't interrupt me or ask any questions. When I completed my statement, I asked, "Can I use the restroom? I have to piss?"

They ignored me, and the younger guy asked, "Is there anything else you remember about the gunmen? Were they light or dark complected? What color hair did they have? Anything else?"

"Uh, they both had sort of dark faces, but they weren't Black or Hispanic. Like I told you, I think they were Russian. They had dark caps over their heads, so I couldn't see what color hair they had. Can I go to the bathroom now? I need to call my mom. The detective at Corky's told me I could call her when I got here."

The older guy asked, "You said you looked at them very briefly from the bathroom door. You were able to get that good of a description?"

"Well, yeah. The bathroom wasn't far from where they were standing, just a short, narrow hallway. Please can I call my mom and go to the bathroom?"

"Did you know the Antonellis very well?" This was the

younger guy.

"Who are the Antonellis?" I didn't know anyone by that name.

This time the older detective raised his voice when he addressed me. "Don't pull that shit on me. You know very well who they are."

I think I jumped when he yelled. I wasn't sleepy anymore. Why were they shouting at me? What was going on? What are they thinking?

I timidly responded. "I don't know what you're talking about. I don't know any Antonellis."

"Listen, Talbott," countered the young guy. "Telling the truth now will make it a lot easier for you in the long run. Why don't you come clean with us?"

"What are you talking about? I told you everything I know. Hell! I just went in there to use somebody's phone. What do you think?"

I'm no dummy. I think that whack on the head slowed my mental capacity somewhat. Now, I don't have this big, important job or anything, but Dad always told me I was wise beyond my years. He said if I'd put my mind to things, I could accomplish anything I wanted. I was beginning to put two and two together despite the head injury. These guys were holding me in this room. They wouldn't let me go to the bathroom. They wouldn't let me call my mother. They're asking things I know nothing about in a very aggressive manner. They actually thought I had something to do with those murders!

The older one spoke, "Okay, Talbott. We know you're lying. Do you know why we know this?"

He didn't wait for me to answer, but I quickly replied, "It's Tank, sir."

"We know this because no pickup truck was found wrecked on the side of the road near Corky's. There wasn't even any evidence of any type of accident."

Okay. What was he talking about? Nobody would have stolen the truck. It wasn't drivable. Did they even look for it? "You must be mistaken. You probably didn't look in the right place. It's several yards from the road on the opposite side from Corky's. You need to look further into the tall weeds. It's down a little embankment. Maybe that's why you didn't see it. Hell, how do you think I got all these cuts and bruises, man?"

"We're not mistaken about the pickup, and we really would like to know how you got banged up. Did Corky get to you before you got to him?"

"This is crazy!" I was getting agitated. Why were they doing this to me?

Then the younger detective chimed in. "And, Mr. Talbott Telek, you told us you live at 15002 Marsten Boulevard with your mother."

"Yeah, I do. Why?"

"Well, Talbott, there's no such address as 15002 Marsten Boulevard in Nawinah."

This was ludicrous. What were they trying to do? "You're

wrong! It's an apartment building. It has about twenty units. My mom and I live on the second floor."

"I said, in case you didn't hear me, Talbott, there's no such building as 15002 Marsten Boulevard. It's a big lot filled with pine trees. Now, come clean with us before it's too late."

Oh, my God! I didn't know what to say. What was going on? No wrecked pickup truck? No apartment building? This was a nightmare! Maybe it really was. Maybe I'll wake up. Maybe I hit my head harder than I thought.

No. No nightmare. My full bladder made me rudely aware of that. It was getting to the point I couldn't think straight. The detectives were confusing me, and I had to piss so badly.

"Please. Let me go to the bathroom, and I'll tell you what you want to know."

The two detectives looked at one another. Then the older one said, "Okay. Mike, take him to the can. But don't let him out of your sight."

At last! The younger detective led me out of the room, down the hall to the restroom. I must've pissed for five minutes. He stood right by my side the whole time until every drop was drained out of my dick. I hope he enjoyed the show. Then he led me back to the same room.

Another detective had joined the older guy. This one was dressed neatly in a police uniform. He looked like he might be the man in charge. As I sat down in the same seat, this new detective spoke, "Mr. Talbott Telek, I'm Captain Ernie Forsythe. My detectives tell me you have something to say."

"It's Tank," I said.

"What?" the captain asked.

"My name is Tank. I told these guys nobody calls me Talbott."

"Well, then, Tank, what are you going to tell us about your part in the incident at Corky's?"

"Sir, I already told them all I know. For some reason, they think I had something to do with killing all those people, but I didn't. I just wanted to use the restroom to wash off the blood from the accident I had in my truck and call my mom to pick me up." I was getting tired of repeating the same thing over and over again.

The captain leaned back in his chair. "Now, Talbott, you know we didn't find any damaged truck along Nawinah Cortland Road; nor did we find any damage to any large tree near the road; and lastly, the address you gave us on Marsten Boulevard doesn't even exist. Can you see why my detectives might come to the conclusion you are lying to them?"

I bent my head down, put my hands over my face, and let out a couple of deep sighs. I looked pleadingly at the captain. "Sir, I don't know what's going on here, but I've been telling the truth. I don't know anything about what went on at Corky's except what I've already told you. That's everything I know."

Before the captain spoke again, his lips were tightly closed and his eyes diminished to narrow slits. "Talbott, ten people were murdered in that bar, and one young woman was seriously injured. She may not survive. You waited forty-five minutes before calling

911, and you were still there when the police arrived, all cut up and bleeding. Do you expect me to believe you had nothing to do with what happened?"

I was breathing very heavily, shaking my head back and forth. This was so unreal. I didn't know what to say.

Then in a harsh voice, the captain addressed the other two detectives as he arose from his chair, scraping it against the cement floor as it almost tipped over. "Read him his rights and book him!"

CHAPTER THREE
Unjust Incarceration

I was roughly grabbed by both of the detectives and marched to a room at the rear of the police station. They took front and side view photos of me holding a sign with a long number on it. Ironically, in those mug shots, I did look like a criminal with all the scratches and bruises on my face and my hair wild and full of blood. Then they took my fingerprints, giving me a paper towel to wipe off the ink residue from my fingers, which still stained them. They told me to empty my pockets into a basket. The problem was, all that was there was a soiled handkerchief. I must've left the keys to Stacey in the ignition. I had been so confused after hitting my head I completely forgot to grab them. My wallet wasn't in my pocket either. While at work, I had this habit of taking out my Fantasy Empire ID, then leaving the wallet locked in Stacey's glove compartment. I had no use for it while I was working. I wouldn't take it out until I got home. I don't know what happened to my ID. It must've fallen from my pocket onto Stacey's front seat or in the weeds when I got out of the truck.

They let me keep the dirty handkerchief. Such kindness!

They put me in a communal jail cell with a bunch of derelicts, who all stared and taunted me when I entered the cell. One greasy guy with tattoos over his entire body yelled, "Hey, fat boy, you want to suck my juicy dick?" Another guy in the corner with a face filled with scars started chanting, *"Humpty Dumpty sat on a wall; Humpty Dumpty had a great fall."* Then he burst out laughing as he slithered closer to me.

"Get away from me, asshole!" I yelled at him as I tried to distance myself from him.

About eight guys started to surround me, poking at me and getting much too personal. I was scared shitless! "Leave me alone! Get away from me, you assholes!" I flailed my arms around my body to chase them away.

Finally, the guard yelled, "Alright, you creeps. Leave the kid alone, or I'm coming in there with my stick."

One guy advanced to the front of the cell and tightly grabbed the bars. "Oh, his stick! Is it a *big* stick?"

They did slowly disburse after the officer yelled at them.

I breathed a sigh of relief and looked around me. There were about a dozen or so guys in the cell. Most of them looked like characters I wouldn't want to meet in a dark alley. The place reeked of urine and other odors similar to what permeated from the dumpsters at Fantasy Empire. As far as furniture, a few stained, worn cots and metal benches were against the walls. A dirty toilet and sink sat out in the open in a far corner. I found an empty space at the back of the cell and leaned against the wall as far from all of those scumbags as possible.

This grungy looking guy was seated on a bench nearby. "Don't pay any attention to them, kid. They won't hurt you in here."

I actually smelled him before I saw him. It definitely wasn't a pleasant odor. With craggy wrinkles mapping his cruddy face, I couldn't even guess how old he was. His clothes were weighed down with grease and grime. The mass of tangled straw atop his head and twisting down his shoulders was a poor excuse for hair. On his feet were running shoes disguised as sandals with his disgusting, yellowed toes protruding from the holes in them.

"What's your name, kid?'

"It's Tank," I answered while I warily looked around at the others in the cell.

This guy seemed to be the only nonthreatening dude in the entire cell. All of the others kept staring at me as if they wanted to rape or maybe kill me.

"My name is Dingo… like the wild dog of Australia."

With the mess I was in, I wasn't in any mood for polite conversation. I didn't know how or why I got into it, and mostly how I was going to get out of it. My head was throbbing, and it hurt to even move. I just wanted to go home and forget about everything that had happened since I left Fantasy Empire.

Then I thought about my mother. She probably didn't even know I wasn't home yet. She was probably in bed sound asleep because she had to get up early for work tomorrow. Why wouldn't they let me call her? I'm sure it would scare her, getting a call in the middle of the night. But what would she think when she got up in the morning and found I wasn't there? Maybe she'd think I was just sleeping in my room. Maybe she wouldn't even know I wasn't home until she got home from work at night. She'd be out of her mind with worry. I didn't need to do that to her. Not after all she's been through.

As all these thoughts were scrambling in my head with the pain pounding my skull, I heard the guy on the bench saying something to me. I finally asked, "Sorry, I wasn't listening. What did you say, man?"

"Why don't you sit down a spell? You don't look so good. You can't go anywhere for a while. I won't hurt you. I'm harmless."

Hesitantly, I left the wall and sat at the other end of the bench. As I lowered my body, I realized how tired and sore I really was. I must've been blocking some of the pain and weariness out of my head when all this other shit was going down. I put my face in my hands and thought about the hopelessness of my situation.

The Dingo guy had been looking at his dirty, broken fingernails. "You want to talk about it, Tank?"

I took my hands away from my face, looked into space, not knowing what to do or say. Is it even worth it to talk to this guy? If the detectives don't believe me, what good would it do to tell some bum in a jail cell? Then what would it matter anyhow? Maybe he could help me make some sense of what was happening to me. Finally, I turned to Dingo and blurted out the words rapidly. "I think I'm in some kind of nightmare. The police are accusing me of killing all those people, but I had nothing to do with it. They keep telling me these weird things, and I don't know what they're talking about. All I wanted to do was to use the telephone. I must be going crazy!"

"Hold on there, Tank. Slow down. How about starting from the beginning. You have plenty of time. Neither of us is going anywhere for a while."

So I repeated my bazaar nightmare to him, starting with Stacey crashing into the oak tree all the way through being put in that cell. When I was finished, Dingo was still sitting, staring at his fingernails. He looked away from his fingers and shook his head. "Well, now, that sure is some yarn."

"You probably think I'm lying, but I'm not. Everything happened just as I told you."

"How about that girl who was shot. Can't she tell the cops what happened?"

"I guess she's in pretty bad shape in the hospital. They probably didn't ask her anything yet. Besides, maybe she thought I was part of it too. I only walked into the bar a few minutes before the gunmen came in to shoot up the place. Maybe she thought I was the lookout guy or something. I don't know. But that still doesn't explain what happened to my truck, why they couldn't find it. And why can't they find my address? That just doesn't make any sense at all."

"Is your apartment building new? Maybe they were using an old map."

"No, it's an old building, probably twenty or thirty years old. In 2011 when I was in high school, I knew some kids on the Nawinah football team who lived there. So I know it isn't brand new."

Suddenly, Dingo turned and watched me with this weird, puzzled look on his face.

"What's the matter?" I asked him. "Why are you looking at me like that?"

After he stared at me for several minutes without speaking, he turned his head and started looking at his fingers again. "Tank, I think you're pulling my leg, here."

"What do you mean? What did I say?" I didn't know why all of a sudden he was acting so cold and distant.

When he looked at me again, I could tell he was angry with me for some reason. "You have yourself a real problem, Tank. Here I am trying to help you out, and you pull this shit on me."

"What shit? What did I say?" I was clueless.

"You know what you said. Do you think I'm a fool, just because I look like this?" He stood, spread his legs and arms, and looked down at his filthy clothes.

"Listen, Dingo. I have no idea what I said to upset you. I know you're trying to help me. I really appreciate it, but I don't know what I said."

He didn't say anything right away. He just looked at me. Then he walked over and pointed his finger at me. "You made that crack about knowing those kids in 2011. *That's* what you said."

He really was confusing me. "So what? What's wrong with me saying that? It's true. I did know some kids from Nawinah? I'm not lying. They played football on the Nawinah team while I played for Evans. What's wrong with that?"

He was still angry as he shook his finger in my face. "Ah, not the kids! You said it was in 2011. Tank, how could you be in high school in 2011 if this is only 1993?"

What?? I think my mouth opened wide enough to swallow a football. I couldn't believe my ears. He said it was 1993! That was the year I was born, not the year right at that very moment! What was he talking about? 1993? This is insane! And here I thought he was on my side. What a jerk! What kind of a game was he playing?

Dingo went back to the other end of the bench and plopped down without saying another word. I sat on the bench, trying to make some sense out of what he had said, but it was impossible. How could it be 1993? Did I hit my head so badly on Stacey's windshield that I was maybe in a coma in the intensive care unit of some hospital, and this was all happening in my mind? But the cuts and bruises on my body felt very real. I dug my fingers into the big gash on my forehead just to verify it was actually there. I yelled out in pain. That injury was definitely real! Could I feel such pain if I were in a coma? Something very wrong was happening to me. I had no explanation, and I didn't know what to do about it. Unless... Dingo and the police were all lying to me. Maybe this was their crazy way to get me to confess I had something to do with the shooting at Corky's.

Now it was my turn to confront Dingo. I stood up and went over to the wall where I had first gone when I originally was led into the cell. I paced back and forth between the wall and the bench. Then I stopped in front of Dingo. I pointed my finger at him. "You're lying. There's no way this is 1993. You're trying to mess me up more than I am already."

Then I went back to my corner of the bench, sat down, and tried to understand how I ended up in this situation. Since my cell phone was broken, I didn't know what time it was, but I was getting very tired and feeling extremely weary. I scooted my ass so my back was against the corner of the cement wall. The entire cell was very quiet. All the other prisoners had apparently gone to sleep. Maybe if I also fell asleep, all this would go away. When I woke up, things would be back to normal. I'd probably be home in my own bed. I rested my head against the wall, cleared my mind of any thoughts, and fell asleep.

CHAPTER FOUR
Knowledge: Not A Waste Of Time

"Tank, I'm so proud of you, graduating summa cum laude. You are my amazing son." Ma was fixing my tie before I got in line to go on stage to receive my Bachelor of Arts degree in History. And she called me "Tank" instead of "Talbott." This was one of the happiest days of my life…. But something was wrong. All of a sudden, it was my turn, but I couldn't walk onto the stage. My head felt like a bowling ball on my shoulders. I looked down at my graduation gown. It was covered in blood. I heard gun shots. The graduates standing near me fell to the ground with blood spewing from bullet holes in their foreheads. I broke away from Ma and ran as fast as I could.

Then I woke up. I was disoriented with a splitting headache. It had all been a dream—or a nightmare. I was not in line to get my history degree. I was not even in my own bed. I was still in the jail cell with a bunch of weirdos where I had fallen asleep on an uncomfortable bench. The smell of food and coffee assaulted my nostrils as a policeman passed out breakfast to the guys in the cell.

I was just as perplexed as when I had fallen asleep and in no mood for any food.

In a daze, I watched as the guys went forward to grab a cardboard tray from the policeman. The scene was so surreal, and I still couldn't wrap my head around my current predicament. I saw Dingo return with a tray. He sat down on the other end of the bench. "Don't you want something to eat, Tank? Free food."

"No, I'm not hungry."

Throughout the cell, I heard the sounds of the men devouring the food as if they hadn't eaten in days. Maybe some of them actually hadn't. Slurps, snorts, gulps, and burps. I felt nauseated from the smells and sounds. I had to get up and walk around to settle my stomach. Maybe a cup of coffee would help. "Dingo, how do I get the guard to give me some coffee?"

"Just go over and yell at him."

I went to the cell bars. The other guys were busy chomping their food, so they didn't bother to harass me. "Hey, guard, can I get a cup of coffee, please?"

I waited at the bars until the guard came over with a paper cup filled with hot, black coffee. He handed it to me without saying a word. I took it from his hands. "Thanks, man." The policeman walked away without any response.

The coffee was actually pretty good. It helped my nausea, but it didn't clear my mind. I still couldn't understand how and why I was in this incredible situation. I sat down on my end of the bench, sipping the coffee.

Dingo had finished his breakfast and was returning from placing his trash on the temporary metal shelf attached to the cell bars. He sat down on the opposite end of the bench, looking again at his dirty fingernails.

I had to get somebody to believe me even if just for my own sanity. Dingo was the only one who showed me any kind of friendship, so I thought I'd try again with him. I moved a little closer to him. "Dingo, listen. I'm not lying. I don't understand what is happening to me. Let me just say some things before you get mad at me again. Okay? Things happened yesterday just as I said they did. I don't know how, and I don't know why I know it's 2015 while you say it's 1993. You think I'm lying, and I think you're lying. Now, I'm good at history, and I have a really good memory. If I can tell you some of the things that happened between 1993 and 2015, maybe you'll be convinced I'm telling the truth. What do you say?"

I knew he didn't believe me, but at least he decided to listen. He looked up from his dirty fingers and said, "Go for it, kid."

So I took a couple of minutes to chronologically think of what had happened in the world between 1993 and 2015 that might have an impact on Dingo's thinking and the way he felt about me. I began pacing back and forth in front of the bench as I looked back in my head at what I remembered.

"Okay. Uh, well, first I'll start with 1993. In April of 1993, I was born. I know you don't believe me and you don't care, but I'll start there and tell you what I had learned about that year. Here goes.

"Well, uh, as far as world events, Czechoslovakia split into two countries, the Czech Republic and the Slovak Republic. There was a raid on the compound of a religious sect called the Branch Davidians in Waco, Texas, lasting for several weeks, and, uh, there was a bombing at the World Trade Center in New York killing several people and injuring about a thousand others. In entertainment history, the television show, *Cheers,* had it final episode."

Suddenly, Dingo put up his hand. "Hold it there, Tank. I know all these things, so what the hell are you doing? You trying to jerk me off again?"

I thought about what he had said. He was right. It was now the end of April, at least in 2015. So if this was 1993, maybe it was the end of April in 1993 also.

"I apologize. Those things happened at the beginning of 1993. Let me think…. Okay, in June of 1993, Lorena Bobbitt cut of her husband's penis."

Dingo looked surprise at that bit of information. I even had to smile a little at his facial expression. Then I continued. "In October, Michael Jordan, the greatest basketball player ever, retired for the first time after his father was killed. Uh, another thing that happened was the Mississippi and the Missouri Rivers flooded causing billions of dollars in damages."

I stopped pacing and looked at Dingo. I had his full attention. So I continued with my historical facts.

"Okay. Let me move on to 1994. The World Series was cancelled because of a major league baseball players strike. A massive earthquake in Los Angeles caused billions of dollars in damages and injured over 5,000 people. President John F. Kennedy's widow, Jackie Kennedy Onassis, died. So did former president, Richard Nixon. The prime minister of Israel, Yitzhak Rabin, was assassinated. "

I stopped and took a deep breath. I also looked around the cell. It appeared I was accumulating quite an audience. My cell mates were also listening to me. Some of them had looks of curiosity on their faces. I continued my recitation.

"In 1995, the Oklahoma City Federal Building was bombed, killing over one-hundred-sixty people. The bombers, Timothy McVeigh and Terry Lynn Nichols, were eventually caught. McVeigh was put to death while Nichols was sentenced to several life sentences. O.J. Simpson, the running back who played for the Buffalo Bills and the San Francisco 49ers went on trial for the murder of his ex-wife, Nicole, and her friend, Ronald Goldman."

I was starting to enjoy this. It even helped me forget about my weird situation and alleviate some of the pain in my head. Apparently, my cellmates were also being entertained. I noticed while I was pacing toward the front of the cell that the policeman on duty guarding us had also pulled his chair closer to the bars of the cell. I progressed to 1996.

"In 1996, a bombing at the Summer Olympics in Atlanta killed two people and insured two hundred. The Unabomber, Ted

Kaczynski, was arrested and is spending several life sentences in the same prison where Terry Nichols is incarcerated. And in 1996 in a very controversial trial, O.J. Simpson was found innocent in the murders of his ex-wife and Ron Goldman."

By this time, I had a completely captivated audience. All my cellmates were sitting down on the various benches, cots, or the floor. A few other police officers stood outside the cell near the guard on duty. I felt empowered. I had never had so much attention before. Not even during my high school football years. I paced the floor a little, searching my brain for the facts on 1997.

"In 1997, the spacecraft, Pathfinder, landed on Mars. They cloned a sheep and named her Dolly. Princess Diana of Great Britain died from injuries received in a violent car crash. Mother Theresa of Calcutta died and was beatified to sainthood in 2003."

My mouth was getting dry. I walked over to the bars, facing about a half dozen police officers. "Do you think I could get a drink of water?"

One of the policemen quickly left the group and brought back a Styrofoam cup filled with cold water.

"Thanks." I grabbed the water through the bars, stood drinking the entire cupful, and then handed the empty cup to the policeman. "Thanks again, man."

I started walking back and forth again and began my 1998 facts.

"In 1998, a hurricane in Central America killed over 10,000 people. The China Yangtze River flooded, killing 3,600 people and leaving millions homeless. President Bill Clinton admitted to having an extramarital affair with Monica Lewinski, one of the White House interns. Kurt Kobain of the rock band, Nirvana, committed suicide with a self-inflicted gunshot."

I heard many comments from my cellmates with those last two facts.

"Whoa, way to go, prez!"

"No shit! Kobain's my man! He killed himself?"

I was on a roll. The information started coming back to me like an assembly line. I was remembering all the historical details I had enjoyed learning previously. And my audience was listening in amazement.

"Let me go to 1999. President Bill Clinton was acquitted of perjury and obstruction of justice. At Columbine High School in Colorado, two students went on a shooting rampage, killing twelve students, a teacher, and themselves. An earthquake in Turkey killed 13,000 people. Off the coast of Martha's Vineyard John F. Kennedy Jr., his wife, and sister-in-law died in a single engine private plane crash."

At that point, I stopped and looked around at my audience: my cellmates, the police outside the cell, and Dingo. I still had their undivided attention. I looked at Dingo. "Should I go on?"

Before Dingo could respond, almost in unison both the cellmates and the police officers shouted, "Yeah, yeah, keep going!"

So I trudged forward.

"I'll start into the new millennium with the year 2000. January 1st of that year was very scary. We didn't know what to expect. It was the first time most of society would experience living in a different millennium. So many advancements had been made since the beginning of the twentieth century to cause many to be afraid of what would happen when the twenty-first century began. Since all computer software only counted the last two digits of the year, it was predicted they would all go haywire at midnight. The issue was called 'Y2K'. People thought computers would stop working or produce incorrect output, causing horrendous problems. There would be a total breakdown of the transportation infrastructure disrupting even food delivery, resulting in mass starvation. Some believed airplanes would actually fall out of the sky. Society would collapse and cause worldwide riots."

Looks of astonishment etched everyone's faces. I even thought I saw fear in some of their eyes. I was beginning to think maybe this strange group of listeners was finally believing me. Or maybe they simply thought I was a good storyteller. Whatever the case, I quickly continued to take away those weird looks.

"But, actually, none of that even came close to happening. Some inconvenience occurred for a week or two involving computer software, but life went on normally. No tragic or end of the world events. I'll just tell you some of the stuff which did happen that year.

"Well, the Republican candidate, George W. Bush, won the United States presidency by a narrow margin over Al Gore, the

Democratic candidate. Air France's plane, the Concorde, believed to be one of the safest planes, crashed and killed one hundred thirteen people. Charles Schulz, the creator of the famous cartoon, Peanuts, died from colon cancer.

"So since we made it through the turn of the century into the twenty-first without the world ending, I'll continue with 2001. Anthrax laced letters were sent to various media and government officials. Several postal workers died after handling those letters. Dale Earnhardt, the famous race car driver, died in a fiery crash at the Daytona 500."

Again, I heard surprise exclamations from both the cellmates and the police.

"No way!"

"Not possible!"

"Not Dale Earnhardt!"

I waited until the mumbling subsided, then I began again.

"On September 11, 2001, nineteen Islamic hijackers from the group known as al-Qaeda and orchestrated by their leader, Osama Bin Laden, coordinated a series of four attacks on the United States. Four passenger airlines were hijacked and flown into buildings in suicide attacks. Two of the planes crashed into the North and South Towers of the World Trade Center in New York City, collapsing both towers. A third plane crashed into the Pentagon, leading to a partial collapse of that building. A fourth plane was targeted at Washington D.C. but crashed into a field in Pennsylvania after its passengers tried to overtake the hijackers. In total almost 3,000 people were killed. As a result of these tragic events, the Department of Homeland Security was created with the primary responsibility of protecting the country from terrorist attacks, man-made accidents, and natural disasters. The Patriot Act was also passed to help detect and prosecute terrorism and other criminals."

Everyone seemed to be affected by this tragedy.

"Oh, my God!"

"Unbelievable!"

I hesitated and looked down at the floor for a moment, remembering those terrible days. When I looked up, I apologized, "I guess I got carried away a little bit, but the 9-11 tragedy, as it is called, has had a profound effect on our nation, including me. My dad's brother was one of the firemen killed when the North Tower collapsed."

I was silent for a while, remembering the day Dad found out about Uncle Andy's death. He was so upset even Mom couldn't console him. They both went to New York for the memorial service and to be with Aunt Biddie. I was only eight at the time. I stayed with Mom's friend, Julie Farnsworth, while they were gone because Mom didn't think I was ready to deal with death and destruction yet, especially something so massive. I was so glad when they got home. Julie Farnsworth was a weird lady! I didn't want to stay with her any longer than I had to. Dad never did get over the loss of Uncle Andy. They were really close.

"Hey, Tank, you okay?"

Suddenly, I realized I had been standing without speaking for a couple of minutes, reminiscing about the past. I looked up and turned toward Dingo, who had called out to me.

"Yeah, yeah. I was just remembering stuff. You know, thinking about the past and all. I'm sure most of you will see for yourself the 9-11 tragedy on television. You'll then know what I'm talking about when I say it affected everyone in this country. People still feel it today. Uh, today in 2015, that is."

My listeners were all watching me, not saying a word. Maybe they were beginning to feel some of the emotion I was feeling. Should I continue? My throat was dry again. I went over to the bars and asked, "Do you think I could have another drink of water?"

As the same police officer who got me the original drink walked to get me another, I noticed the two detectives who had questioned me the day before had joined the group of policemen. The captain was there too. I wasn't sure what that meant, but they hadn't stopped me. I guess they were listening to my monolog also.

The officer brought me my water, and I gulped it down quickly. I walked back to the bench where Dingo was sitting. "Should I go on?"

"Sure, kid. I think we're all enjoying this. Go head. You either got some crazy, wild imagination or you are a great liar."

"I'm telling the truth. Just like it happened."

I saw the captain come over to the bars. He called out to me.

"Come over here, boy."

I walked over to him. Everyone in the cell was very quiet. So were all the policemen nearby. "Yes, sir?"

"I've been listening to you for a while. My men tell me you've been going on like this for about an hour. Is that true?"

"I guess it's been about that long, sir."

"Well, I'm just wondering what you're trying to do here, and why my men are so captivated by what you're saying."

"I'm just trying to convince Dingo I've been telling the truth about everything. He told me this is the year 1993 and got angry with me when I told him it wasn't. That can't be true, sir. I was born in 1993. I graduated from Evans High School in 2011, and it's now 2015. Nobody seems to think I'm telling the truth. I thought if I could convince Dingo, maybe you and the other detectives would believe me and take me seriously. Then you'd let me out of this cell so I could go home."

The captain sternly looked at me. "Well, Talbott, suppose I let you finish your little history lesson, or maybe science fiction story, whichever. Then we'll talk."

Timidly, I asked, "Sir, I'm getting kind of hungry. Do you think I could get something to eat before I finish?"

Without responding to me, the captain walked away, saying to one of the policemen as he exited the area where the police were standing around, "Get that boy some food."

CHAPTER FIVE
Accolades For A Slacker

I sat down on my end of the bench waiting for the food and considering my surreal predicament. I didn't know what time it was. I may have lost all track of hours and minutes, but I hadn't lost track of years. I was positive it was 2015. It couldn't be any other year. No one could convince me otherwise. I guess it was my job to convince everybody else.

As I sat waiting, my cellmates started to move around and talk amongst themselves. One guy came over to me. "Hey, man, how you know all that shit? You some kind of genius? You don't look like no genius to me."

"No, I'm not a genius. I just like history and learning about the past. I do have a good memory, though."

The guy looked confused. "Whatchu mean history? You been talkin' bout shit that ain't happened yet. You a fortune teller or somethin'?"

The guy with all the tattoos came over to me. He wasn't acting in a threatening manner as when I had first arrived in the cell.

"What you doin' in this place if you know all that shit?"

"It's just stuff that has happened. That's all. I just have a good memory."

"I believe you, kid. Nobody could make up all that crap that fast. You got me really intrested. Specially that crap 'bout those airplanes killin' all those people."

Then the policeman showed up at the cell carrying my food. I got up from the bench to walk over to the bars. The two other cellmates moved out of my way to let me walk by.

The food was a wrapped sandwich and a bag of chips. Nothing like a fast food hamburger, but I was hungry, and it tasted good. I ate all the food and drank most of the water. As I was finishing up, the officers outside the cell were beginning to gather in the area again. This time they each had grabbed a chair for themselves. I guess they figured this was going to take some time. I took my paper trash over to the bars, and the guard took it away. Then I saw the captain walk into the area. "Are you ready to continue, Talbott?"

"Yes, sir, but I really would appreciate if you'd call me Tank."

"I can do that, Tank."

So I started back on my dissertation.

"I also want to mention the war in Afghanistan, which started after the 9-11 attacks in 2001. US invaded the country searching out the al-Qaeda, who were responsible for the 9-11 attacks. I won't go into a lot of detail, just to say many of our troops were lost. It's still going on today, uh, I mean in 2015.

"Let's see, in 2002, in Pennsylvania nine miners were rescued after seventy-seven hours in a flooded mine shaft. Two snipers preyed on the Washington DC suburbs killing ten people and wounding others. Ozzie Osbourne, the heavy metal singer, and his family appeared on an MTV reality show series. FBI agent Robert Hanssen was sentenced to life imprisonment without parole for selling secrets to Moscow for over a million in cash and diamonds."

I heard some "oh's and ah's" with the mention of all that money. I stopped pacing, thinking ahead to 2003, trying to get my facts straight in my mind.

"Oh, yeah, in 2003, the space shuttle, Columbia, exploded while it was reentering earth's atmosphere, killing all seven astronauts on board. In March, President Bush ordered an attack on Iraq. In April, Bagdad was occupied by US troops, and in December, Iraq's former dictator, Saddam Hussein was captured. Arnold Schwarzenegger, the actor, was elected governor of California.

"In 2004, George W. Bush, the son of George H.W. Bush, was reelected as president of United States. His brother, Jeb Bush was governor of Florida from 1999 to 2007.

"Okay, what else? Ah, yes, Facebook was launched. Let me tell you, Facebook is a really big thing in 2015. It was created by Mark Zuckerberg and his college roommates when he was only a sophomore at Harvard. Actually, he was born in 1984. So if this is 1993, like you think it is, he'd only be nine years old. Well, in

2015 he is now thirty years old and is probably one of the youngest billionaires in the world. As for Facebook, it's the most popular social networking media in the world."

Guys were looking at me with their mouths open. I guess if I were in their shoes, and somebody started rattling off all these facts, I'd react the same way. Just maybe this would help me. Just maybe I could convince them it was 2015. Even if I did, how could I then come to grips with it actually being 1993? I didn't want to think about it at that moment. I was enjoying myself too much, spouting off my history lesson.

"A lot of natural disasters occurred in 2004. An enormous tsunami in Asia killed 200,000 people. And Florida was hit by four hurricanes that year: Bonnie, Charley, Boris, and Jeanne. Oh, gay marriages were legalized in Massachusetts, the first of many states to do so.

"In 2005 the USB flash drive replaced floppy disks for storing computer data outside the hard drive of the computer. Hurricane Katrina flooded New Orleans killing more than 1,000 people and leaving thousands homeless. Pope John Paul II died."

I took a deep breath and looked around at my audience. Everyone still seemed to be very interested in what I was saying. I started on 2006.

"Okay, in 2006, Twitter was launched, which is another form of social media that has become very popular. Pluto was demoted to a dwarf planet status. Saddam Hussein, the former Iraqi prime minister, was executed. The annual Rose Bowl Parade was drenched with rain for the first time in fifty-one years. Because of all the terrorist activity, all the airlines began having very strict rules on liquids and gels carried onto aircrafts.

"On to 2007. Apple debuted the iPhone, becoming quite the sensation in the country. United States sent 30,000 troops to Iraq to stem the deadly attacks during their civil war. Later in the year, 20,000 more troops were deployed to Baghdad. The minimum wage was increased to $5.85, the first increase in ten years.

"Let's see… Uh, 2008 was a dismal year for the US economy. Banks failed, many big corporations went under, real estate value plummeted, and the government had to bail out banks as well as some of the big auto manufacturers. We were in the grips of a recession that resonated to the rest of the world as well. Also in 2008, three men stole four pieces of artwork worth $163 million from the Zurich Museum in Switzerland in broad daylight.

"In 2009, Barack Obama, our first black president, was sworn in as the forty-fourth president of United States. Africa's population reached one billion. Michael Jackson, the pop star died at the age of fifty. Senator Edward Kennedy, brother of John F. Kennedy, died of brain cancer. Chrysler and General Motors both filed for bankruptcy."

I again stopped and looked around the area. I walked over to the bars to address the captain. "Sir, I don't have a watch, but maybe it's lunchtime. Do these gentlemen in the room need to be fed?"

I heard remarks from my cellmates. "Wow! He called us

'gentlemen'! Ain't that classy?"

There were snickers from the policemen on the other side of the cell bars. Captain Forsythe got out of his seat and came over to me. "You might be right, Tank. I think we all can use a little break." He turned back to the police officers. "How about it, men. Let's feed this group before Mr. Tank finishes his speech. Does anyone need to be processed out of here yet?"

One of the officer's spoke, "No, sir. Nobody leaves until two o'clock."

So all the police officers disbursed to their various duties. My cellmates started talking among themselves. Several of them came over to ask questions or comment on some of the things I had told them. They were looking at me with an entirely different perspective. I no longer was the "Humpty Dumpty" fat boy to ridicule. I had gained their respect.

Several policemen brought in the lunches. I took another sandwich offered to me. Instead of water they gave each of us a can of soda. The cellmates were really impressed. I was also. Even the police were treating me with respect. But I was still worried about how this was all going to end. Would any of it make any difference?

After we ate and our trash was taken away, the police and the cellmates returned to their former seating arrangements. They looked at me in anticipation, waiting for the continuance of their history lesson. I got up from the bench, wiped the crumbs off my lap and started on the year 2010.

"Okay. I'm up to 2010 now. Since I was a lot older in 2010 than I was in the nineties, I actually vividly remember much of what happened. One of the huge natural disasters that year was the devastating 7.0 magnitude earthquake striking Haiti, killing over 230,000 people, and displacing over a million and a half others. Some of those people are still living in tents under deplorable conditions. The oil company, BP Oil, had a massive spillage in the Gulf of Mexico. Over two hundred million gallons of oil was pumped into the water, and it went on for eighty-seven days affecting 16,000 miles of US coastline and killing over four thousand animals. President Obama introduced his controversial health care plan still in effect today, but still being criticized.

"Well, I only have a few more years to go, but it doesn't get any better. I sure wish if it really is 1993, I could change so many of the things that have happened since then. But all I can do is tell you what I know.

"In 2011, Japan had a 9.0 earthquake and tsunami, but by 2015 they had almost completely rebuilt the damaged areas. Osama bin Laden, the mastermind of the 9-11 attacks I told you about in 2001 was captured and killed. Kate Middleton married Prince William of Great Britain. Penn State defensive coordinator, Jerry Sandusky, was arrested on charges of forty counts of sexual abuse. Oh, by the way, I also graduated high school in 2011. Thought you might want to know that."

I got some weird looks from everybody with that comment. I think with me personalizing my narration, they were beginning to realize how bizarre this entire scenario had become. Up to this point, they were taking it all in as if I were simply telling a story. Now maybe they were beginning to think about why I was telling them all these facts. I started on 2012.

"In 2012, a gunman opened fire in a theater in a Denver suburb killing twelve people and wounding fifty-eight others. He was arrested in the parking lot behind the theater. Hurricane Sandy hit the east coast spreading a thousand miles wide of destruction. At Sandy Hook Elementary School in Connecticut a twenty year old gunman killed twenty-six people. Twenty of them were six and seven year old children. There was a massive wild fire in New Mexico burning 190,000 acres. Colorado also had one covering sixty square miles.

"Wow! We are at 2013 now. The royal baby to Kate Middleton and Prince William was born. They named him Prince George Alexander Louis of Cambridge. How's that for a name? Okay. What else? Uh, Pope Benedict XVI announced his retirement. He was the first pope to do so since 1415. The new pope, Cardinal Jorge Mario Bergoglio of Argentina, chose Pope Francis as his name. There were two bomb explosions during the Boston Marathon. Three people were killed and over two hundred and sixty were injured. During the manhunt for the two Muslim brothers responsible, one of the brothers was killed, the other was injured. Illinois had its deadliest tornado outbreak on record."

I paused and looked down at the floor, remembering the big tragedy in my life. "On a personal side, my dad was murdered in a drive-by shooting outside our house in Pine Hills. That's why my mom decided to move us to Nawinah. To this day, the murderers were never caught."

When you lose a loved one who is very close to you, every time you talk about it or even think about it, you become emotional. I think I was beginning to make friends. I heard comments like, "Sorry, kid." "What a bummer." "No shit!" After a moment, I stood up straight, shook my head a little, and I continued.

"We are now up to the year 2014. What a year! Gay marriages have been legalized in most states. In Nigeria two hundred seventy six female students were kidnapped from a government secondary school. Authorities believe they were forced into unwilling marriages. The girls have not yet been found. A Turkish mine disaster, the worst in the history of underground mine fires, killed three hundred one people. Actor/comedian Robin Williams committed suicide. One encouraging and even miraculous event happened in Australia. A man's leg was trapped between a train and the platform. All passengers on the train got out and jointly lifted up that train and freed the man's leg. It was amazing!

"Well, I am now up to 2015. There are some significant things that have already happened this year. Remember that Boston Marathon bomber from 2013 who was wounded? Well, he went on trial in January and was found guilty of all thirty charges. Oh yeah, the New England Patriots beat the Seattle Seahawks twenty-eight to twenty-four, winning their fourth Super Bowl. I watched that game, man. It was great! The Patriots actually came back from a ten point deficit. You guys won't want to miss that game. Uh, oh, Hilary Clinton, the wife of former president, Bill Clinton, announced her candidacy for the 2016 presidential election. A German jetliner carrying one hundred fifty people crashed into the Alps. From the voice recorder it was determined the co-pilot deliberately crashed the plane after he locked the pilot out of the cockpit."

I stopped walking back and forth and looked around the cell at my fellow prisoners and at the police outside the cell. "So that's it guys. I've led you up to now—by my calendar, anyhow."

I walked over to the bench and sat down. Then suddenly, everyone in the entire place stood up and started applauding. I was shocked! I don't know if they believed me, but they sure must've enjoyed my so-called presentation. I was really humbled.

CHAPTER SIX
Accepting The Impossible

Several of my cellmates came over and asked to shake my hand. It was as if I were a celebrity. Many of them asked me questions about some of the events I had mentioned. They were intrigued by so many tragic disasters and senseless crimes. Nobody was harassing me anymore. After everyone had disbursed again, I sat down on my end of the bench to finish my soda. Looking around the cell, I felt good. Sure, I was in the most challenging and unbelievable predicament of my life, but the past couple of hours had also been very fulfilling. I felt I had gained a lot of respect from both these cellmates and the police.

Other than when I had asked him if I should continue, Dingo hadn't said one word to me the entire time I was reciting my facts. I knew by the look on his face he had listened, but I didn't know what he was thinking. As I was taking my last swig of soda, he said, "That was quite impressive, Tank."

I put down the soda can and turned to him. "Do you believe me now? You know I couldn't just make up all those events that

59

quickly on the spot. You know that, don't you? To *me*, it really *is* 2015. I can't believe it either. But if everybody who I've talked to since I was in that crash with my truck thinks it's 1993, then something unbelievable happened to me when my truck hit that tree, and I lost consciousness. I don't know how, and I don't know why, but I think I have actually gone back in time. It just doesn't make any sense. And I have no damn idea what to do about it!"

I sat back, looked down at the floor, and shook my head.

"Here's the thing, kid. As crazy as it sounds, I think you're telling the truth. I'm as dumbfounded as you are. But what I think is this crazy stuff has happened to you for a reason. I don't much know what the reason is either, but I think you got to find out what it means, or who knows what kind of mess your life will be in?"

I thought about what he said. "But what reason could there be for something like this to happen to me? I'm just a nobody. I have a low-level, nothing job. My life is going nowhere. I don't know anybody important. I'm just your typical loser who will probably be collecting minimum wages for the rest of my life."

"Tank, don't sell yourself short. The way you rattled off those facts like you were reading them from some book at that very minute, you aren't a loser by any means. Believe me. You got something special. We just have to figure out what good it'll do you."

Did I hear him correctly? Did he say "we"?

"Dingo, you said 'we'. Does that mean you're willing to help me figure this out?"

"Well, kid, this situation intrigues me. I know, I know. You look at me, and you think I'm just a bum. What help can a deadbeat like me be? But like the old saying goes, 'don't judge a book by its cover'. When something sets my mind to thinking, I need to find out why. It's been a long time since something interested me enough to take notice, and you did just that, my boy. You did just that!"

I don't know why, but I was elated. Here I was in a jail cell with some low life criminal saying he believed me. Not only did he believe me, but he was willing to help me find out why I was in this bizarre situation. It gave me some encouragement. Bum or not, I needed help, and he was offering.

I was about to thank Dingo for having faith in me when the guard came to the cell and called out, "Talbott Telek. Captain Forsythe wants to see you."

I quickly got up. I gave Dingo a puzzled look as if to ask what he thought this was about. He scrunched his shoulders to his head and turned up both his hands as he shook his head. I picked up the soda can and walked over to the cell door. The guard unlocked the door to let me exit, then quickly closed and relocked it. He told me to walk in front of him to the captain's office down the hall. I threw the soda can into the wastebasket next to his desk as I walked by.

At the captain's office, the guard went back to his position near the cell, and another policeman knocked on the captain's door. "Sir? Talbott Telek is here."

"Please come in, Tank, and take a seat."

I walked in and sat in one of the two leather chairs in front of the captain's desk. The policeman closed the door, but stayed inside the captain's office.

"Tom, you can go back to your other duties. I won't need you here."

The policeman left the office, closing the door behind him.

The captain put down the ink pen he had been holding and pushed the papers before him to the side of his desk. "Well, Tank, you gave us a fascinating recitation today. I must say you had everyone captivated. But I am in a bit of a quandary. You have a unique ability. I'm just not sure what that ability actually is. Were you able to conjure up those facts in your head from your wild and disturbed imagination, or were you truly reciting events you *thought* occurred in the future? If the first of my statements is true, then I think you should go to Hollywood and write scripts for the movies. However, if you provided us with an account of what really happens in the future, I am simply astounded! I don't know what to do with you. You have presented me with an unprecedented challenge."

The captain picked up the pen he had previously been using and started tapping it on his desk while he stared at me. I didn't know what to say to him. He had heard most of my speech back in the cell. What else *could* I say? I gave it a try. "Sir, I'm more confused than you could possibly imagine. I didn't ask for this. I was just on my way home from work during my usual early morning hour, and now my entire world has been turned up-side-down. I don't know how to deal with it. Dingo says this has happened to me for a reason, but how the hell am I supposed to know that reason? I can't go home. You guys tell me my home isn't where it's supposed to be. I can't call my mom. Where can I find her? According to you guys, I should be only a couple of weeks old now. I don't even know where my parents lived when I was a baby. Even if I did know, would I be able to go home to them? How could I be an adult and a baby at the same time and confront myself? That's so bizarre!"

I put my hand on my forehead, and just shook my head back and forth in frustration, actually causing my headache to flare up again.

Maybe the captain was starting to understand how I was feeling. He took a deep breath and moved forward, placing his elbows on his desk. "Tank, here is my dilemma. I don't know what to do with you. I have a mass murder case to solve. If you were not involved in the crime, then you are my only witness until we find out if Gina Mariani will survive. If she does survive, I don't know how much she will remember of what happened. So I need you. I need you to help me out here. Now, *if* you are actually telling me the truth, how do I keep you around to help me solve this case? Are you going to suddenly jump up to 2015? This is simply preposterous! I can't wrap my mind around it either."

"I know it is. That's what's so baffling. How can anybody know what to do when this is unprecedented? I'm really sorry, sir.

I surely didn't mean to put you in the middle of this and complicate your investigation any more than it already is."

The two of us looked at each other. Our minds were trying to come up with some sort of solution. The captain kept tapping his pen on his desk, trying to drill a solution into his head or perhaps the desk. I closed my eyes and lifted my head, thinking maybe an answer would be on the back of my eyelids.

Soon the captain spoke, and I immediately opened my eyes. "Okay, Tank, do you have any money?"

"No sir. Not really." I reached in my pockets, retrieving what remained of my change. "I have less than a dollar in change. My wallet was in my truck. I had about twenty or thirty dollars in it, but God only knows where my wallet or truck are now."

He was silent again.

"Here is what we'll do. I can't justify using too much public funds right now for any of this, so I'll set you up in a cheap motel for the time being. I'll give you one of the mobile phones we recently requisitioned for some of our men. I'm sure the technology of these phones are not what you're used to, but at least we'll have a means of communication. I'll also give you access to one of the abandoned cars we have at the vehicle morgue. You don't have your driver's license either, I suppose."

"No, sir, it's in the truck too."

"I suppose it wouldn't be a good idea to use it even if you did have it, what with the dates on it being inconsistent with this period in time. Instead, I'll give you a personally signed document you must carry. I'm hoping you won't need to use it for anything, but you'll have it just in case. My dilemma is what date I put on it as far as your birth date. I can't put your real birthday, but I also can't put any false information on it either. What I'll do is use today's date. If for any reason, you need to show it to some authority, I'll put my direct telephone number on it. Have them call me immediately. If it's a state or federal authority, I'll deal with it."

He hesitated while staring at me and then said, "I'm also going to give you eight hundred dollars in cash for living expenses."

Surprised and puzzled, I asked, "Excuse me, sir, you're doing all this for me, but what do you expect me to do for you?"

"Well, Tank, I'm not exactly sure of that myself. My men are currently out looking for the two men who murdered those ten people at Corky's. I have an idea who they might be and who they are connected with, but you mentioned to the detectives you might be able to identify them. If that's the case, I at least need you around for that purpose. I'm also hoping you could help us with something else. Maybe Dingo is right. Maybe you are here for a reason. By the way, do you know who Dingo is?"

"Uh, he's that guy I just met in the cell. Other than that, all I know is he's the only one who originally showed me some courtesy when I was arrested, including your detectives and *you*, sir."

"I apologize, Tank, but you have to understand where I'm coming from too. You, yourself, know your story is totally beyond belief. Yes, you have convinced me it is more than a story, but you have to agree, we had good reason to suspect you had something to do with the murders. Your situation just didn't add up. You were at the scene of the crime where multiple murders had occurred. You looked like you had been beat up. We could not confirm your report of a truck accident, and the personal information you gave us about your address could also not be corroborated. Put yourself in my shoes. What would you have thought?"

"Yeah, I guess you're right. I wouldn't believe me either if I wasn't actually *living* it. So what am I supposed to do now, sir?"

"Well, you need to be processed out of here. We'll correct your file so this arrest doesn't appear on any record, like it never existed. Hell, I'm not sure if we were even able to put this on your record. Did you give them your social security number when you were booked?"

"Yes, sir, I did. But since according to your calendar, I'm only a few weeks old, I don't know if my parents had a social security number for me yet. I know they had to have it before they filed their 1993 tax return, but that wouldn't be until 1994."

"I guess I might get a call from the Social Security Administration. Probably not. They are years in arrears on investigating any discrepancies. So you let me deal with that situation.

"After you're released, have a seat in the waiting area until we can get all the paperwork taken care of as far as the car, the mobile phone, and the motel are concerned. The car is about a half mile away. It'll take an hour or so for everything to get processed. Better yet, why don't you go to the coffee shop down the street? I'll send a patrolman there when everything is completed.

"Oh, another thing. You need to go to the hospital and have that forehead looked at. That gash is pretty deep. In fact, I'll give you an extra two hundred dollars for the emergency bill. You won't be able to give them any insurance card."

"Yeah, I have insurance with Fantasy Empire—in 2015. In 1993, I'm sure I was covered under my mom and dad's insurance. I guess it's best if we don't try to claim anything on theirs. Who knows what repercussions that would cause? Is it okay if I go to Nawinah General Hospital? That's where I was born."

"Sure. That'll be fine. It's the closest. That's also where Gina Mariani is hospitalized."

"I thought her name was Gina Antonelli."

"Corky's name was Carl Antonelli. Gina is his daughter. She is married to a Vince Mariani. He also worked at Corky's. He wasn't among those killed at the bar. Thus far, we haven't been able to locate him."

"Do you think it's okay if I stop by to see her at the hospital?"

"I don't see why not. They have her in an induced coma right now, and we have a guard posted outside her room twenty-four seven. Currently, for her protection, the only visitors she can see are family members. I'll include a letter with your paperwork to show the hospital employees and the guard so they'll give you access to her room. You should probably have a picture ID made and attach it to the letter. Tom will take care of that. I don't want to use the mug shots we took when we booked you. Those will be purged."

The captain was quiet for a few minutes, looking out the window.

"Will that be all, sir?" I waited for him to continue.

"That's it. Stop at the desk to pick up your belongings and sign the release forms."

"Well, I actually have no belongings. Everything was in the truck."

"Oh, yes. That's right. Then just sign out. Stop to get the contact telephone numbers so you can keep in touch with me. The officer at the front desk will give me the number of the mobile phone issued to you. That's it, Tank. I'll be getting in touch with you soon."

"Thanks for everything, Captain Forsythe."

"Don't thank me, Tank. It's been a horrible and unusual mix-up."

The captain got on his phone. "Tom, come back to my office to take Mr. Telek through his release process."

So I left the captain's office. Officer Tom took me to have my photo taken and to sign the release papers. Then I stopped at the front desk and told the officer I'd be at the coffee shop waiting for whatever stuff they were going to give me. The officer handed me the mobile phone and an envelope with the money and telephone numbers in it. He said he had already been informed of my destination. Someone would be at the coffee shop in about an hour with everything else.

CHAPTER SEVEN
Partners In The Unknown

I walked to the coffee shop just a few doors from the police station. I sat in a booth along the wall while I looked at the contents in the envelope. There was a card the size of a business card with a few phone numbers on it; the captain's mobile number, the captain's home phone number, the Nawinah Police Department, and the Orange County Sheriff's Office. The business card of the Garden Motel was also in the envelope. One thousand dollars was in a smaller envelope within the large one in denominations of twenties, tens, and fives. I had never seen so much cash at one time in all my life. I'd need to buy a wallet to hold all this money. While I was putting everything back in the large envelope, the waitress approached my booth.

The tall, thin woman took out an order pad from her apron pocket. "What'll it be for you this afternoon, sir?"

"I'll just have coffee, please."

"Are you sure you don't want a piece of our delicious homemade pies? My favorite is the peach, but the cherry and key line are also very tasty."

"Okay. Maybe I'll have that peach pie."

She didn't bother writing the order down. I guess it wasn't too hard to remember. Look who's talking! I just got through reiterating world history for over twenty years. I'm sure she could remember two items.

She brought me the pie and coffee. The coffee was hot and steamy, and she was definitely correct about the delicious peach pie. I wondered if this coffee shop was still around in 2015. I'd have to check it out and see if the pie was still as good. Well, that is, if life ever got back to normal, and I ever returned to 2015.

As I was devouring the pie, who should enter the coffee shop but Dingo. I was quite surprised to see him walking over to my booth.

"What are you doing here, Dingo?"

"I told you, Tank. Your story intrigued me. I want to help you."

"But how did you get out of the jail?"

"Oh, hell. I'm in and out of that place all the time."

'I don't understand. What were you in there for? How could you get out so soon?"

Just then the waitress approached our table. She gave Dingo a look of disgust. "Excuse me, but you need to leave. We don't allow any transient people in here."

"Oh, ma'am, it's okay. He's with me. Please bring him a cup of coffee and some of your yummy peach pie. Oh, and can you refill my coffee too?"

She looked at me rather skeptically, but she did leave the booth.

Dingo didn't seem to be bothered by the waitress' reaction to him. I was more upset than he was. I had blood all over me. Why hadn't she said the same thing to me? "That was rude of her. Do you run into her kind of treatment often?"

"Well, I don't usually frequent any of these kind of places, but the captain told me you'd be here."

"The captain told you?"

"Yes."

"Why would the captain tell you where I was?"

"Well, he knew I could help you deal with your unique situation. Remember I told you that 'you can't judge a book by its cover'?"

"Yeah, you said that, and I know it's an old saying, but what does it mean as far as you're concerned?"

"I guess the captain didn't tell you about me, did he?"

"He did ask me if I knew who you were. I said you were the only one who half way treated me decent from the beginning."

Before either of us could say anything else, the waitress brought a mug for Dingo and a piece of peach pie. She also set a thermos of coffee on the table. She set them down without saying a word, but scowled at Dingo as she walked away.

My curiosity was getting to me. "So who are you? Apparently, you are more than just a vagrant spending the night in jail."

"It's a long story, kid. Are you sure you want to hear it?"

"Yes, I'm sure. I can't go anywhere until I get the paperwork and the car keys the captain promised. Even then, who knows where I'm going? I certainly don't know!"

Dingo first poured himself a cup of coffee. I noticed his hands were no longer filthy, although the rest of him looked as grubby as in the jail cell. He took a sip of the coffee. "My real name is Darrell Crockett. Years ago I was a high powered criminal attorney."

I couldn't help it. I interrupted him. "You're kidding, right?" There was no way this guy could've been what he said he was. However, who was I to question him? Look what I wanted people to believe about me.

"No. I'm not kidding. I really was a prominent attorney in Chicago. I graduated with honors from the University Of Chicago Law School, and directly after graduation, I got a job with a prestigious law firm near Chicago's Magnificent Mile. I was a hot shot, young attorney who had many clients, some guilty, some innocent. I got most of them off with very light sentences, even some of the guilty ones. But my illustrious career came to a screeching halt when in 1965 I stupidly decided to enlist in the army and was sent to Vietnam. As smart of a guy as I thought I was, reality kicked me in the ass the day I landed in Vietnam. I could've avoided the inhumanity that I saw over there, but smartass that I was, I thought I owed it to my country to fight for her. I saw atrocities I never dreamed mankind was capable of committing. The images are imbedded in my mind forever.

"And when I finally returned to the states, I was treated like shit. As soon as my troop disembarked our aircraft carrier, we were bombarded by these young, punk, anti-war protestors, spitting at us and chanting every inflammatory and vile remark the English language possessed. Worst of all, the nightmares I had were horrific. I was afraid to go to sleep at night because I'd relive the horrendous sights and sounds of the war all over again. I became a basket case. I went back to my old law firm, but I could no longer handle the job. One day when I was in the courtroom before the judge, I suddenly was transformed back on the battlefield witnessing the death and destruction of both my fellow soldiers and our enemies. I lost it. I started yelling and screaming as if I were in a battle zone. I grabbed the prosecutor, twisting his arm around to his back. I wrapped my other arm around his neck and started choking him. The judge had to call in three policemen and the bailiff to restrain me. I was sedated and taken out of the courtroom on a stretcher. It was too much for my brain. I was hospitalized for a while, but I never fully recovered. Lucky for me, that prosecutor I attacked realized I was sick and dropped all the charges. He was a good guy.

"I guess I wasn't alone either. About half a million Vietnam vets came back with similar issues. They called it Stress Response Syndrome. I don't really care what they call it. It has been hell living with it. Depression, loneliness, alienation. Most of us have drug and alcohol problems..."

Dingo seemed to withdraw from me. He stopped explaining. I finally spoke, "Wow! I'm so sorry, man. I read about all that stuff, but I never knew anybody who actually *lived* it. In 2015 they call it Post Traumatic Stress Disorder, but the VA is really trying to help guys out now. It must've been awful coming home after risking your life for everybody in this country and then to be treated like crap. I truly feel for you, man."

Dingo seemed to be returning from whatever far off place he had gone in his mind. He turned from staring blankly into space to looking at me.

I was concerned for him. "Are you okay now? You seem to be pretty much together."

"I have had some help. Ernie, you know, Captain Forsythe, he's actually a good buddy of mine. I knew him when I worked at the law firm. He was a young detective back then. He sort of keeps an eye on me. When I have no place to go, he lets me stay in the cell and feeds me. I think he sees this thing with you as an opportunity for me as well as for you. That's why I'm here. He thinks we can help each other out."

"That's really something. I never would've guessed." I hesitated and looked affectionately at him. "I tell you, Dingo, I'm glad you're here."

A smile broke out on his craggy face as he nodded his head up and down. "Same here, Tank. Same here."

As we both were finishing our coffee and pie, a policeman entered the restaurant. He walked over to me. "Are you Tank?"

"Yes, that's me."

"Here are the keys to the vehicle Captain Forsythe is loaning you. It's in the impound lot down the street. It's a tan 1985 Buick Electra Sedan. There are a few dents on the passenger side, but it runs good. You shouldn't have any trouble with it. Also, here is the envelope with the papers Captain Forsythe wanted me to give you. He told me he wants you to call him after you've been to the hospital to get stitched up, and you get settled in your motel room."

The policeman shook hands with both Dingo and me. As he was walking out the door, he turned to us. "Good luck, men."

I drank what remained of my coffee and put the money for my tab on the table. "What do you say, Dingo? Shall we start our adventure?"

"Let's go, kid."

CHAPTER EIGHT
Scoping Out A New Reality

This was the beginning of something where no one could even speculate what the outcome would be. Virgin territory. I couldn't change what had happened; I had to embrace it for now and hope for the best.

Dingo and I walked the half mile to the police impound lot to find the Buick. It was surreal, looking around the lot at the weird vehicles parked in the various rows. I was so used to seeing late model cars, maybe from 2000 to the 2015, but that lot was like being at some car museum. My dad really would've enjoyed wandering through it. He knew every car ever manufactured and all the different models. In fact, before his death he had been saving his money to buy this 1942 green Packard Clipper somebody was trying to sell on eBay. He had shown me a picture of it. I'm not much into cars, but it was a beauty. He never got the chance to save enough money. Those bastards!

Dingo took me out of my reverie when he suddenly shouted, "There it is!" He pointed to a vehicle in the next row. We walked between two beat-up cars to get to the Buick. I was speechless looking at it. Was I actually going to drive this car? What an experience! The two of us rubbed its exterior as we circled around the vehicle, admiring it.

Dingo bent over to pet the car with his cheek almost touching the metal. "This is nice! This is real nice!"

I meandered back to the driver side, took the keys out of my pocket, and opened the door. I slid into the driver's seat and reached over to unlock the door for Dingo. As he was getting into the car, I sat there, hands on the steering wheel, my mind trying to come to terms with where I was. Then I looked down at the buttons and knobs on the dashboard, testing some of them out: radio, air conditioner, heater, air vents, speedometer, odometer, gas gauge with a full tank of gas, clock, and cassette player. Everything looked so different from what I was used to. I put my left hand back on the steering wheel, inserted the key into the ignition, and started the car. The motor began to hum immediately. I looked down at the gear shift console between Dingo and me and moved the gear shift knob to reverse, slowly backing the car out of the parking space. When I was out of the space, I looked over at Dingo. "I guess this is it. Where to first?"

"I think you'd better get to the hospital and get that head gash taken care of."

"Oh, yeah, with everything else going on, I kind of forgot about it. I guess you're right. Uh, I know the way there. That's our first stop. But before we go to see the young woman from Corky's,

I'd like to get cleaned up a little. You probably should also."

Dingo's reply to that suggestion: "Humph!"

At the hospital emergency room, I received eight stitches in my forehead. They took x-rays, but nothing was broken. The ER doctor yelled at me for not taking care of the wound sooner. I would now probably have a big scar. Oh, no. There goes my good looks. I also got a couple of stitches on some of the cuts on the arms and legs, and they cleaned and bandaged some of the other open wounds.

Then we went to Carneys to buy some clean clothes for both Dingo and me. I bought some body hygiene products for us also and a cheap wallet in which to keep all my recently acquired cash and papers. I also bought some bandages and tape to redress my wounds when they got wet or dirty.

I found the Garden Motel where the captain had told me to get a room. We stopped by the office to register and pick up a couple of keys. Our unit was on the second of two levels at the end of the building. I pulled the Buick through the parking lot and parked in front of the lower floor unit below ours. Dingo and I grabbed our packages and went up the stairs to Unit 220.

As expected, it was not a fancy room. It did have two double beds with blue and green plaid bedspreads on them. Dingo was happy about the beds. "I haven't slept in a real bed in years. The closest thing to a bed I've slept on has been those uncomfortable cots at the local homeless shelter."

The night stand between the beds held a lamp and a weird

push button telephone. Facing the beds was a bulky television set quite different from the flat screen I watched at home while loafing on Ma's couch. The TV rested on a combination desk/bureau. Along the same wall, a small table in the corner near the front window had a couple of small chairs pushed up against it. In the opposite corner was a worn but comfortable, upholstered chair.

Dingo watched the TV while I took my turn first to shower and shave in the attached bathroom. I had also purchased some plastic wrap and adhesive tape to wrap around my wounds in order to keep the water from getting the bandages wet. Some I'd have to redo.

The shower was amazing. I had felt so cruddy with both my blood and Gina Marianis blood caked on my body and my clothes. Then being in that jail cell all night, I'm sure I smelled as bad as I looked. Maybe not quite as bad as Dingo, but close.

With a clean, white towel wrapped around my lower half, I came out to the bedroom to get dressed. Dingo took his stuff into the bathroom while I removed the tags from my new clothes, fixed some of the wound bandages, and got dressed. I felt a hundred percent better with my clean body and new clothes, although their style appeared a bit odd to me. As I waited for Dingo, I lay against the bed's headboard and watched a very old episode of *Hawaii Five-O* on TV. The actors were totally different from those in 2015 and the storyline and clothes seemed sort of weird. Even make-believe had changed in the last twenty years.

While I was putting on my socks and shoes, Dingo came out

of the bathroom. I couldn't believe the transformation! Besides the dirt being washed down the shower drain, he had shaved and neatly cut his curly, sand colored hair. I swear he either cut off with the shaver or washed away half of the wrinkles on his face also. He literally looked like a different person.

"Dingo! You look amazing!"

"I clean up pretty good, don't I?"

"You sure do. I can't believe you're the same guy who went into that bathroom a half hour ago. You're almost as good looking as I am."

"Ha! Sonny boy, I got you beat by a long shot."

We then decided to get something to eat before going back to the hospital to see the Corky woman. I didn't want to carry all the cash with me, so we searched the room to find a suitable hiding place for some of it, not the typical places like in the desk drawer or under the mattress. This wasn't the most prestigious motel in the area, and I couldn't afford to have this cash stolen.

Dingo suggested, "How about hiding it in the air condition return vent. It's close to the ceiling, so it's not easy for any of the cleaning staff to reach it—in case they are inclined to be the dishonest type."

I counted the money I had left in the envelope. The ER had cost me one hundred ninety-five dollars, the clothes, bandages, and toiletries had cost around ninety dollars, and the coffee and pie had been around ten dollars. I also had paid the desk clerk at the Garden Motel one hundred dollars for the room for four days. I had about six hundred five dollars left. I put a hundred dollars and the change in my new wallet and left the five hundred five dollars in the envelope. I also folded up the two letters the captain had given me, one to use in place of a driver's license and one to get access to Gina Marianis room at the hospital. I put both of them into the wallet. Then I pulled up one of the chairs near the table. Standing on the chair with Dingo holding it to balance me and using the scissors I had purchased for Dingo to cut his hair, I opened up the vent and placed the envelope on the metal tubing. I closed the vent back up and cautiously got down from the chair.

"There! That should keep it safe. That's all the money we have."

"Hey, I'm sure Ernie will give you more if we help in solving these murders."

"Well, I don't want to count on it. We have enough clothes for now. We can wash them at a laundromat, mine *and* yours. Since I know what you really look like in normal, clean clothes, I think you should stay that way."

"Yes, master," Dingo mockingly said as he bowed to me.

"Oh, get up! I didn't mean to be bossy, but you have to feel better since you washed all the crud off your body and put on some fresh clothes."

"I guess I really didn't care what I looked like or how I felt. But, you're right. That shower did feel invigorating. I could get used to those."

"I hope so," I jokingly told him as we left the room.

We went to a fast food restaurant close to the hospital for dinner. Then I drove back to Nawinah General, going through the main entrance and up to the front desk. I asked the receptionist behind the counter, "Could you tell me what the number of Gina Marianis room is?"

She looked in her computer. I could partially see the screen and noticed their operating system was the old fashion DOS version with the black screen and the amber type. How strange it looked! All the operating systems I have ever used were different versions of Windows. I guess in a sense, if nothing else, the experience I was having would help me appreciate the advanced technology since 1993 that I had formerly taken for granted.

After finding the room number, the receptionist asked, "Are you family members? She is only allowed family member visitors."

"No, but I have a letter from the Nawinah police chief allowing us access to her room." I took out Captain Forsythe's letter from my wallet and handed it to her.

She read the letter and looked at my photo, then looked at me to verify it was my picture. "I'm afraid I need to call my supervisor. I have never had a situation like this before."

We waited while she dialed a number on her phone.

"Mrs. Grady, could you come to the front desk please?"

We waited a few more minutes for Mrs. Grady.

From a door behind the reception area a stern faced, gray haired woman dressed in a navy blue suit came over to the desk.

"What is the problem, Amy?"

"Ma'am, these gentlemen wish to visit a patient who, according to our records, is only allowed family member visits. He has shown me this letter he says should allow their visit. I've never seen anything like this before. I didn't know how I should handle the situation."

Mrs. Grady took the letter from Amy, looked at my photo, and read the letter. "What is the purpose of your visit, gentlemen? We are under strict orders to permit only close family members to visit her?"

Dingo took over. "Mrs. Grady, we are aware the patient's room is guarded twenty-four hours a day. However, the captain of the Nawinah Police Department knows it is crucial we speak to this woman. I'm sure his phone number is on that letter if you think you need to call him directly. However, since he is probably home enjoying his dinner with his family, he may not appreciate the interruption. The purpose of that letter is specifically to give us access to Mrs. Marianis room without any hassle."

Mrs. Grady was contemplating what Dingo had said. She handed the letter back to Amy, who in turn, handed it back to me.

Then Mrs. Grady spoke with some reluctance, "Well, I suppose it's okay. Amy, give them passes. Gentlemen, you will probably need to show the guard this letter for him to let you into the room."

Dingo answered, "Ma'am, he is part of the Nawinah police force. He probably already expects our visit."

Amy gave us our passes, and we walked over to the bank of elevators and pressed the "Up" button. Getting off on the fourth level, we found our way to room 415. As expected, a uniform police officer was seated directly outside the door to Gina Marianis room. When we approached, the officer stood up and even put his hand on his revolver. "Gentlemen, this patient is not allowed visitors."

Dingo responded, "Officer, we have a letter from Captain Forsythe allowing us to speak to Mrs. Mariani."

Again, I took the letter out of my wallet and handed it to the officer, who opened and read it. "It seems to be in order. However, I can't permit you access to the room without another police officer present."

He got on his walkie-talkie and called another officer in the hospital. "Officer Merkin, please come to Room 415 immediately. It is not an emergency, but I need your assistance."

The officer gave me back Captain Forsythe's letter, and we stood awaiting Officer Merkin's arrival. He appeared ten minutes later and accompanied us into Mrs. Marianis room.

The room was dark and quiet. The patient was on a ventilator with countless other gadgets, wires, and tubes attached to her. She looked delicate and pitiful, not like the vibrant woman I first had seen at Corky's, full of life and waiting on her customers. A nurse was writing statistics on Mrs. Marianis chart. "Nurse, on behalf of the police department, we are here to talk with Mrs. Mariani. Is that a possibility?"

"I'm afraid at this time it is not. She is currently under an induced coma to help her heal. We're not sure how long that'll take. She was seriously injured. One bullet missed her heart by less than an inch. If she makes it, she'll need months of recuperation."

"Do you think I can talk to her, anyhow? I've been told sometimes comatose patients are more aware of their surroundings than we might expect."

"I see no harm in it."

I approached Gina Marianis bedside, taking her small, fragile hand into mine. Even as pale as she was, she was attractive. "Gina, my name is Tank. I'm the guy who came into Corky's a few minutes before the shooting. You remember? I told you I had been in an accident. You let me use your bathroom to wash up. When I was in the bathroom, I heard those men come in and shoot up your bar. I even got a look at them. I'm sort of not from around here, but I'm going to stick around a while and help the police find the guys who did this to you, your dad, and those others in the bar that night. I know you probably can't hear me, but I'll be back again to talk to you. You get better. I want to see you smile again."

Then I turned to the nurse. "If I give you my phone number, will you call me as soon as she is out of the coma? I've been given permission to talk to her by the Nawinah police captain."

"Do you have any documents from the captain giving you that permission?"

"Yes, I do."

"Leave your telephone number at the nurse's station. Show

them your letter of permission. They'll make a copy for our records."

"I appreciate that. Thanks."

I went back over to Gina. I took her hand again. "Gina, I'll be back. Take care."

She looked so defenseless and alone in the hospital bed. I didn't know much about her life, but I know her dad had been killed. If and when she came out of the coma, she'd have a lot to deal with. The captain had said she was married. I also wondered about her husband. Where the hell was the guy? Shouldn't he be constantly by her bedside? Maybe they still weren't able to find him, which was strange. They said he worked at Corky's too. I'm sure he would've heard about the shooting by now, wherever he was.

Dingo and I left the nurse alone to finish her chores. Officer Merkin returned to his other duties. We left the phone number and a copy of the letter at the nurse's station and went back to the motel.

It was about nine o'clock when Dingo and I were relaxing in the motel room. I was wiped out from the emotional and physical strains since my truck hit that tree. I wasn't able to concentrate. "Dingo, what do you think we can do now? I feel helpless. I don't know where to start. This stuff is all new to me. Since you've been a lawyer, you've probably had to help solve all sorts of crimes, right?"

"Yes, but look how many years ago that was, Tank. And I

never had any case even remotely like your predicament."

"I know. I know. But think about it. I don't know one single thing about living in 1993 except what I've read in history books. Where do I even start? I think the captain is placing too much faith in me. I don't know if I can live up to his expectations."

"Right now, the best thing for us, especially you, is to get a good night's sleep. Try to put everything out of your mind, the murders *and* your unique time travel experience. Tomorrow your mind will be fresh. You're a bright young man, and I'm not so stupid myself. Between the two of us, we'll find some answers. The captain wanted you to get in touch with him. You saw the faces of the gunmen. That's where we'll start. You can call the captain tomorrow, and we'll go back to the police station to look at the mug shots on file. Hopefully, you'll recognize those bastards."

"I guess you're right. I'm not thinking straight. I am really beat. I didn't sleep well last night, as you already know."

I got up from my chair, stripped to my tee shirt and boxers, and crawled into the bed. Dingo turned the TV down low. I was fast asleep within five minutes.

CHAPTER NINE
Mission Impossible

As Ma often told me, "Sometimes, Talbott, you get yourself in a pickle." If she ever finds out about this "pickle," she will definitely say, "I told you so, young man." Whether or not she could help me get out of it, presented another "pickle" in itself.

The next morning I called Captain Forsythe, but he was in a meeting. Dingo and I went to the Nawinah Police Station anyhow. The captain was still at the meeting when we arrived, but he had assigned Detective Ben Carruthers to assist us. Carruthers led us back to a file room. I sat at the metal table while he produced piles and piles of binders containing mug shots. I spent all morning looking through thousands of photos, but I didn't recognize any of the unsavory looking characters. Dingo had eventually wandered off somewhere while I was held captive by the staring images of a bunch of scumbags. At noon Captain Forsythe arrived while I was perusing my endless gallery of revolting individuals.

"Tank, let's take a break and get some lunch."

I welcomed that opportunity. My legs and back were stiff as I arose from the pain-inflicting chair, and my weary eyes were definitely ready for a break.

We went to the same coffee shop where I had waited the day before. Dingo and Detective Carruthers joined us. After we had ordered, Captain Forsythe said, "Guess you haven't had any success so far looking through those photos. Are you sure you'll be able to recognize them when you see them?"

"I'm not positive, but I'm ninety percent sure their faces were not among those I've already seen. My eyes were getting extra tired, Captain, so thanks for this break. I know there are more binders to look through. I'm ready to try again after lunch."

"Well, actually, we have a fairly good idea who those killers might be. When we get back to the station, I'll have Carruthers pull out a special binder in which I think you might find who you're looking for."

I was a bit irritated. Why did I need to wade through all those countless other binders all morning before this "special" one was given to me? "Uh, why didn't you have me start with that file in the first place?"

"I didn't want to influence your judgement in any way. However, since you seem to be fairly certain you'll recognize the men when you see them, I'm going to help you out a little. Here's the thing, Tank. When we first suspected you of the murders, I must admit, I was baffled. I couldn't figure out what your motive would've been to do such a horrible act. But then the more I got to know you while listening to you spout off your knowledge from that cell, my mind kept telling me you had no reason to kill those people. You had no money on you, so you didn't rob the place. You stuck around during the entire time the police were investigating and cleaning up the scene. You answered every question we asked, albeit we couldn't verify your answers. If you were guilty, I would think you would've taken off immediately with the gunmen. I doubt very much if they would've let you stay behind if you were part of their group. You didn't even have a vehicle in the parking lot. Also, if you were guilty, why would you even call 911 in the first place? So once I discounted you as one of the perpetrators, I tried to figure out who would have reason to kill Corky."

He stopped explaining and was staring at me. What?? Was something going on I should know about? Detective Carruthers and Dingo were staring at me too.

"What?? Why are you guys looking at me like that?"

The captain decided to enlighten me. "Tank, we're fairly certain who the gunmen are. I don't want to tell you at this time because I don't want to prejudice your judgement. However, as soon as we're done here, we'll go back to the station, and I'm a hundred percent sure you'll pick out the gunmen within an hour."

Okay. I had to accept they weren't going to tell me anything just then.

We finished our lunch with very little conversation and walked back to the police station. Detective Carruthers led me back to the file room. I sat down on the hard, metal chair while he brought out one more binder filled with more disgusting characters. He laid it in front of me without saying a word. I looked up at him before opening the binder. He nodded at me and walked to the other side of the table to sit in another torture chair with his arms crossed.

I opened the binder. Page one. Twelve images were on each page. I spent several seconds looking at each photo. Nobody familiar. Page two. Again, I studied each image. Nobody I recognized. Page three. The same. I turned the binder to page four. There they were! Staring right back at me from the middle of the page, those cruel, evil faces of the thugs who had slaughtered everyone in the bar that night. I immediately recognized their hard, threatening, unshaven faces. I jumped out of my seat and pointed directly at the two photos. "There they are! These are the guys. No doubt in my mind."

Carruthers also jumped up and quickly walked over to me. "Are you absolutely sure?"

"Yes! Yes, I am. These are the guys who I saw at Corky's. I'm positive."

Carruthers picked up the phone and called the captain. "Captain, he has made a positive identification."

Within a few minutes the room was filled with policemen, some uniformed some in plain clothes. The captain burst into the room and came over to where I was standing with the binder in front of me open to pages four and five. I didn't know what was going on. There seemed to be so much activity. What did it all mean?

"Tank, which men have you identified?" the captain asked.

I pointed to the photos in the middle of page four. "These two men are definitely the men I saw in Corky's who shot Corky Antonelli and Gina Mariani. I didn't see them shoot the other men, but I definitely saw them shoot Corky and Gina."

A lot of commotion and activity started to take place at that point. I wasn't sure what I was supposed to do. Then the captain said, "Dingo, take Tank to my office. I'll join you in a few minutes. Get him a soda or a cup of coffee. We have some discussing to do."

Bewildered, I followed Dingo out of the file room to the captain's office. "Do you want a soda or coffee, Tank?"

"I guess I'll have a soda."

I sat in the captain's office and waited for Dingo and the captain, wondering what would happen next. I identified the bad guys. What more could I do? Maybe the captain wanted me to return the money I had left and the keys to the Buick he had loaned me.

Dingo came back with sodas for him and me. We sat silently drinking the sodas and waiting for the captain.

I was getting impatient with the awkward silence. "Do you know what's going on, Dingo?"

"Yeah, I have an idea."

"Well, are you going to tell me what it is?"

"I'll let the captain explain."

Okay, now I was intrigued. Why wasn't Dingo talking? I even had the goofy idea that maybe they finally found my truck.

About fifteen minutes later the captain came striding into his office. He plopped on his seat behind his desk and expelled a big breath. "Tank, I want to thank you for that ID. You don't know how important this will be. Let me explain a little."

The captain leaned back in his chair. "For the past four or five years, the Russian mob has moved a faction of their organization into Central Florida. They are strong-arming many of the small businesses in the area: bars, restaurants, pawn shops, tattoo parlors, any place where they can get a hook. They're offering *protection* to these businesses for a price, a *big* price, even though the businesses never needed the protection in the first place. They tell the shop owners the police can't protect their businesses any longer, that it's just a matter of time before New York sends in their big guns to take over the area. Of course, the small businesses have no choice. Some of these owners are people who may have been involved in some type of illicit dealings in the past or they might be in the country illegally. They might even be new shop owners who are clueless to what the mob is doing, or they could have had some minor problems in the past with thieves or vandals. So they are ignorant or hesitant about contacting the law on their behalf. They fall right into line and start paying big bucks for that *protection*. You've seen what happens if a businessman reneges on the deal he made with the Russians. We've had several clues and leads as to who is fronting the organization in this area but have never been able to actually charge him with anything. We think something went wrong with Corky and the Russian mob. Maybe he didn't pay them what they thought he owed. Maybe he was late in paying. I don't know. Whatever, we're sure it involves the Russians.

"So this is a big break in the case. We know the two men you identified, Boris Petrov and Viktor Kozlov, are both part of the Central Florida mob. With you identifying them, we can arrest them, bring them to trial, and probably be successful in getting the death penalty for them. But as they say, we have bigger fish to fry. We would like to set our sights on the big guy, Ivan Kerchenko, the dirt bag who runs the entire organization in Central Florida. He has eluded us all these years, but I think we now have a chance to take him down. Not only is he involved in this protection extortion, but he is also the kingpin behind most of the drug and sex trafficking in this area."

The captain stopped explaining, but remained focused on me. I wasn't sure why he was telling me all this. "Well, I guess you're through with me now since you know who the gunmen are. Do you want me to stick around to ID them at their trial? As you know, I'm not sure what will happen to me. I'm not sure how long I'll be stuck in 1993. If I knew how, I'd like to get back to 2015 as soon as possible. I don't know how or why I'm here in the first place."

The captain and Dingo were both acting strangely. It was if they were not really hearing what I was saying; as if they wanted to say something but were afraid to say it. For the life of me, I couldn't figure out what the captain of the Nawinah Police Department would be hesitant about saying to me. Oh, was I ever in for a surprise!

"Tank, I believe your destiny is to help us. I know. I know. Neither you nor I, hell, nobody, knows how long you'll be around. However, I'd like to take advantage of you while I can."

"So you do want me to identify the gunmen in person?"

"Well, yes, I do want that, but I also have another agenda for you. That is, if you agree."

The captain looked over at Dingo again, so I turned to look at Dingo too.

I had finally had enough games. They had to tell me what was bugging them. "Okay, spit it out. What is going on?"

Dingo moved his chair around to face me. This must be serious.

"Tank, I've been doing a little research into your family history."

"My family history? What does my family history have to do with those killers? I can identify them. That's it." Nobody needs to know about my family. "What the hell for, Dingo?"

Dingo opened a folder he had in his hands. I hadn't even noticed it before. He pulled out the top sheet of paper. "Your great grandfather, Dmitri Telekhov and his wife Marta, emigrated from St. Petersburg, Russia, to the United States back in late 1910 when the cholera epidemic was widespread in Russia. They went through Ellis Island in New York, but soon settled in the Chicago area.

Your grandfather, Leonid Telekhov was born a year later. He too eventually married a Russian woman, Eva Aristova. Your grandfather changed the family name to Telek when he and your grandmother married and moved to Florida. Your dad, Stefan Telek, who went by Steve, married your mother, Cheryl Sawyer in 1991. Your dad's sister is named Katarina. She married an American named George Wainwright. As of today, they have no children."

"Uh, why are you telling me all this? Why is my family history any concern of yours if you know I wasn't involved in those murders? Besides, Aunt Kathy and Uncle George actually have two kids. Devin is two years younger than me, and Katlin is four years younger. Oh, that's right. They were born *after* 1993. You wouldn't know about them. So why are you giving me my family genealogy, Dingo?"

"Let me finish and Captain Forsythe will answer any of your questions."

"Okay, but I know all this anyhow. You don't need to tell me."

"Just bear with me, Tank."

And Dingo continued telling me what I already knew.

"Your dad was fluent in Russian. I understand you are fairly knowledgeable in the language also."

"I can get by. I can understand it better than I speak it. So what difference does that make? I only have to identify these Petrov and Kozlov dudes. I don't have to carry on a conversation with them."

The captain interrupted, "There's more to it than that. But let me preface what I'm about to ask you by saying that your participation in this will be purely voluntary. You will not be obligated to accept any part of it. You can merely identify these two hoods and be on your way—wherever and whenever that will be. However, we are about to ask you to step completely out of your comfort zone and help us solve this case. Since you were actually at the location when the murders were committed, we know you have a personal interest also. Plus, we think you could be a great asset to us."

I had no idea what the captain or Dingo were talking about. Why were they spouting off my family tree as if they were logged onto some internet ancestry website? I figured I'd identify these creeps and be on my way. I thought I could go back to the scene of the accident. Maybe that would help me find a way to get back to 2015. That's it. Done here. On my way.

The captain and Dingo looked at each other as if neither of them wanted to go forward with their suggestion as to how I could be such an asset to them.

After looking back and forth between both of them, I finally said, "Okay. What do you want me to do? It can't be that bad."

Dingo cautioned, "I think you'd better hear it, then decide how bad it is."

He cleared his throat. "Ahem." Then he told me their very weird idea.

"Here's what the captain has in mind. As you can imagine, Ivan Kerchenko has a large turnaround of hired help in his line of work. Two of his men were killed by FBI agents last week in a shoot-out near a bar in Apopka. Last month his right hand man drowned in a boating accident on Lake Monroe. Then a few days later two other bodies washed up on the shore near Daytona Beach. We think these last two double-crossed Kerchenko in some way, and he had other associates get rid of them. He is trying to hone the skills of his son Luka, who is somewhere around your age. But Luka isn't the brightest crayon in the box. His focus is partying and drugs. I wouldn't be surprised if his father eventually writes him off and gets rid of him too, although I doubt if that is in the near future. Kerchenko's second wife, Ludmilla, handles their personal lives. The family lives in Isleworth on a thirty-five million dollar property. Two walls actually surround the property to keep out unwanted guests. One is around the entire land owned by Kerchenko. The other surrounds the main resident and most of the other structures."

"Wait a minute," I quickly cut in. "I think I remember my dad talking about him. I was young at the time, maybe eight or nine. When he would drive us to Fantasy Empire, he'd point out the area where this rich Russian mobster used to live. I bet he was talking about Kerchenko. He never went into detail about him, or maybe I was too young to remember or care. I don't know. But, yeah, I think I remember some stuff about him."

The captain asked, "So you don't remember what happened to

him? Was he still around in 2015?"

I thought about the question. "No, I don't think so. In 2015 I was reading current events in newspapers and online. I would've been aware if he still was wreaking havoc in the area."

The captain asked, "You don't remember what your dad said about him when you were a boy? Was he still living in the house then?"

I wrinkled the side of my face and looked up toward the ceiling, trying to remember those conversations in the car with Dad. "No, I think some real estate mogul had bought the house and remodeled it by then. I remember Dad describing the two separate walls on the property. So, no, he was gone by the time I was, let's say at least nine, which would be in 2001 or 2002. Although, as I mentioned in the jail cell, the 9-11 event occurred in 2001. The devastation of that event overshadowed anything else for months. We didn't even go to Fantasy Empire during those times. So I doubt if much focus would've been on Kerchenko even if he were still around."

Dingo and the captain let that information sink in. Maybe Kerchenko had disappeared from the area by 2001 or 2002. I guess that was a good sign. Maybe whatever the captain was planning would be successful. I waited for them to tell me how I entered into their scheme of things.

"So what do you want me to do? If you want me to be a Russian interpreter, I'm a little rusty with the language."

Dingo looked straight into my eyes. "We want you to infiltrate

Kerchenko's organization."

I wouldn't have been more surprised if he had told me he wanted me to take a spaceship to the moon or to repaint the Sistine Chapel. My lower jaw must have dropped far enough to land on my chest. "You're kidding, right?" I even snickered at his joke.

The captain spoke very seriously, "No, Tank, we are not kidding. With your background, your command of the Russian language, and your uncanny memory, we think you'd be an excellent candidate for this. Like I told you when we started out, you *can* refuse. You're under no obligation to accept this assignment. However, if you do agree to the job, we'd train you in the areas where you are weak or lacking, and we'd take every precaution to keep you safe."

I was speechless. They were serious. Think about it. Here I was twenty-two years from where I should be, unable to come to grips with that predicament itself. Now they wanted me to be a guinea pig for them. It was so ridiculous I actually laughed out loud. Then I looked around the room. No one else was laughing. Their faces were focused on me, waiting for me to speak. I had to find out more about their ridiculous plan.

"Tell me how it would be possible. First of all, this Kerchenko dude knows nothing about me. How could I even get into his organization? And if I did, how in hell could you ever protect me? I can't wear a wire of any kind. I'm sure the first time he meets me, he'll immediately check me for a wire, probably *every* time he meets me. This is a very bad idea."

The captain argued, "We know this won't be easy, and it isn't a sure thing. Most of all, there's a hell of a lot of danger involved and a hell of a lot left up to your instincts. But we know you're the right man for the job."

I stared at him, shaking my head. "I'm glad you're so confident. You can be. You won't be going into that lion pit. *I* will."

"I know, Tank. You'd be taking a huge risk. I can't tell you it won't be dangerous. You know that already. But we need you here, son. Kerchenko won't believe any of our undercover detectives. He's too smart for that. But you? You'd fit right in with his organization."

I quickly objected. "What do you mean? I act like a criminal or something?"

"No, I didn't mean that at all," the captain swiftly refuted. "I mean, first of all, you're a very intelligent and astute young man."

I interjected, "Don't give me that crap! There are any number of 'intelligent and astute young men' around here?"

"You're right. I'm not trying to patronize you. There *are* a lot, but you're different. You have a unique ability to remember facts and events. I have no one who has any ability remotely like that. It's a gift, and I want you to use it. Sure, it's for a selfish reason, but don't you want us to solve these murders?"

"Why should it be your concern if I use my 'gift', as you put it? I think that's my business, not yours."

The captain wasn't giving up on me yet. "Yes, it's your

business. But think of Gina Mariani and the families of all those men who were in the bar that night. Don't they deserve some answers? Some retribution? So it's not just for me or the Nawinah Police Department. It's for them also; so they can be satisfied we have done our due diligence in finding and convicting those responsible for the deaths of their loved ones."

"Now you're trying to lay a guilt trip on me. What else do you have up your sleeve?" I was getting irritated with the entire conversation.

I sensed the captain was exasperated too. He fell back against his desk chair. "Okay, Tank. How about if we give it a rest until tomorrow? Spend the remainder of the day however you want, but think about it. Think about what it would mean. Come in here tomorrow and give me your answer. Whatever it is, I'll accept it without any discussion, argument, or pleading. What do you say? Do we have a deal?"

I looked first at him, then at Dingo. I clasped my hands together and lowered my forehead onto them. After a few seconds, I looked up. "It's a deal."

CHAPTER TEN
Beauty And The Beast

Dingo and I left the police station with neither of us speaking. We got into the Buick, and I drove back to the Garden Motel. In the room Dingo switched on the TV, then lay back in his bed. I couldn't sit down. I paced back and forth in front of the TV, tossing the captain's stupid idea around in my head.

Finally, I said to Dingo, "I'm going for a walk."

As I was opening the motel door, Dingo asked, "Do you want me to come with you?"

"Definitely not," I practically yelled. "I need to be by myself and think about this scheme you and the captain have laid on me."

The motel sat back several yards from the main highway. I walked toward the street, then turned right toward Orlando. I had no destination. I just needed to think and clear my mind of all thoughts, my strange situation, and the captain's outrageous request. However, my surreal surroundings were hampering my thought process. I knew this highway. I would drive down it probably every other day of my adult life. But now it was so weird.

Most of the stores, restaurants, and shops were different from the way I remembered them. Vacant lots gapped before me where gas stations or restaurants should be. Plus, the vehicles traveling up and down the highway looked like a blast-from-the-past, massive car show, seeing nothing newer than the 1993 models. Even the outfits of people I saw as I walked seemed so strange and out of place. How could I think while I was being bombarded by this creepiness? I had to get away from all of it. Where could I go?

When I approached a fast food restaurant, I went in and purchased a large cup of coffee, then went back to the motel to sit in the Buick. While in the driver's seat, I closed my eyes and leaned back on the headrest. I was in an impossible set of circumstances. Time travel? How absurd! Russian mob? Undercover infiltration? How did this happen?

I couldn't sit there any longer. It wasn't helping. Not realizing it, I started up the Buick and pulled out of the motel parking lot. Turning onto the highway, I headed toward Nawinah Hospital. I hadn't received any phone calls but I'd see if there was any change in Gina Marianis condition.

The same girl was at the reception desk as the day before. She remembered me and gave me a pass without any questions. I took the elevator to the fourth floor. A different officer was on duty outside Mrs. Marianis room. I showed him my letter from Captain Forsythe, and he immediately gave me access to the room without calling for another officer.

Inside her room, the drapes were drawn. The sun peaked

through the very edges where the drapes didn't cover the windows completely, casting streaks of light across the floor and the bottom of her bed. No one was in the room, and she was still sleeping. The ventilator wheezed in and out as she breathed. I pulled the upholstered chair closer to the left side of her bed and sat down.

Staring at her still, silent face, I realized again how beautiful this woman was. Her deep brown hair billowed out against the pillows in shiny ringlets. Her skin looked like heavily creamed coffee without as much as a freckle or flaw. The blanket was pulled over her chest, but her arms lay straight down by her side outside of it. IV needles were inserted in her right wrist, and constant, slow drips of fluids crept down the long, plastic tubes attached to the needles and flowed into her veins. Hopefully, all this equipment was not just keeping her alive but was actually healing her, making her whole again.

I looked at her left hand, laying on top of the blanket. It seemed so tiny and fragile. With my clumsy hands, I awkwardly, but gently took the small hand into mine. It was as soft as a kitten's fur. The nails were perfectly manicured and painted with muted peach nail polish. All thoughts of my unusual predicament temporarily left my brain. I could only stare at this beautiful woman while I held her hand.

Finally, I was shaken out of my reverie with the sound of the door opening. I quickly replaced her hand on the bed as a nurse entered the room.

"Oh, I'm sorry! I didn't know she had a visitor," the startled nurse spoke as she saw me in the chair. Then she walked to the IV bottles and started changing out the fluids.

"How is she doing? Is there any change?"

"No, there isn't. She's still in the coma. You must be the gentleman who had been given permission to see Mrs. Mariani. Otherwise, I guess the officer wouldn't have allowed you in the room."

"Yes. I'm Tank Telek."

The nurse took care of whatever duties she had to do. I had to leave the room while she changed the bedding. I waited down the hall in the visitors' room drinking my coffee and remembering the soft touch of Gina's hand. After finishing the coffee, I went back to Gina's room and asked the officer if the nurse was done. With his positive reply, I went back in the room and returned to the chair.

She was lying in the same position with the blanket over her chest and her arms by her side. I could smell the faint odor of bleach as I reached down to take her hand in mine again. Instantly, I thought I felt a slight movement in her hand. I sat perfectly still, waiting to see if I would feel it again.

No. It must have been some kind of reflex reaction.

So I sat there, holding her hand, staring at her face. She was mesmerizing. Why hadn't I noticed that before? The first time I saw her behind the bar at Corky's so lively and active, I knew she was pretty. But now, looking at her lying on the bed next to me, she was absolutely gorgeous.

A strange feeling came over me. What's wrong with me? This

is a married woman. I shouldn't even be holding her hand. Where is her husband anyway? Surely he knew about the shootings. I'm sure it was on TV, probably all the national networks as well as local stations. The radio and newspapers too. He couldn't have missed it. So why wasn't he here by her side? He should be in this chair instead of me.

I had to get her out of my head and start thinking about the dilemma Captain Forsythe had forced me to consider. I gently put her hand down and pushed my chair back. I went over to the window and moved the drape aside enough to look out.

Below I saw the traffic on the highway, people traveling here and there with definite destinations. Again, I thought of my current situation: stuck somewhere in limbo in the year I was born. I wished I could go to sleep and wake up in my own bed, in my own room, in my old life. I didn't want to be involved in all this stupid time travel stuff, these murders, or this Russian business any longer. I wanted my boring existence back. I kept staring out the window, feeling sorry for myself.

Then I began to actually think about that life I had in 2015. What life did I want back? I had a nothing job anybody with half a brain could do. Cleaning up other people's garbage. Some job. I made next to nothing for that job. I'm overweight and lazy. When I wasn't working at that nothing job, I crashed on the couch all day or hung out with other nobody's like myself. My own mother doesn't respect me, and rightly so. I think it's time I did something to get off my fat ass. Here is my opportunity, dumb jerk. Here is the chance for me to do something worthwhile with my life. Something unselfish for a change. Who else would ever get a chance like I have? *Probably nobody.* So what am I going to do about it?

I turned around, let the drape close, and looked at the beautiful woman in the bed. Captain Forsythe was correct. She does have the right to know who put her here, who killed her father, and essentially, who ruined her life. I have a chance to make that happen. At one time I had wanted to enlist in the Army, but I was too overweight. They refused to take me. Back then, I thought I could do something to show my life wasn't useless. But I didn't even try to lose the weight: I simply gave up. Well, here is my chance again. It may be even riskier than hand to hand combat with a foreign enemy, but I won't know until I try it.

I walked to Gina Marianis bedside and took her hand again. "Gina, I don't know if I will ever get to know you. If not, I'm sorry I didn't have that opportunity. But I'm going to do everything possible to find out why they did this to you and to make them pay."

Then without even thinking, I lowered my lips and gently kissed her forehead.

CHAPTER ELEVEN
Acquiescing And Accepting

Never in my wildest dreams would I have ever imagined myself in this situation. When I was a kid, my buddies and I wanted to be superheroes and save the world from all the bad guys. I'd pretend I was "Tankman." I'd ride around in a gigantic, army tank that could travel on land, air, and water to search and destroy the villains. If I didn't crush them under the tracks of my tank, I had such super strength in my arms and legs capable of pulverizing them with one punch or kick. Boys. The games we'd play. I don't have any of those imaginary super powers, but maybe somehow I could use the God-given talents I do have to help catch these real life bad guys.

When I got back to the motel, Dingo was napping with the TV still on. Some soap opera was just ending. The clock on the bedside table showed it was almost three-thirty. I didn't want to wake him. Like he had said, he has not had the opportunity to sleep on such a bed in a long time. I laid on my back on my bed, folding my arms behind my head. Even though I really didn't know what I was getting myself into, I actually felt more content than I had since this fiasco began. I looked at Dingo while he lay there on his side with his belly overlapping his underwear. His mouth was wide open, and he was snoring, not loudly, just steadily. Spittle dribbled from his mouth. I thought of how his life had changed since I met him in that cell. He had a purpose now. The captain even had faith in him. So maybe my being back in 1993 would positively affect many lives. Whatever the outcome, I decided I was in it until the end, whenever and wherever that would lead me.

As I stared at Dingo with the TV changing programs to a *Who's the Boss* rerun, he started to wake up. The snoring turned to wiggles, grunts, groans and farts. Soon he opened his eyes and stared back at me. "What the hell are you looking at?"

I smiled and snickered. "I was just watching you sleep."

"Why? Am I some kind of freak show or something? Pervert."

I decided not to go into his sleeping habits any further. "No, not at all. I just got back. I've made my decision about Captain Forsythe's proposition."

"Yeah, yeah. I knew you wouldn't do it? Young kid like you. Why would you want to risk your life?"

"Actually, I am going to do it. I've been a slacker all my life, and you guys showed me I'm better than that. I don't know how this will turn out, but I'm willing to give it my best."

Dingo sat straight up in the bed and loudly yelled, "What the hell!"

I called the police station to make an appointment with the

captain for the morning. The front desk said he'd pencil me in for nine o'clock.

Dingo and I went to some country style restaurant for dinner. He told me more about Viet Nam, his return to the United States, and, eventually, to his life on the streets. He had led a very interesting, but sad life. I was so pleased to see him now cleaned up and with a purpose. It was all good.

After leaving the restaurant, we bought a six pack of beer and went back to the motel to await our morning appointment with the captain.

****

We were waiting in the captain's office when he strode in like he usually did, bounding behind his desk to his chair.

"Well, Tank, what is your decision. As I told you, I'll accept it no matter what it is." He looked at me, anticipating my response.

I blurted it out without mincing words. "I'll do it."

Surprised, he sat up straight at his desk. "You will?"

'Yes. I thought about it long and hard. Whether you know it or not, my life has sucked since my dad died. My poor mom had been carrying all the weight with me just hanging on to her. I figure no matter how this turns out, at least I can say I tried to make her proud of me."

"Well, Tank, you have pleasantly surprised me. And I want to thank you for your decision. Uh, I actually thought you would say no, so I've been remiss in setting up your training. I'll call Caruthers in here to show you around the police station. That'll give you a feel for our equipment and what we do. I'm sure it won't be as advanced as the technology you are used to, but it's what we have to work with. Do you know how to use a gun?"

"Yeah, sort of. My dad and I used to go target practicing at this range, but I never went hunting. So I've never shot anything living. I'm not sure I could, like a deer or a rabbit—or a man."

"Well then, that's one area where you'll need some work. Believe me. You won't be dealing with innocent deer or rabbits. If your life depended on it, I know you will have what it takes to shoot.

"Dingo, you should probably hone your skills a little. It's been a long time since you held a gun in your hand too.

"You'll need some different clothes, Tank. Those Carneys specials are okay for hanging out at the motel, but Kerchenko will not be impressed by them. I'll give you money to work on a new wardrobe."

I was a little bewildered. "How do you want me to dress?"

"I'll let Caruthers take care of deciding your attire. He has an eye for fashion, if you haven't already noticed."

Now that the captain had mentioned it, I did recall Caruthers was a sharp dresser for a police detective with tailored suits and Italian shoes.

He gave further instructions. "Caruthers also knows more about the Russian mob in Central Florida than anyone else in the department. He can fill you in on what you'll need to know about them."

I was still not quite clear how we'd pull this off. "So, Captain, how will I penetrate the organization?"

The captain sat back and relaxed in his chair. "We'll set you up with a false ID and a false criminal record. Dingo will also be given a new ID. Corky's Bar will be reopened as soon as it is remodeled. The process has already been started. We are creating a different atmosphere in there. We know we'll get thrill seekers wanting to actually see the place where so many people were murdered, but we want it to be a working bar. Eventually, it'll gain its own regular clientele. Dingo will be undercover as Carl Antonellis brother from Cleveland, Dominic Antonelli, who has come to restore the business and help out his niece. A couple of our undercover detectives will assist him and work at the bar too."

I looked at Dingo. "Did you know about this, Dingo?"

He gave an affirmative head shake. I guess he was okay with that plan.

The captain continued. "After we get you trained and ready, you'll start hanging out at the bar. I don't think it'll be too long before Kerchenko begins to harass and threaten Dingo to pay for protection. Then it'll be up to you to impress his men enough so they will want to introduce you to Kerchenko himself. We know this is a long shot, but I think it'll work. However, you'll have to really submerge yourself into your character. You'll have to make it believable, or you and Dingo both will be in trouble. I don't want that to happen. Do you?"

"Uh, no, sir!"

"We'll train you for a couple of months. By that time the bar should be remodeled and already open for business. If you need more time, tell Caruthers. You'll be in his hands for the duration. Once you're ready and you step into character, Dingo will be your contact until you establish yourself with the Russians. You can't come near the police station after that. Hopefully, it won't be too long after your character change for you to get the Russians to accept you. Once that is done, you'll need to cut all ties with Dingo also. We'll then set you up with a new contact.

"How does all this sound to you, Tank?"

"It sounds feasible but worrisome. I just hope I can get it to work."

"I've gone over all this in advance with Dingo, hoping you'd agree. Do you have any questions?"

I thought about yesterday afternoon and how my visit to the hospital had actually helped me make my decision. "Well, I was wondering about Gina Mariani. Do we know anything more about her prognosis? How about her husband? Has he been found yet?"

The captain looked down at his desk, then back up at me.

"Yes. Vince Mariani has been found."

"Why didn't I see him at the hospital yesterday? He should be by his wife's side."

"He was found in his car in the Ocala forest with a bullet in his head."

Wow! I didn't see that coming. This Kerchenko was really a bad dude. "Uh, do you know anything about his murder?"

"We know he was shot with a Russian PSS silent pistol. That may give you an idea who we're dealing with here. We also determined he was supposed to deliver Corky's protection money to the mob. It appears he hadn't been doing so for several weeks. He was on his way out of the state with the money Corky had given him for the mob when we assume some of Kerchenko's men caught up with him."

Poor Gina Mariani. Her father and her husband brutally murdered. Maybe she'll recover. Maybe not. I looked down at the floor and shook my head.

The captain ended the silence. "I'm sorry to bring you such bad news. I hope this hasn't changed your mind. Do you have any more questions?"

"No, it hasn't changed my mind. If anything, it has given me more resolve. I can do this. I know."

"Well if that's all, I'll turn you over to Caruthers to start your training and indoctrination. He's a strict disciplinarian. Believe me, you might be happy to be free of him and join the Russians when he gets through with you. Good luck, men."

Dingo and I rose from our seats and walked to the door of the office. As I was opening it, the captain called out, "Oh, one more thing. Gina Mariani is four months pregnant."

CHAPTER TWELVE
Fat Boy Transformation

The training and weight loss was grueling and took four months instead of just a couple. I was in pretty bad shape. Since my high school football days, I had done nothing to keep physically fit—unless you consider lifting garbage cans at Fantasy Empire as a workout. I was overweight; I ate greasy, fatty, starchy food; I loafed in front of the TV for hours; and I had no incentive to do anything with my life. Caruthers really had a challenge. He worked my ass off from six in the morning until eight at night. Then I was so tired I crashed until the next morning. I actually roomed with him in his condo so he could monitor my every move and every bite of food I ate. I was under his supervision twenty-four seven. He said I'd get sick of seeing his face. He definitely was right about that. I must've cursed him out at least twenty times a day. Of course, it didn't bother him in the least. He'd often smile and say, "Tank, there will come a day when you'll get down on your knees and thank me for this."

"No way!" I'd bellow as I called him every fowl name under the sun. During those four months, it was impossible for me to even consider that any good would come from all this torture. "Hell, no! Never!"

Gradually, I realized he was absolutely right. I started losing weight right away. As far as the diet he forced on me, I learned I actually could live without the starch and grease I had been accustomed to eating regularly for too many years. Caruthers was an excellent cook. He made broccoli and cauliflower, which I detested, even taste palatable. I ate a lot of skinless chicken and fish served in so many different ways with various kinds of seasonings. They didn't taste terribly awful either. As for the beer, well, I never found a great substitute, but I did find a healthy alternative in sparkling, fruit flavored water. I had a can in my hand almost all the time.

Captain Forsythe also hired a teacher to help me brush up on my Russian. Once I started with Olga Bakova, I was actually surprised how much I still remembered from my younger days. I was able to master the language sufficiently within the first three weeks. Olga congratulated me on my ability to pick up the language so well and so quickly. I secretly thanked my grandpa for being such an excellent teacher.

Caruthers changed my wardrobe drastically. At home in 2015 when I didn't have to wear my Fantasy Empire uniform, I'd hang out in baggy blue jeans worn below my big gut and tee shirts usually with a sport team logo on them. If the weather was hot, I'd wear cargo shorts with my belly overlapping at the waist. That type of apparel was gone from my new wardrobe. Black. That was my new color. Black jeans. Black tee shirts with white heavy metal band logos stenciled or embroidered on the front of them. I also had a couple of studded belts that were dangerous if my arm hit them too suddenly. Caruthers also decided a black leather jacket was a necessity to the wardrobe. On my feet I wore combat boots. They were actually quite comfortable once I broke them in. Probably the hardest thing to get used to was the chain wallet Caruthers told me I needed.

In April when I was thrown back to 1993, my sandy colored hair was fairly short. Fantasy Empire rules wouldn't have it any other way. Caruthers made me grow it long. I had never worn it long before. During high school the coach also suggested we keep it short. He said it was much more comfortable under the football helmets. I was surprised the longer hair had a nice wave to it so I could push it behind my ears. Caruthers said I had to let it grow even longer.

The tattoos that Caruthers forced me to get were the most disturbing part of my new look. I had a fancy skull on my right arm and an intricate snake on my left. On my back, left shoulder I had one of an eye in the middle of a sword dripping blood. Hell if I knew what any of them meant. My main concern was what would happen to them if and when I ever got back to 2015. I knew I wouldn't be able to work for Fantasy Empire with these things showing. Caruthers said they weren't exactly permanent and would fade away in time. However, he said it may take a year or so before they would be gone completely. Oh, well, I couldn't worry about how they might affect my employment in 2015 because I was then living from day to day, not expecting or anticipating anything. Life was so uncertain for me that I didn't know if I would suddenly be dashed to 2015 without warning. Plus, if by chance the Russians accepted me into their fold, would I even get out alive?

So after the four months of exhaustive training and starvation, I was in good enough shape to pass Caruthers and Captain Forsythe's inspection. When I started the program, I weighed three hundred ten pounds. At the end of the training, I was down to two hundred thirty five and still losing. That's an average of almost six pounds a week. I never thought I could do it. Thanks to Caruthers, I accomplished it, even though I didn't appreciate him at the time. I'm actually very muscular now. If I must say so myself, my tattoos look great on my upper arms.

Caruthers set me up in a cheap furnished studio apartment on the east side of Nawinah. He told me they also set Dingo up in a pad on the other side of town close to where Carl Antonellis widow lived. Caruthers also told me Corky's Bar reopened after three months, and Dingo was able to establish himself as Dominic Antonelli, Corky's brother. The bar had been running smoothly and was beginning to pick up a regular client base. Most of the staff consisted of undercover police personnel. Surprisingly, the place hadn't had any visits from the Russians thus far. The captain had expected them to approach Dingo as soon as it had opened.

As for Gina Mariani, she finally came out of her coma about a week into my training. Thankfully, they said she didn't lose her baby. Gina stayed in the hospital for another couple of weeks then was released. Apparently, she didn't remember much of what happened at Corky's that terrible night. She didn't remember the Russian guys coming into the bar or the shooting. She didn't even remember me. That doesn't matter to me anymore since Captain Forsythe finally believed my farfetched story of what happened. I guess finding out both her dad and husband were dead really affected Gina. I hadn't seen her or Dingo since I started the training. Maybe it was a good thing she didn't remember me either. Maybe Captain Forsythe didn't want her to know who I was when I started hanging out at the bar trying to get accepted by the Russians. I looked different with my weight loss and other changes, so she probably wouldn't have recognize me anyway.

I moved into my new place and had begun to establish my new identity. I had to memorize my new life history. At first they were planning to have me use my real name. Then they had second thoughts. Since in actuality, I was just recently "born" in 1993, they didn't want to cause any danger to my mom and dad.

My new name became Maxim Gorelov, nickname Max. My parents were Leonid and Maya Gorelov, first generation immigrants. I was born and raised in Highland Park, a Northshore suburb of Chicago. The captain picked this community because it had an almost sixteen percent Russian population. My parents still lived there. I graduated from Highland Park High School in June of 1989 and went to work for a manufacturing company on the north side of Chicago. Since graduation I had been in and out of jail for petty crimes, like drug possession, stealing cars, and fighting. I moved to Nawinah in June of 1993 because my dad wanted me to get a fresh start where nobody knew me. My dad's brother, Nikolay Gorelov, Uncle Nick, and Aunt Inga lived in a small bungalow on Porter Avenue. Caruthers told me they had lived at that address for several years, and those were their real names. They were to be my new contact with Captain Forsythe when it was no longer safe to talk to Dingo at Corky's.

Caruthers also got me a job in a wholesale food warehouse near Nawinah where I loaded and unloaded trucks. I guess given enough time the police can do just about anything. Then all I had to do was develop the cocky attitude of a criminal.

****

My first day at Stanton Food Distributors was on a Wednesday. The day went well. The work of unloading and loading boxes was easy enough for me with the physical training Caruthers had made me suffer through. I didn't act too friendly with my co-workers. I wanted to present a surly, tough guy image even at work. In addition, with my situation, I wasn't going to have a lot of time for friendships.

I worked through Friday, and then decided to make my first stop at Corky's Bar since the shootings. It was time to get started on my assignment. I still had the Buick loaned to me by Captain Forsythe, so I didn't have to worry about transportation. I went back to my apartment, showered, and changed into my all black, badass uniform before driving to the bar. I parked in the parking lot, which had been repaved since my last visit. Grabbing onto the steering wheel and taking a deep breath, I psyched myself into character. This was big. I *had* to act the part. "You can do this, Tank. No, you can do this, *Max*. You are a badass Russian dude. You are tough. You are the *MAN*!" My life and probably the life of others depended on my pulling off this act.

When I felt I was ready, I got out of the Buick, stood up tall and swaggered to the entrance of the bar. The front door had been replaced as well as a new neon sign, still reading "Corky's Bar & Grill." Opening the door, I walked in and stood still, looking around the room. It was very different from that fatal night. The bar was made of high polished walnut. The heavy plastic bar stools in front of the bar were a complimenting brown tone. Booths and small Formica tables were scattered throughout the space. The walls were painted a light beige with beer, whiskey, and heavy metal band posters and photos strategically placed around the room. Probably a dozen or so patrons were in the place, most of them dressed similar to me. A couple of women were included in the mix with their long, poofed hair, black leather skirts, and heavy makeup. The thick, and distorted sound of intense heavy metal electric guitars was playing in the background.

My eyes drifted to the short hallway where I had stood on the night of the murders while police and paramedics bustled about the room. For just a moment, I was a bit dizzy, remembering the horrid scene. But then I stood up straight with my legs spread, head held high, chin jutted out, and began to strut to the bar.

I took a seat midway at the bar with no occupied seats on either side. The bartender, who I didn't recognize, came up to me. He had on a black tee shirt with the word "Corky's" stenciled on it. He said in a friendly enough voice, "What'll it be, man?"

"Gimme a shot of Jack Daniels and a cold beer."

"What kind of beer?"

"Make it a Bud."

He went back and got my drinks and placed them in front of me. Neither of us said another word. I gulped down the shot, and then slowly started sipping my Bud as I turned sideways on my stool to look around the room.

Most of the patrons were talking to their friends. A couple were singing along with the thick vocals coming through the speakers. I figured my first time here I didn't want to call too much attention to myself. When I finished my Bud, I ordered another. The place was beginning to get more crowded. A couple of guys sat down on the stools to my right. I nodded at them, and they returned with similar gestures. I didn't speak, just continued to sip my second beer while trying to hone in on the two dudes' conversation. They seemed to be eyeing up the hot chicks in the place and making comments to each other about them. I finished my beer, paid the bartender, and sauntered out of the bar as if I owned the place.

So that was it for my first visit to the renovated Corky's. Come the following Monday I went back again, trying to keep the same persona. Tuesday, Wednesday, Thursday, and Friday I did the same. By then the bartender was conversing a little with me. When I told him my name was Max Gorelov, I noticed a glimpse of recognition in his eyes. He must've been one of Captain Forsythe's men. Of course, I wasn't going to show my hand to him. No reason to. If he really was the captain's man, he'd know why I was there and wouldn't blow my cover.

It was the Saturday of the following week when things started to happen. I arrived at the bar about eight-thirty. The place was hopping by then. Dingo, aka Dominic, was bartending along with Donnie, the regular guy. When I sat down at the one open bar stool, I realized Dingo had noticed me. However, he hadn't seen me since I had lost weight and let my hair grow, so I could tell he was a little surprised at my appearance. He came over to serve me and asked, "What'll you have?"

I responded with my usual. "Give me a shot of Jack and a Bud."

He brought me my drinks and then went off to help other customers, not saying anything else or giving me any weird looks.

Since it was Saturday night, I planned to hang out a little longer than on the week nights. However, I was concerned about my alcohol intake. I didn't want to get the least bit drunk. As it turned out, I didn't have to worry. When I asked for my second round of drinks, my Jack Daniels was a Coke and my beer was a ginger ale. Problem solved.

So I continued to order my drinks and sip my "beer" for several hours, just hanging out, talking occasionally to some of the other regular guys. I didn't exchange any personal information, simply talked about the music, sports, or the fine chicks in the place.

About ten-thirty two guys walked into the bar and Dingo gave me an odd, knowing look. I nonchalantly turned around to look at them. My heart skipped a beat! They were the two Russian gunmen who had shot up the bar that night. I nearly pissed my pants! I had to act cool. I turned back to face the bar and continued to sip my mock beer.

No vacant stools were left at the bar, but these two dudes went up behind two guys seated about three stools down from me. The Russian dudes tapped the seated guys on their shoulders. When the guys on the seats turned around, the two Russians indicated with their thumbs to get off the stools. I was wondering how the guys on the stools were going to react, but they got up and walked away, not even looking back at the Russians. The two gunmen then sat down. Dingo went over to them. I heard him ask them what they wanted to drink. The tall Russian said, "Stoli". When Dingo went back to get the drinks, he quickly glanced my way. I nodded my head as he took the drinks to the gunmen.

As Dingo placed their drinks on the bar, I heard the taller gunman closest to me ask in his Russian accent, "You, Dominic Antonelli?"

Dingo stepped back slightly from the bar. "Who's askin'?"

"We need to talk."

"What do you want to talk about? Make it quick. We're kind

of busy here."

"We need to talk privately, *now!*" The Russian's voice tone sounded threatening.

"That's not gonna happen. I'm too busy right now. Come back later."

So this was my dilemma. I had to get these gunmen's attention away from Dingo and focused on me. I knew what their private conversation was going to be. So did Dingo.

Donnie had just given me another fake Jack Daniels. I had a plan. I quickly bolted off the stool, slammed the drink on the table, actually spilling it on the guy next to me, and yelled very loudly at Donnie. "Damn it! I said I wanted a vodka! What is this shit?" Then I cussed at him in Russian.

Donnie was taken aback by my outburst, but immediately, I knew he realized what I was doing. "Sorry, man! My bad."

I had the attention of most everyone in the bar, including the Russians. I took a twenty out of my wallet, threw it at Donnie, and walked out of the bar. I felt all eyes on me as I trotted briskly out of the place.

Once outside I stepped a few yards away from the door and took out a cigarette. I'm not a smoker. I hate the things, but while training with Caruthers, we both thought it might be a good idea for me to take up the habit, giving me more of a tough guy image.

As I was lighting up, out of the corner of my eye, I saw the Russians come out of Corky's. I pretended not to notice them and kept puffing on the cigarette, looking into space. I was hoping I looked relaxed instead of as freaking nervous as I actually was. The two dudes came over to me. The tall one asked me for a cigarette in Russian. Without replying, I took out my pack of Marlboros, slapped the pack so a couple of cigarettes appeared, and offered one to each of them. After putting the pack back in my jacket, I offered him a light and continued to puff on my cigarette while looking straight ahead. The two Russians stood beside me doing the same. For a couple of minutes, no conversation took place. I was definitely having a difficult time controlling my nerves and acting casual.

When I was done with the cigarette, I tossed it on the ground, stepping on it to put out the embers. Then as casual as I possibly could act, I said in Russian, "See you."

As I began to walk away, the shorter dude grabbed my left arm. In my head, I quickly had to decide how to respond. With my right hand I forcefully whacked the guy's arm, saying in English, "Hey, get your freaking hands off me!"

The shorter guy quickly removed his hand while the taller guy came in front of me about a foot from my face. I was completely terrified, but I knew I couldn't show it. "Look, I don't want no trouble. What's your problem?"

In a non-threatening manner, the tall dude said, "We see you in the bar. We like way you handle yourself. We like to talk to you about job."

In my toughest voice, I replied, "No thanks. I already have a job."

"I bet this job you have won't make money like job we have for you."

So I hesitated and pretended to be interested. Well, I guess I was interested. Why else would I be in this situation? "How much money are you talking about?"

"Big money."

I nodded my head, sticking my chin out. "I'm interested."

"Let us go back in bar. We talk."

"Alright. We can do that." I kept using my rough voice.

The tall one led us back into Corky's. He walked over to an occupied booth in the far corner of the room. Two guys and a chick were already seated at the booth. When we approached, the tall Russian dude said to them, "Out!" They immediately halted their conversation and looked up at us. One of the men snickered, "Who says so?"

The Russian dude grabbed the guy's shirt under his neck and twisted it. "I do."

Immediately, the three vacated the seats and quickly walked away, looking back at us several times. The tall Russian sat on one side. The shorter guy motioned me to get on the other side. He sat next to me.

After we were seated, the tall one signaled for Donnie, who had been observing our entrance. Donnie came over directly. "What can I get you gentlemen?"

The tall one ordered three Stolis. Donnie walked away, and no one spoke until he brought our drinks to us. I was hoping my drink was either watered down or substituted with something non-alcoholic. I watched as Donnie placed them on the table, being specific about who got which drink. We each took a sip of our drinks. Mine was *not* Stoli.

Then the tall one began to talk in Russian. I figured he didn't want any eavesdroppers to know what we were discussing. "Your name?"

"Max. Max Gorelov,"

"Where you from?"

"I moved here from Highland Heights outside Chicago a couple of months ago. Where are you guys from?" I also spoke in Russian.

The tall guy had a smirk on his face. He looked at the shorter dude, then back to me. "I ask questions first. Then you get chance. Where you work now?"

"Stanton Food Distributors."

"You quit tomorrow."

I quickly leaned back in my seat, gave him an intrusive look, and laughed. "No way! Not until you tell me about this job you have for me."

"Ha, ha," he also laughed. "You a bold son o bitch, aren't you? You see how we be treated in here? You see how everybody afraid of us? Why you not afraid?"

Did he think I wasn't afraid? I was petrified! But I knew I had to pull this off. That's why I was in this situation. Believe me. I had practiced and practiced how I'd react at such a meeting like this. I was prepared to disguise that fear with brashness. So I lowered my body, put my elbows on the table, and put my hands on my cheeks with my chin jutted forward. I used a deep, gravelly voice. "Listen, dude, *you* should be afraid of *me*!"

He laughed even harder. Then he got serious and brought his face just inches from mine. I was having extreme difficulty controlling my terror. He said very seriously, "You don't know who you are talking to, Max Gorelov."

He stayed in my face for several seconds before he straightened up with a grim smile on his face.

I also sat back in my seat, staring at him for several seconds and keeping my face as blank as possible. "Well, tell me who you are so I know who I'm talking to and who I'm supposed to be afraid of."

He puckered his lips, put his elbows on the table and folded his hands together. "Mr. Gorelov, have you heard of Ivan Kerchenko?"

I looked at him with a mock puzzled expression. "No, I don't think I have. Is he some sort of celebrity or something?"

The short guy next to me chuckled at my answer. "You could call him that."

I was beginning to wander if the short guy could even speak. That was the first thing he'd said since I first encountered these dudes.

The tall guy resumed the conversation. "I will introduce us to you. I am Boris and my friend is Viktor. We work for Mr.

Kerchenko. He is entrepreneur looking for reliable assistant. We like how you handle yourself at bar earlier this evening. I think Mr. Kerchenko would be interested in talking to you about position with his organization."

"That asshole gave me the wrong drink!" I said with conviction because I wanted to show them what a badass I was. Then I responded to his last statement. "About that job. You have my interest. What type of a job does an assistant do for Mr. Kerchenko?"

"We will let Mr. Kerchenko tell you duties of his assistant," answered Boris.

I accepted the invitation. I can't say I was willing, but this was the beginning of what I had trained for, ready or not. We arranged to meet back at Corky's on Monday night at nine o'clock, and they would take me to meet Kerchenko. Then Boris and Viktor left, leaving me alone in the booth.

When I was sure the Russians were gone, I caught Dingo's eye as I looked over at the bar. He tipped his head toward the hallway, indicating I should go into the restroom. I wanted to tell him what just transpired, but I also had to piss after all the liquid intake of the night.

I casually arose from the bench and swaggered to the short hallway. I kept up my tough guy act in case someone else was in the bar watching me. As I drew closer to the bathroom door, I was struck by déjà vu of that horrible night. Strange, it actually gave me more resolve to keep in my *Max* character. These bastards had to pay for what they had done.

I opened the restroom door finding Dingo already inside. He greeted me with a big bear hug. "How you doin', kid?"

I returned his embrace. "I tell you; it's been a harrowing couple of hours, but I think they bought it. I'm supposed to meet Kerchenko next Monday night."

"That's good. That's good." Then he stepped back. "Are you holding up okay?"

"Yeah, pretty good." I turned around, pirouetting like a ballet dancer. "Do you like my new bod? I've been working hard losing weight and getting into shape."

"I see. I see. You look like a different man."

Then I gave Dingo the once-over. "You still look pretty good too. How are things going here? I guess Donnie knows who I am, right?"

"Yeah, he's undercover from Forsythe. He kind of likes the gig. He says maybe after all this is over he might work part time here anyway. I like it too. It's been challenging and a lot of responsibility, but very fulfilling, trying to get the business started back up again. We've gotten a lot accomplished since the place was remodeled."

"I see that. The place doesn't even look the same. I'm glad they changed it up. Makes it easier." Then I paused. "By the way, what's the word on Gina Mariani? Has she been back yet?"

"Funny you should ask. No, she hasn't been back to the bar yet, but she had a baby girl a couple weeks ago. Named her Carla after her dad. She sold the condo she owned with her husband and moved back in with her mother. Both of them have so much to deal with right now. Being together probably makes it a little easier. At least they have each other's support. Forsythe has a patrol car go by there every couple of hours to check on them. So far the Russians haven't tried to get to her. We aren't sure why they haven't. Maybe they heard she didn't recognize the shooters. Forsythe tried to get her and her mother to go into the Witness Protection program, but they refused. I hope they don't regret that decision." Dingo shook his head compassionately.

That worried me. Two helpless women at the mercy of the dangerous Russian mob. I wished I could help out there, but I had another job planned for me.

I thought we'd better talk a little more business. "So will you be telling the captain about my meet and greet with Kerchenko next week?"

"Yeah, I'll get word to him. Caruthers will get word to you if the captain has any special instructions or advice for you."

Just then a patron walked in the bathroom. I walked over to the urinal to piss while Dingo washed his hands at the sink before going back to the bar. It had been great talking to him, but I had to get back into my new personality. I left the bar and went back to my apartment.

CHAPTER THIRTEEN
Meet The Boss Man

I was nervous all day Sunday anticipating the meeting with Kerchenko. What would he ask me? More importantly, what would he ask me to do? Was I supposed to be a henchman like Boris and Viktor, killing those who disobeyed his mandatory requests? I couldn't shoot anyone, especially somebody innocent. But what if I was expected to be a murderer? How could I get out of it? I knew I shouldn't get all worked up before I even knew what was in store for me. But isn't that human nature? Sometimes you just can't control those things.

Sunday afternoon I went over to Porter Avenue to meet my new uncle and aunt. I needed to get familiar with their location and get to know them a little. I happened to arrive when Uncle Nick and Aunt Inga were eating *oped*, which is what the Russians call lunch. Aunt Inga invited me to join them. She first served us borsch with dark, homemade rye bread and then beef stroganoff. They were delicious. Then over a hot cup of black tea, we discussed the relationship I was to have with them. They were to be my go-between with Captain Forsythe after I was inducted into

Kerchenko's organization.

"Can I ask how the two of you got involved with the captain?"

With a solemn face, Uncle Nick said, "Max, you do not need to know that information."

I was curious but realized it was none of my business. I was actually grateful I'd have some contact in case I got myself into serious trouble. So I guess Uncle Nick was right. I didn't need to know their relationship with the captain.

They gave me their phone number and told me someone would always answer the phone. Uncle Nick instructed, "If a man answer the telephone, he will say, 'Anno, Nick Gorelov.' If a woman answer, she will say, 'Anno, Inga Gorelov.' If telephone answered in any other way, it means it not safe to talk business or come to house."

After my visit with them, I took a long walk on the West Orange Trail, contemplating and planning for the meeting with Kerchenko. Mom had always told me I shouldn't worry about things before they happened. Be prepared, but don't fret about it. As difficult as that was, I had to psyche myself to do just that. I had to have confidence in my own instincts and hope I did the right thing when the time came.

I didn't sleep much Sunday night, and I was groggy when I got up for work Monday morning. I had an extra cup of coffee to keep me awake, which wasn't such a good choice. My stomach was already doing flip-flops from my nerves, and the coffee on an empty stomach caused more flips than flops. Luckily, I kept busy at work and didn't have a hell of a lot of time to think about the meeting.

When I got back to my apartment, I showered and put on my heavy metal uniform. I hadn't shaved that morning. I thought a scruffy face might make me look more badass and confident. I had talked to Caruthers on Sunday night to see if the captain had any further instructions for me. Caruthers said, "Captain Forsythe trusts your judgement, and he wishes you luck."

Great! I was definitely on my own. No lifelines. Sink or swim or *die*! No, I wasn't going to die. I was smart. I had done a good job so far. There was no reason I couldn't continue that attitude and that success. Before I left for Corky's, I stood in front of the mirror scrutinizing my appearance. I definitely looked the part. I started mock punching my image. *I could do this. I'm strong. I'm intelligent. I'm Max Gorelov. I am ready!*

Out the door I went.

I got to Corky's about eight-thirty, walking into the bar with my tough guy arrogance. I ordered my usual Jack and Bud from Donnie. I was especially grateful he gave me the fake drinks. I didn't want to be the least bit incapacitated that evening. Too much depended on my ability to think and act clearly.

So I drank the Jack and nursed the Bud for the next half hour, occasionally partaking in small talk with Donnie or a couple of the regular customers. Dingo was there too, but we didn't talk. The Russians walked in the bar at ten after nine. They took empty stools on both sides of me.

"Good evening, Mr. Gorelov," Boris said as he sat down.

I first looked at him on my left side and then at Viktor on my right. Then I looked at the clock on the wall in front of us. "You're ten minutes late."

Both men snickered and Boris said, "You must excuse us. We had some very important business that could not be postponed. Are you ready to go?"

"Yeah, I'm ready." I didn't want to think about what their "important business" could have been.

We walked out to the parking lot, Viktor, me, and then Boris. Viktor led us to a black SUV with dark, tinted windows. He got in the driver's seat, Boris got in the front passenger seat, and I got in the back seat behind Viktor. No one spoke as Viktor pulled out of the parking lot, heading north onto Nawinah Cortland. Road. He maintained the speed limit all the way to Isleworth, and we maintained silence too.

At the gate to the Isleworth property, Viktor showed his ID to the security guard, who then electronically opened the wrought iron gate. The SUV drove through the gate opening and proceeded down the winding road to the right. On each side setting a distance back from the road were elegant, magnificent mansions owned by affluent celebrities and entrepreneurs who made Central Florida their home. It was surreal, and I was a bit envious to know people actually lived on these estates compared to our little bungalow in Pine Hills or the apartment in which my mom and I lived in Nawinah. In fact, our entire apartment building could fit comfortably within some of these mansions. Yes, I admit it. I was a little jealous.

Viktor drove to an area with no dwellings. The road was landscaped with lush shrubbery and colorful flowers and plants, all tastefully illuminated with bright lanterns and spotlights. The drive itself was lined with tall, thin trees on both sides. Between the trees I was able to see a few small buildings lit up in the distance and scattered yards apart. Soon he approached a wide, expansive, decorative gate with stake-like metal projections protruding from its top. The gate and the attached sand colored cement wall must have been at least ten feet high. The wall itself also had wrought iron protrusions emerging from its top about every six inches. However, these were pointing outward toward the street. In other words, no way could anybody climb that wall without being impaled or killed on one of those spikes.

Viktor stopped at the gate. Two armed men exited the guard station and approached the SUV, one on each side. The one on the driver side recognized Viktor, and in Russian, Boris told the one on his side I had an appointment with Kerchenko.

The guards opened the gate, and Viktor drove for about two tenths of a mile when we came to another wall and gate very similar to the first ones. Another guard station was attached to this wall. Two armed guards exited this station as Viktor pulled up to it. Viktor and Boris both showed the guards some sort of circle with a red star on it. Boris told the guard on his side about my appointment. One guard went inside the station to mechanically activate the gate. The other guard stood at attention until we were through the gate, and it was closed again. Once inside this second gate, Kerchenko's residence was visible. I wouldn't actually call it a house. I didn't know a place like this could even exist. It was massive! Lit up like the 2015 Super Bowl game in Arizona, it looked like the Taj Mahal. Once Viktor pulled in front of the entrance and I exited the SUV, I stood and stared in awe. Boris noticed my amazed expression. "You like Mr. Kerchenko's humble dwelling?"

"I guess it's okay." I wasn't fooling him. He knew I was impressed.

Viktor then proceeded to check me for a wire. I let him do his touchy, feely thing with my arms and legs spread out so he could reach all the necessary body parts.

Boris smirked as he watched the invasion of my physique. Although I tried my best not to show any discomfort, Boris definitely enjoyed observing the procedure. Then he ordered, "Come. Let us not keep Mr. Kerchenko waiting. He is not a patient man."

I straightened my jacket and followed them up the marble steps leading to huge ornate, metal double doors. I saw armed guards in various locations around the property, some standing still and some walking back and forth. When we reached the top of the stairs, the doors were opened by another armed guard, who said in Russian, "He will see you in his office."

I first looked around the entrance hall, which was amazing in its beauty and style: gold marble floors, massive high ceilings, and extravagant crystal chandeliers. Apparently, the office was not on the first level, for we entered an elevator on our right. Viktor pressed the gold number three on the shiny elevator panel. The door closed, and we ascended to the third floor. Then a door behind us opened, and we exited into a deep, lush carpeted hallway. We walked three abreast down the hall, our shoulders almost touching. Various closed doors were on either side, but our destination was at the end of the hall where a set of double doors awaited us. When we reached them, we stopped, and Viktor pressed a code on a keypad on the left wall. I heard a faint ringtone coming from the other side. We waited for about fifteen seconds while I nervously switched my weight from right to left and back again. Then I heard a buzzing sound and Boris reached to open the door.

The plush carpet continued into this room, which was about the size of Ma and my entire apartment. The room was tastefully furnished in rich ebony and stunning gold tones. A glistening, stark black desk was placed in front of the wall before us with a gold leather chair behind it. A young, good-looking, Russian dude about my age was seated in front and to the far left of the desk. I assumed he was Kerchenko's son Luka. Kerchenko himself was standing with his back to us, admiring a painting of Saint Basil's Cathedral, the Russian multi-colored domed sixteenth century cathedral on Red Square. The painting was amazing. Immediately, I thought of my way to introduce myself to Kerchenko. Captain Forsythe was right. All those random facts I knew were once again going to prove useful for me.

I spoke in Russian. "Ah, what a magnificent painting The Cathedral of Vasily the Blessed. I'm not familiar with this painter. May I ask who the artist is?"

Kerchenko slowly turned to face me. He was a tall man, actually about my size. My guess was he was possibly in his early sixties and in great shape for his age. He had large, hard facial features and coarse, thinning, white hair which contrasted against his ruddy complexion. I saw a glint of surprise and pleasure in his dark eyes. After several seconds, he remarked, "So, Mr. Gorelov, I see you have some knowledge of Russian history. I commissioned Anton Fedorov to paint the cathedral. I, too, am pleased with his work. Do you know why I would want such a painting, Mr. Gorelov?"

My brain instantly searched my historical facts on the cathedral. Ah! I remembered! "I cannot say definitely. However, I know your name is Ivan, and it was Ivan Vasilyevich, the first tsar of Russia, who ordered the construction of the cathedral. It was his grandson, also named Ivan, who completed the construction."

"Very good! Do you know anything else about my favorite architectural masterpiece? Please sit." He gestured toward a black and gold brocade chair on the right side in front of his desk. Kerchenko sat at his chair behind the desk.

I ventured over to the offered chair. Boris and Viktor took two similar seats between mine and the guy on the left, who was staring at me as if he wanted to knock my teeth out.

I placed my palms on my thighs, leaned forward with my head scrunched to my shoulders in order to observe the painting. "I know it was named after Vasily, the fool, who is buried in the cathedral. I know it has had several other names, among which are Church of the Intercession, Cathedral of the Intercession of the Virgin of the Moat, and Pokrovsky Cathedral. I know the brilliant colors on the façade and the domes were not added for over two hundred years. I know it was saved from extinction by an architect named Pyotr Barnovsky during Stalin's time as head of the Soviet Union."

Kerchenko continued to stare at me with his elbows on his desk and his hands folded at his chin. I leaned back on the chair. Out of the corner of my eye, I could see Boris and Viktor's amazed faces. The other dude was giving me a very hostile look.

Finally, Kerchenko spoke, "Mr. Gorelov, to my surprise and delight, you are a very astute young man. I must think further about the job I had planned for you. I do not want to waste your talents."

Great! I was feeling a lot better. I had been fairly sure I'd be cast in a similar role as Boris and Viktor, and I was quite apprehensive about how I could handle that type of an occupation. However, I was yet to find out what Kerchenko had in mind, so I couldn't get too comfortable yet.

Kerchenko continued, "First, let me introduce my son Luka to you." He gestured toward the dude next to Boris. "He is learning about the business. I like to include him in some of my decisions."

He paused as I nodded to Luka. In response, this Luka dude stuck his chin in the air and frowned at me. I knew I was in for some flak from this guy. I'd have to watch my back around him. Just from this initial introduction, I had a feeling that Luka would never replace Kerchenko's former right hand man who had recently drowned in Lake Monroe.

I turned to Kerchenko as he continued, "I have checked out what Mr. Petrov has told me about your family. You seem to be someone who could do well in my organization. Of course, I will continue to dig further into your past. However, now I want to get acquainted with you and you to get acquainted with the organization. Get your affairs in order this week. Quit your current job. Move into a suite on the West Wing of the house. Do what you need to with your present living arrangement. You will work with Mr. Petrov and Mr. Kozlov next week to become familiar with their operations. I will keep my eye on you also. Everyone I hire is a potential risk to me. Make no mistake. If you are or will become a threat to my organization, you will be terminated."

I knew "terminated" didn't simply mean getting fired from the job. The Luka guy had a sneer on his face as he looked over in my direction.

Then Kerchenko glared at me. "Before I continue, are we clear on these statements? If you disagree, Mr. Kozlov and Mr. Petrov will take you off my property, and you will be advised never to speak of this meeting to anyone. If I find out you have opened your mouth, you will pay the consequences, which are not at all desirable."

He was threatening me. I had to remain calm and not think about consequences of any kind. I also had to be steadfast in my conviction to be Max Gorelov and not Tank Telek.

"Mr. Kerchenko, since you have checked into my background, you know what kind of a man I am. I come from a good Russian family, and they have taught me to be loyal to our mother land. Even though I was born in the USA, I feel I owe no allegiance to this wretched country. Since I am new to the Central Florida area, I do not know much about your organization, but I am willing to learn. And you will find I will be a very loyal employee (liar, liar, pants on fire), willing to do whatever job you think will help your organization and further my career. However, I am concerned about the money. If I am to take risks working for you, will I be sufficiently compensated?"

Kerchenko leaned back on his chair with an obvious grin on his face. "I must say, not only are you an intelligent young man, but you have balls, Mr. Gorelov. You have balls. I pay well for jobs well done. If you do a good job, you will be amply compensated. If you do not, well..."

I thought I had to say something. "That's fair enough." I wasn't going to think about what would happen if I didn't do a good job, or even more serious, what would happen if he ever found out what I was really doing under his nose in his very home.

Kerchenko ended the meeting by shaking my hand. I offered

my hand to his son, who accepted it but acted as if I were contaminated.

It was midnight when Viktor dropped me off at Corky's. The bar was still open, and I decided to go in for a *real* drink to unwind after that intense meeting. I also wanted to see if I could talk to Dingo about what transpired so he could relay it to Captain Forsythe. We couldn't take any chances, though. Kerchenko could've planted one of his goons in the bar to check up on me. I still walked into the bar with my defiant attitude. I needed to keep up the act at all times.

Donnie asked me what I wanted. "Give me a Miller Lite." I hoped he'd take the hint and give me a real beer. He came back with a tall, foaming glass. It was real.

I sipped the cold beer slowly, going over in my head the last couple of hours. I really pulled it off—so far, but I couldn't pat myself on the back just yet. This had been only the first step of how many I could only guess. I knew I had to keep my eyes open at all times and be alert to anything. Anything that could bring Kerchenko down but also anything that would endanger my safety. I sure wished somebody who I could trust was on the inside. When this all started, I thought Dingo would be that liaison. But the role the captain had for him was definitely not going to help me out much once I was entrenched in Kerchenko's organization.

I was beginning to doubt if I was the right person for the job. After all, I had no police training. I had no training in covert operations other than what Caruthers had given me in a couple of months. Doesn't it take more like years to get good at this kind of stuff? Not only that, let's not forget how I got here in the first place. I belong in 2015, not 1993.

I was staring into space, regretting my decision to take part in this caper when Donnie came over and asked if I wanted another beer. I told him "no", but as he was wiping up the bar in front of me, he lifted my glass and slipped a small piece of paper under it before walking away. I let about a minute pass by, then I picked up my glass to drain the rest of the beer and casually slid the paper along the bar into my hand. Then I got up, got my money out of my wallet while also slipping the paper into it. I placed my money on the bar, saying, "See you later, Donnie."

I did my strut out to the car. Several other cars were still in the parking lot, and I didn't know if any of Kerchenko's men could be lurking in any of them. I decided to wait until I got to my apartment to look at the note.

After I had been approached by Boris and Viktor to join Kerchenko's organization, the captain had my apartment searched for hidden cameras and bugs. It came up clean, He had also placed a couple of undercover cops around the building to make sure the devices weren't added later. So I felt confident it was safe to view the note in my apartment. I locked and bolted the door, took another shower, then sat on the side of the bed to read it.

"Meet 6:00 AM Clubhouse. Use back door".

CHAPTER FOURTEEN
Plans, Schemes, And Stalking

In the morning, I put my work clothes on, then drove over to the apartment complex's clubhouse. I parked on a side street and took the back way through a few neighbor's yards. I didn't want to take any chances. Maybe I was being paranoid, but it was better to be paranoid than dead.

The door to the clubhouse was unlocked. I walked into a dimly lit, large room. At first I saw no one, but eventually as my eyes focused, I saw the captain, Caruthers, and Dingo seated at a table in the back of the room. I went over to them and sat in the fourth chair.

"How are you holding up, Tank?" asked the captain.

"I guess alright, considering this covert shit is all new to me."

"That's what I wanted to talk to you about. Do you think this thing is more than you can handle? I know in the beginning you were all primed to catch these guys. Now that you've actually met them, do you still feel the same?"

"Truthfully, Captain, I don't know. I think I did a great job convincing them of who I wanted them to think I am. But, I got to tell you, I'm scared shitless! These guys are brutal. For instance, the patrons at Corky's keep away from Petrov and Kozlov at all costs. And Kerchenko is really a scary dude. Then there's his son Luka. I think I'm in for some trouble from him. Like I say, I held my own; I just hope I can keep up the charade."

"What exactly does he want you to do?"

"Well, that's the weird part. At first I think he had plans for me to be another bill collector and head chopper like Kozlov and Petrov. I remember you had said his employee numbers had diminished lately. However, I impressed him with my historical knowledge just like I did you."

I told the captain about the Saint Basil's Cathedral conversation. Then I added, "So I think he plans to put me in a different capacity. He was not specific. I have a feeling it'll be a more informative position where I can obtain more evidence against his organization, but it will also be much more dangerous for me."

"Yes, I'm inclined to agree with you."

"I have another concern, sir. This thing about being in 1993 when I should be in 2015, we don't know how or when that will change. What if in the middle of this sting, I suddenly find myself back in 2015? What then? All of this will be in vain."

"Tank, as far as that situation, you've been here now for what, about five months? I'm willing to risk the time element if you are."

"Yeah, I guess I agree with you. Not much we can do about it, anyway. I suppose if somehow I am transported ahead to 2015 while still involved in Kerchenko's organization, I then won't have to worry about him killing me. I won't be around."

They all smiled at my remark. Dingo said, "Yeah, Tank, your worries about being shot by the Russians will no longer be a concern. You'll then have to worry about explaining yourself to your people in 2015. One problem solved; another one added. You just can't win."

After the chuckling died down, the captain asked, "Is there anything else worrying you, Tank?"

"Well, my main concern is being out there on my own, not knowing what to do, if I'll make things better or worse, and nobody around to help me out."

"I know, son. It's asking a lot of you. That's why I wanted to make sure you were prepared to go through with it."

I twisted my mouth to the side, nodding my head slowly. "Let's say I back out now, what could I do? I can't go home since my home isn't here yet. I don't have any friends except you guys because they haven't been born yet or are still babies. Who knows what would happen if I tried to see my mom and dad? Plus, Kerchenko told me if I decided not to work for him, he'd be sure I kept my mouth shut, one way or another. I didn't like the sound of that. You know what? I don't think I have a choice anymore."

Caruthers asked, "What is your next step as far as Kerchenko is concerned?"

"I have to quit my job and move onto his estate. Then I'm

supposed to tag along with Petrov and Kozlov for a while to see how that part of the operations works. After that, I don't know."

The captain leaned back on his chair. Caruthers, Dingo, and I waited for his next statement. "Okay, here is how we'll handle this. You close out your apartment. Leave nothing personal behind. Move into Kerchenko's estate, like he said. When you're situated and get a telephone, I want you to call or visit your Uncle Nick as often as possible to let us know how you're doing and feed him important information you learn. Do not under any circumstances discuss directly with him any issues you're having. If you need to speak with us, tell him you will be visiting him at a certain date and time. Then someone will discreetly meet you at his house. With any luck, the Russians won't follow you. Keep an eye out for them, and if they do, park on the street. If you park in the driveway, our man will know it is safe for him to come out of hiding. Now, if we need to get in touch with you, your Aunt Inga will call you to tell you your uncle is ill. Hopefully, that ruse will not seem suspicious to the Russians. I think if you keep normal contact with Nick throughout this entire operation, we should be okay. What do you think?"

"Yeah, sounds like a plan. Besides, my Aunt Inga is a great Russian cook. Maybe I can get a meal over there every so often."

The captain smiled. "Yes, the more you treat them as family, the more normal your communications with them will appear."

It was getting late. I had to get to work. I didn't want to interrupt my routine in case I was being watched. I stood up. "I need to get to work. Do I tell my boss I quit, or is that something you will handle?"

"Go ahead and tell him. We want to stick to protocol for appearance's sake. Just tell him you got a better job. He'll know what that means. Tell Kerchenko's men you'll be moving into his place on Friday. That will give you a couple of days to get more acquainted with Nick and Inga. Oh, how about the telephone? Do you have it on you? We can't have you carrying that around while you're in the company of the Russians."

I returned the telephone to the captain, and I went out the back door to my car. I went to work and told the boss Friday would be my last day. As Captain Forsythe mentioned, my boss understood and asked no unnecessary questions.

That night after work I went to Corky's. I assumed Boris and Viktor would eventually show up, and I would tell them about my moving plans. As suspected, they came in the bar about nine o'clock. We went over to a booth where I told them I quit my job and I'd be moving out on Friday. Boris said they'd meet me at my apartment building at noon on Friday with ID for me to get into the Isleworth development.

Wednesday night and Thursday I packed my clothes and limited personal belongings and put them in the Buick. I cleaned out the fridge and kitchen cabinets and straightened up the place a little. About seven, I went out to dinner, and then I went to Corky's. I wasn't sure how often I'd be able to get back there once I was under Kerchenko's men's scrutiny.

The bar was fairly empty, so I had my choice of barstools. Donnie automatically gave me a *real* Jack and Bud. I could handle one without any mind altering effects. Dingo was behind the bar washing glasses. When he saw me, he signaled to meet him in the restroom. Leaving my beer on the counter, I arose and walked casually to the restroom. Dingo was still working on the glasses. In the restroom, I waited for a couple of minutes before Dingo came through the doorway. No one else was in the room.

"The captain wanted me to check with you to see if you have destroyed all the papers he had given you that would link you with the police."

"Oh, yeah. I actually burned them before I even met up with the Russians. When I got the Max Gorelov ID's, I figured I didn't need the captain's paperwork anymore."

"He also wanted me to tell you about the safe house in case you end up needing to hide out somewhere. We can't be too prepared. You never know."

"Hey, you're right. I don't know what to expect when I get a hundred percent involved in this sting. I'll feel better knowing there's a place I can go if I need it."

"He doesn't want you to write the location down. However, knowing what your mind is capable of, I'm sure he realizes you'll be able to remember the directions quite easily."

"Yeah, I'll remember," I said with a smile.

"Okay. If you go south on Nawinah Cortland Road past Corky's Bar for about three miles, on the left side is an unnamed dirt road. There's an abandoned, two story house on one corner and a large *For Sale* sign on the other. Take that road for about three more miles. You'll see a small, block house off to the right and back about fifty yards. The porch light is kept on. Go around to the back of the house. Next to the back door steps and extending the length of the house are two rows of pavers. On the left underneath the fifth paver in the first row closest to the house is a key in a flat, red plastic box to open the back door. Remember, on the left, fifth paver, first row. That's it."

He paused as he gave me an anxious look. "You okay?"

"Yeah, yeah, I'm fine. Nervous and a little worried, but fine. Don't know when we'll get to talk again, but thanks for everything, Dingo."

"Hey, kid, we'll talk when this is all over. Mark my word. This will be a success. How can it not be with two brilliant guys like us working on it?"

Dingo gave me a big bear hug before going back to the bar.

It was still early, about eight o'clock, when I finished my beer. I didn't have anything to do, but I was so nervous thinking of the prospect of this second great change in my life. First, being thrown back in time and now being thrown into a pack of wolves. How or why did I get myself into these two very different and dangerous situations?

Sitting in the driver's seat of the Buick, for some reason I had the urge to see Gina Mariani. Of course, that was impossible. What would I do? Walk up to her door and tell her who I was? Then tell her I was going to bring down the murderers of her father and her husband? It was a stupid thing to even think about. The captain said she didn't remember me. She didn't even remember being shot or who shot her, so no way could she identify the gunmen. Although I wondered if Boris and Viktor were aware of that. Probably her life was already in danger no matter what she remembered.

I couldn't help myself. I drove to the nearby convenience store and looked up the address and telephone number of Carl Antonelli in the phone book. Dingo had said she was living with her mother now. The listing gave the address as 12840 Millstone Lane, Nawinah. I remembered there was a housing development about a mile from Ma's Marsten Boulevard apartment. One of the guys I knew when I worked at Carneys for that short duration said he lived on Millstone Lane. Before I got fired, we were planning to car pool to work. What the hell? I could drive by to look at the place. No harm in that. I could also check out the area where Ma's apartment complex would be built.

I got back in the Buick and drove to Marsten Boulevard. It felt so weird seeing some familiar things, like the gas station on the corner of Lowry Road and Marsten. It looked the same, maybe a little newer. But when I drove further down Marsten, half of the businesses that were there in 2015 had not been constructed yet. As I drove a little further, I verified what the detectives had told me back at the police station when they were interrogating me. The space where the apartment complex should've been was a lot full of tall pine trees. I pulled the car over and parked on the side of the road. Getting out of the Buick, I walked into the lot among the trees. I was dizzy from the reality of the scene. This was impossible, simply impossible. I was probably standing on the very spot where the walkway led to the main building of the complex. If I went down the imaginary walk and turned right, I'd be approaching our building, Ma and my home. How could this be? I probably stood there for fifteen minutes, staring into the woods, trying to come to terms with what was happening. Finally, I turned around and went back to the Buick.

After driving again for about a mile, I arrived at the Millbrook development. I remembered Millstone Lane was either three or four streets off Millbrook Avenue, the main road into the development. Luckily, the street signs were very clear, and I found the street quite easily. Since the mailboxes were at the curb, as my headlights hit them, I was able to search for 12840 with no difficulty. The houses on this side of the street had even numbers. Thus, I was on the correct side. I passed about seven or eight houses before I saw 12840 on the white mailbox.

So now that I found where she lived, what did I plan to do about it? I noticed parking was only allowed on the other side of the street. I kept driving until I came to a house with no lights on and turned around in their driveway. A parking spot was open one house up from the Antonellis on the opposite side. I pulled into the spot and turned off the engine.

For several minutes, I stared at the house. The front picture window was lit up, and occasionally, I saw a shadowy figure go back and forth in front of it. What was I doing here? What did I plan to do? I knew I wasn't going to be a peeping tom and go up to that window, crouching down, and peeking over the window sill. As much as I wanted to, I couldn't do that. So I just stared at the window, watching the shadows sometimes walking by.

About five minutes into my observation, I saw a woman pulling a trash container from around the side of the house and dragging it to the curb. I slithered down in my seat so she couldn't see me. From the light of the street lamp, I recognized Gina Mariani. She looked different, actually more beautiful than when I saw her in the hospital bed. Her skin was more radiant. Under the light her dark hair shined like it was sprinkled with tiny flecks of gold.

Why was I so fascinated with this woman? I didn't even know her, yet I found myself thinking about her often. Was it because I witnessed her almost losing her life? Did I feel sorry for her because she bore the loss of both a father and a husband while having to be a mother to a newborn? I've had crushes on several girls in my life, but this was different. This was something I totally didn't understand. And if by chance I even thought something could result from this strange infatuation, what about the 1993 versus 2015 thing? This woman is twenty-two years older than I am!

Gina positioned the trash container and then ambled down the walkway on the side of her house. Soon she was pulling a second container to the curb. It took all my willpower not to jump out of the car and run over to assist her. But I merely watched her struggle and straighten the container and then walk back the way she came, unaware of my peering eyes on her every move.

After she disappeared from my sight, I drove away. If anyone saw me, they might think I was a stalker. Well, I guess in a way I was. More importantly, if the Russians knew I was hanging out there, it could be disastrous not only to me but for both those women in that house.

I slowly drove to Millbrook Avenue, still thinking about Gina Mariani. As I was stopped at the stop sign, checking to turn left onto the street, making a right turn onto Millstone Lane was a big, black SUV with tinted windows. My heart skipped a beat. Could that be one of Kerchenko's cars? Instead of turning left to get out of the development, I turned right and went up to the next street, Maple Drive, which ran parallel to Millstone Lane. As soon as I saw a parking place, I pulled in and hurried from my car. What next? I had to see if that black SUV belonged to Kerchenko's men. I tried to gauge how far up the block the house would be that was in line with Gina Marianis house. I walked up about three houses, then cut through a back yard, making my way over to Millstone. Staying as close to the houses as possible, I crept around to check how far I was from her house. I had to think about what distinguished her house from the others on the block. Then I remembered that a gas lamp post stood at the end of her driveway. Realizing I happened to be at the house where I had parked earlier,

I knew her house was just across the street and down one.

As I was debating what I should do, I saw the SUV slowly drive by her house. Maybe I was wrong. Maybe it was somebody who lived in the neighborhood. After all, other people owned black SUVs besides Kerchenko's crew. I waited to see what happened next. Sure enough, the SUV went up to the very same driveway as I had used and turned around. Then they parked in the same space as I had parked, directly in front of the house I was hiding next to.

I was freaking out! I was not equipped to confront these guys. I had no weapon. Plus, these guys were professionals. I didn't stand a chance with them even if I would've had a gun or a knife.

At that moment a police cruiser was driving up the street. Okay, Dingo had said they were checking on Gina Mariani every couple hours. But would the police notice the black SUV? Since it was merely parked on the street with several other vehicles, they probably wouldn't think it was a threat at all. I had to somehow get the attention of the officers in the cruiser. Quick! What to do?

I ran back to the Buick and drove in the opposite direction as the SUV on Millstone, hoping to find a street to cut over to Millstone. Yes! There it was. Birch Drive. And the police cruiser was coming toward me!

I stopped the car, threw it in park, jumped out, leaving the driver door wide open, and ran over to the cruiser. "Officer! Officer! Stop!"

The driver stopped abruptly when he saw me approaching. He got out of the vehicle with his weapon drawn. "Hold it right there, mister!"

I stopped and threw both my arms up into the air. "Officer, please! This is an emergency. My name is Talbott Telek!" Wait! My ID reads I'm Maxim Gorelov. These guys won't believe me. I had to try. "I mean Max Gorelov. There's a woman in danger on Millbrook. Gina Mariani."

As soon as I mentioned Gina's name, the officer interrupted me. "What do you know about Gina Mariani?"

"I know at this very moment there's a black SUV parked across the street from her house. I don't know what they have in mind, but I know it isn't good. Could you just go back and check on her?"

The officer hesitated. The second officer also got out of the police car with his gun drawn.

How could I get them to *move*? "Please! Please! I'll get in your car. Just go over there immediately. Her life is in danger."

The second officer put his gun away but brought out a set of handcuffs. He snapped them on my wrists. "Get in the car." He pushed my head down and shoved me in the back seat.

The officer who was driving got back in the car, backed up and went back to Millstone Lane. As soon as I noticed the SUV was still there, I said, "There! That's the car." I hunched down in the seat so its occupants couldn't see me. I didn't want to be recognized by any of Kerchenko's men.

The officer saw the SUV. He said to the second officer, "I'm going to pull in her drive and check on them. You wait in here with this deadbeat."

He slowed the cruiser and pulled into Gina's drive. I raised my head slightly to look out the back window. The black SUV was pulling away. Amen.

Since the SUV was now gone, I sat upright in the back seat. The officer who was driving got out and walked up to the porch. He knocked on the door, and the porch light turned on. Gina opened the door and invited the officer into the house. While he was inside, the second officer said, "Okay. We saw the SUV, but it pulled away. What makes you think the occupants planned to harm Mrs. Mariani?"

I couldn't explain my situation. I couldn't blow my cover. Not after all I had done so far. "Please. Just get in touch with Captain Forsythe. He'll explain."

The officer laughed at me. "So you are on speaking terms with the big man, are you?"

"If you just call him, he'll tell you all you need to know."

"Oh, he will, will he? Should I call the mayor or the governor too?"

I figured I wasn't getting anywhere with this guy. Maybe the other officer would be more reasonable.

The first officer was exiting the house, saying final words to Gina. Then he came back to the police car. When he got behind the steering wheel, he turned to me. "You. We're taking you in for questioning."

At first I was about to protest. Then I thought otherwise. This wasn't all bad. If I'm arrested, it might look bad for Tank Telek, but for Max Gorelov, it'll just add to his character. I said to the officer, "Can we go back so I can lock up my car first?"

****

Déjà vu. Back at the police station again. Same procedure as before. They took all my belongings, Max Gorelov's belongings, and put me in an interrogation room. This time was different. I wasn't scared and confused like the last time. This time might work out to my advantage.

I waited in the room for about a half hour. No big deal. Soon a detective I didn't recognize came in the room. "Maxim Gorelov. Is that your name?"

Here was my dilemma. Should I try to get him to call the captain or Caruthers, or should I play it cool and act my part as Max Gorelov? I decided to do the latter. This would look good to the Russians, me being arrested. I'd have to come up with some make believe charge to relay to them. It couldn't be stalking Gina Mariani. Not a good idea. I could think about the charges as I rot in the cell until the captain realizes I was in his care again. So I grumbled, "You know my name. You saw my ID."

Apparently the officers who had brought me in had made out a police report. This guy was looking at it while questioning me.

"So what were you doing snooping around the Antonelli house?"

"Me? Snooping? I was just out for a pleasant, nightly drive."

"That's a strange place to be out driving."

"So what? I like looking at all the ticky tacky houses in that area."

The detective looked down at the paper again. "Why did you stop those police officers?"

"I am a concerned citizen."

"A concerned citizen? What were you concerned about? Were you planning to break into the Antonelli house?"

I figured I had said enough to this guy. I didn't know who in the police force knew my situation, and I didn't want to say more than I should. So I said what I had seen all the scumbags on TV say. "I want to see my lawyer."

That shut him up. I was taken to the holding cell.

Some of the deadbeats in the cell looked familiar and looked at me a little strangely also. Perhaps they thought they recognized me. I hoped not. I'd spend the night in the cell. By morning the captain would hear about my arrest. And Boris and Viktor would find I am not at my apartment.

CHAPTER FIFTEEN
Indoctrination

The next morning after sleeping on the hard cell bench, I awakened cramped and sore. I looked around as all my cellmates were also awakening. Since they had taken my wristwatch, I didn't know what time it was. I knew I had to wait until the captain or Caruthers arrived before I could get out of this place.

About an hour later, we were served breakfast. As I was finishing up my congealed scrambled eggs, an officer came over to the cell door and shouted my name. "Maxim Gorelov, This way."

I got up from the bench, carrying my cardboard tray, and followed the officer. I dropped my tray into the garbage can as the officer turned around. "The captain wants to see you."

When we entered his office, the captain was behind his desk writing on some papers in front of him. He looked up with a surprised expression on his face. "Tank, what the hell are you doing here?"

I sat on one of the chairs in front of his desk. "It's a long story, sir." Then I explained about the night before and the incident at the

Antonelli house.

"Well, well. This was totally unexpected. I guess you were at the right place at the right time. Now we undoubtedly must do something with those ladies. They are unsafe where they are. I don't know what possessed you to be in their area, but I'm glad you were there.

"As for how to handle your arrest, you must have decided to spend the night here on your own. Otherwise, you would've had the officers get in touch with me."

"Actually, sir, I tried to convince the two officers in the patrol car to contact you, but they thought I was a big joke. When they refused, I decided on another plan. In the eyes of Kerchenko's men, my arrest could be a good thing. It simply adds to my badass image."

The captain agreed with me. Then we had to decide how he was to handle the arrest as far as the Russians were concerned. I couldn't admit I was near the Antonellis house. The captain called Caruthers into his office to help devise a plan. Caruthers had searched the prior night's criminal activity docket before coming to the captain's office. "As it turns out, there was a fight outside a bar in downtown Nawinah early this morning, and several men were arrested. Tank, you have become one of those men."

The problem was I didn't look like I had been in a fight, so Caruthers fixed that issue for me. He punched me in the left eye. He did a good job. Yeah, it hurt like hell, but the flesh around the eye started to bruise and turn purple, which was the exact effect I needed. Then I slammed my right fist against the outside wall of the police station so my fist looked like it had hit a couple of faces.

I was released from the police station around eleven o'clock. Caruthers drove me to pick up my car. Then I went back to the apartment and took a quick shower. The eye was increasingly turning purple and black, and my fist had cuts and bruises on it.

At ten past noon, Boris and Viktor were at my door. "Late again. Do you guys make a habit of this?"

Both men's eyes widened when they saw my face. Boris asked, "What happened to you?"

"Oh, I had a little misunderstanding with some assholes outside a bar this morning. If you think I look bad, you should see the other guys. I spent a couple of hours in jail, that's all. Actually, I just got out before you guys got here."

Neither Boris nor Viktor said anything more, but they both had sneers on their faces as I locked the door to the apartment.

I had to drop off the apartment keys at the management office. They followed my Buick in their black SUV. While walking back to my car after dropping off the keys, Boris signaled me over to him. "Okay. Here is your ID to get on Isleworth property. You must be behind our car when we reach Mr. Kerchenko's gates. I will give guards permission to admit you on property. We get you settled in room, then you meet with Mr. Kerchenko. Follow us. Don't get lost."

I got in the Buick and let them pull out first. Since I knew the way to Isleworth, I wasn't going to get lost, but keeping up with them was a challenge. I swear they were traveling sixty miles an hour through Windemere. I wasn't sure how things worked in 1993, but in 2015, if you even went three miles over the speed limit in Windemere, the cops would stop you and give you grief and a hefty ticket.

Safely arriving at Isleworth, I followed the SUV to the guard station. Showing my new ID, the guard permitted me to go through the gate right after Viktor. When we arrived at Kerchenko's first gate, the two armed guards came out of the guard station. One went to the driver's side of the SUV; the other to the passenger side. I saw both Kozlov and Petrov show the same gold circle/red star ID to the guards, and the guard on Kozlov's side went into the station to mechanically open the gate. The SUV moved forward, and Petrov signaled with his hand out the window for me to follow them. When we came to the second gate, the same procedure was followed, and as the SUV drove through the open gate, I did also.

On the Kerchenko estate, the Russian vehicle took a side drive and drove around to the back of the property. As I drove behind it, I admired the size of the buildings and structures on the estate. On my right we passed a tennis court. In the distance I saw a golf course. I knew a swimming pool existed somewhere, but it must've been on the other side.

Finally, we reached the back of the main house. We drove onto a parking lot capable of holding about seventy cars. A dozen black SUVs just like the one Viktor was driving were parked in the first and second rows. Viktor parked in the first spot in the second row. I pulled up next to him. Getting out of my car, I opened the trunk and retrieved my bags. Then I followed Petrov and Kozlov to the house.

Two guards were standing on each side of the entrance. One patted my body down for weapons or wires while the other checked my bags. When they were satisfied I had no wires or recorders, Petrov punched a code into the box next to the door. We entered a large room with tables and chairs set up like a school cafeteria. A kitchen area was located to my right. On the left wall directly near the door was a large key rack holding several sets of car keys all with corresponding numbers to the numbers on the rack. Next to the rack was a bank of lockers also similar to a high school hallway.

I followed the two Russians across the room and through a set of double swinging doors entering a wide hallway with lavish, muted green carpet and walls painted a sandy, beachy color. Several metal doors lined each side of the hallway. Each door had a tiny door at eye level that opened from the inside. Below each of these small doors was a brass nameplate engraved with what appeared to be someone's last name. Petrov stopped at a door on the right with the name, Babin, on the plate. As Petrov opened the door, he said, "This is your suite. There are no keys or locks to any of doors on this wing. Your life belongs to Mr. Kerchenko now. All of staff will respect your privacy. If you should show reasons for Mr. Kerchenko to deem you as untrustworthy, your privacy will be gone in instant. Do you understand?"

I was gazing around the room, thinking how this would be my home for a while, but I was also listening to Petrov. "Yes, I understand completely. I will give Mr. Kerchenko no reason to mistrust me."

"Well, then, you get settled. At two o'clock, someone will knock on door to escort you to *oped* with Mr. Kerchenko."

"I'll be ready."

As they went out the door, Petrov stopped. "Oh, yes. The name plate will be changed today. Babin is no longer with us." They closed the door and walked away.

And there I was. I can't say I was nervous at that time. Maybe apprehensive would be a better description. Maybe after I found out what my job would be, my reactions might change drastically. Or maybe if I found out what had happened to Babin, I might run away as fast as I could.

The space was adequate. Actually, it was like a small apartment, not quite a studio because the bedroom, though small was separate. A tiny bathroom with a shower was off the bedroom. The common area had a comfortable chair, a two seater couch, a desk, and an entertainment center with a bulky TV and a video tape player. I found several tapes in one of the drawers. I couldn't help but think of my broken iPhone on the front seat of my truck— in 2015. I had often watched movies on it when I was bored. Big change in technology here.

The kitchenette had a couple of well stocked cabinets with food and dishes, a sink, a small fridge, mini dishwasher, a two-burner stove with a tiny oven, a microwave, a coffee maker, and a table with two chairs.

Everything was in neutral tones, very generic. The walls, however, were adorned with photos of various Russian historical architectural sites, the Kremlin, several shots of Red Square, the Bolshoi Theater, the Winter Palace in St. Petersburg, and St. Basil's Cathedral.

The place was also very clean. I hoped I didn't have to be responsible for keeping it that way.

I took my duffle bags into the bedroom area and put my stuff away. I had absolutely nothing on me to tie me to the police or the Antonellis, so I didn't have to worry about concealing anything. The fact that the suite couldn't even be locked was a blatant clue it was probably searched on a regular basis. Maybe it was already bugged. Well, no way did I plan to try anything to jeopardize my safety while in this place. I would play by the rules.

By the time I heard the knock on the door, I had completed my tasks of unpacking and organizing my meager personal items. I opened the door to a dude about my age dressed in khaki shirt and pants. He had a blank expression on his face. "Mr. Gorelov, come. I escort you to dining room."

I followed him down the never ending hall to a huge entranceway, a different one from the one on my first visit to the estate. It must face another part of the property. He then led me down another long hallway to an expansive, unbelievable dining area. The lengthy table covered with pure white linens had to seat at least fifty or sixty people. The room was as big as a banquet hall but much more lavish. The walls were covered with maroon and sparkling gold brocade cloth. The backs of the shiny mahogany chairs were ornately carved in infinite scrolls and patterns. The place couldn't be more opulent.

At the head of the table, which seemed to be a mile into the room, sat Kerchenko. Several other men were seated on each side of him. When my guide and I entered, Kerchenko's voice echoed as he spoke and pointed to the vacant right seat next to him. "Come, Mr. Gorelov. Sit."

I walked across the hardwood floors with the sound of my shoes clicking on them in the silent, resonating room. I quickly looked around at those seated at the table as I took my seat. I only recognized Kerchenko, Boris, Viktor, and of course, my good friend, Luka.

After I was seated next to Kerchenko, he began his introductions. "Mr. Gorelov, I would like to introduce you to our colleagues. You will be working closely with some of them; others you may not see often."

He started with Luka, who was sitting to his left. "This is Luka, my son. I believe you met him on your last visit to my house. I will call him my vice-president."

Luka frowned at me and said nothing. From his demeanor then and the last time I had met him, he seemed like some young punk who thought he was a big shot. The captain had warned me that I needed to watch out for this major player. He could cause me some headaches during my stay here.

Kerchenko pointed to the second person on his left. "This is Yury Gorsky. He is head of security."

Gorsky was a very large dude. I could see why he held that position. His biceps were almost bursting out of his shirt.

We exchanged nods and Kerchenko introduced the third guy on his left. "This is Oleg Dudin. He is the field supervisor. When you are visiting our clients, if you have any concerns or issues with them, go to Oleg. He will help you solve your problem."

Reading between the lines of what Kerchenko said, Dudin was probably the dirt bag who ordered the hit on the Antonellis. I would have to keep him in my radar also.

Kerchenko indicated the next man on his left. "And this is Bogdan Makarov. He is my chief accountant. You may be dealing with him in the near future."

So maybe Kerchenko was considering putting me in the financial part of the organization. That would give me a great opportunity to obtain the needed evidence to bring all his and his cohorts' illegal activity to an end. Captain Forsythe would be very pleased if I was put in such a position.

Indicating the last man on the left side, Kerchenko said, "The last gentlemen is Anatoly Oleshin. He is the grounds maintenance supervisor, taking care of my beautiful property on which we all comfortably reside."

Kerchenko turned his head to his right. "Sitting next to you is Leonid Martinovich. He is mechanical maintenance supervisor. If you have any issues with your vehicle, talk to Leonid."

My vehicle? Am I going to get a big, black SUV?

"Sitting next to Martinovich is Iosif Fedkin. He is supervisor of housing staff, including cooks, servers, and cleaning crew. Next to him are Boris Petrov and Viktor Kozlov. Of course, you know these gentlemen already. They will be your immediate supervisors for duration of your road training. My lovely wife, Ludmilla, who is also my personal secretary, could not join us for lunch today."

After the introductions, our first course of the meal was served. Many times grandma Eva Telek used to make *shchi*, this Russian cabbage soup. Aunt Eva still made it, but Ma, being English and Scottish, just doesn't have the knack to cook good Russian food. Don't get me wrong. She's a great cook. She just cooks different types of food. Her chicken and dumplings are out of this world.

Very little conversation occurred during the slurping of the soup. Then the waiters brought out the *shashlyk*, which is a form of shish kabab. My serving was marinated and grilled to perfection. Boiled potatoes and pickled cabbage were served with the meat. As for our beverage, we were served *kvass*, a Russian bread-based drink only slightly alcoholic.

I was stuffed by the time the dessert arrived. I hadn't enjoyed such a unique Russian meal since visiting Grandma Eva's house as a young teenager. The dessert of *pastila* was served with hot, black tea, a perfect way to top off the meal. By then I felt like taking a nap, especially after the night before on the cell bench. However,

Kerchenko had other plans for me.

After lunch, Boris and Viktor gave me an extensive tour of the estate, first showing me what was in all the surrounding buildings. They showed me the garage, which held Kerchenko's private vehicles: a Porsche, a Lamborghini, a Bentley, an Aston Martin, a Mercedes Benz, and a Rolls Royce. A few more conservative cars rounded out the ten. I bet there were several millions of dollars in vehicles just in that garage.

They also showed me the armory. Shit! I swear enough artillery was in there to take down all of Central Florida. I tried to remain calm and not show my amazement *and* concern.

After we finished touring the grounds, they showed me through the mansion itself. The only area I was not permitted to see was Kerchenko's private wing. Remembering how his office was decorated, I'm sure his personal wing was even more luxurious than the rest of the house.

Next on the agenda, I met with the various head honchos. Yury Gorsky, the security supervisor, told me the rules and regulations regarding inside and outside security. "I will give you five number code to memorize enabling you to enter various areas of property. This number will change at midnight on last day of every month. There is sequence to follow for change in code. For example, this month's number is #54836. Please memorize number. Never write it down anywhere. For next month each digit will increase by one number. So November's number will be #65947. An entirely different sequence will start at midnight on

December 31. It will be your immediate supervisor's responsibility to inform his staff of new code.

"I am also giving you gold emblem. This is your means of identification as member of organization. It will permit you to come and go on property and will also recognize you to other men and women in our employment. Do not lose emblem, or serious consequences will be administered. Keep it on your person at all times, but well hidden. Some team members hide them in shoes, socks, or underwear. Others tape theirs to hidden parts of their bodies."

The emblem was a two inch circle with a red star taking up most of the circle and a gold, double headed eagle engraved in the middle of the star. I surely didn't want to lose this thing. I wasn't sure what "serious consequences" would occur. The way this group worked I wouldn't even venture a guess. I'd have to think about where I planned to hide the emblem. Taping it to my armpit was not an option. It would be too hard to access and quite painful to remove. Taping it near my crotch would even be worse.

Gorsky was also in charge of weapons. "You will not be issued handgun until probation period is over."

The thought of surviving in this place without a weapon gave me concern. If something should happen to blow my cover before the probation period ended, I would be up shit creek. "How long is the probation period?"

"That will depend on you, Mr. Gorelov. You will be monitored during probation, and we will continue to check your background. Sometimes it takes months; sometimes it is weeks; and sometimes only days. But if I were you, I would not wish for days. If it is days, then we have found something we do not like about you, and you will be eliminated from organization."

It seemed like everyone in the organization wanted me to realize how serious was my employment and commitment. I took the word "eliminated" to mean gone from the face of the earth, not just the organization.

After my meeting with Gorsky, I was given directions to the office of Leonid Martinovich, the mechanical maintenance supervisor. I made a few wrong turns, but I eventually found his office. Martinovich was mainly in charge of the vehicle fleets. After my illusive probation period ended, I would be entered into the pool for the use of the SUVs. "You will not be given vehicle exclusively for your own use, but vehicles are assigned according to availability. Then you will be able to use any one of them not in use or specifically assigned to someone of higher status."

As for my Buick, I could either sell it or store it in one of the garages on the property. I thought it best to keep the Buick until I received my own SUV—if that ever happened. I needed to have an available means of transportation at all times. I hoped my keeping the Buick didn't put up a red flag. However, I wasn't a prisoner on the property. I would have my own personal time when not working on a job. So I would think at least during my probation period, there would be no issues with the Buick.

I was next directed to the office of Iosif Fedkin, the housing staff supervisor. He was actually located near the area where my private suite was situated. "A staff member will be assigned to clean your apartment and do your laundry every Friday. He or she will also restock refrigerator and cupboards. If you have any special requests for food or other household items, dry marker board is attached to refrigerator for any comments or requests. You may eat meals in your suite or in common cafeteria, whichever you prefer. You may also leave the property to take your meals when time is available for you. However, every Sunday morning, you will be required to attend breakfast meeting in cafeteria where various supervisors will update their staffs of any concerns. At these meetings, you can also voice any general issues you might have. I must warn you; Mr. Kerchenko often attends breakfast sessions. Mr. Kerchenko may also invite certain men or women to mandatory meal with him. Be prepared."

After leaving Fedkin's office I went to see Bogdan Makarov, the chief accountant. Makarov was in charge of all office and accounting functions of the organization. "Mr. Gorelov, I understand you are quite intelligent young man."

I didn't want to sound like I was bragging. "Well, I know a little bit about a lot of things."

"Does that include knowledge of mathematics?"

"I'm okay with regular math and algebra, but don't ask me about calculus or trigonometry."

"I may be able to use your mathematic ability. After you finish field training, I will speak with Mr. Kerchenko to see if you would be good fit in my department."

In all my visits with the various supervisors, no one had discussed money with me. Makarov should be the guy in charge of payroll. Even though I had no idea what I would do with the money I had to pretend it was a big factor to me. "So how and when do I get paid?"

Makarov stared at me for a few seconds. I didn't know if I said something wrong or if he was determining what to tell me. "Ah, yes, your pay. Well, of course, that is concern, isn't it?"

He again paused and stared at me. I didn't see why this should be an issue, so I simply stared back at him.

Finally, he said, "During your probation period, one thousand American dollars will be placed in top drawer of your desk every Sunday morning while you are attending breakfast meeting in cafeteria. When you are no longer on probation and still with organization, Mr. Kerchenko and I will discuss where your permanent position will be and what you will be paid."

Makarov excused me and gave me directions to the office of Oleg Dudin, the field supervisor. Boris and Viktor were also in his office. "Mr. Gorelov, you will be under my supervision until I am satisfied you are very familiar with our operations, and I feel you are capable to take over should I need you to replace someone else."

There's that hint of "elimination" again.

"For a while you will accompany Mr. Petrov and Mr. Kozlov to our clients' facilities. Sometimes you may be partnered with only one of these gentlemen. You must observe their actions and learn from them. They are responsible for collecting our fees from our various sources of income. Their territory consists of Orange and Lake County suburbs primarily south of West Colonial. However, they will take you to all our territories and introduce you to supervisors in charge of each. You may eventually be needed anywhere in our area. One never knows."

He hesitated with a slight smirk on his face. Then he began again.

"At this time you only need to be concerned with one phase of Mr. Kerchenko's organization: collecting our Protection Fees from local businesses in each territory. If Mr. Kerchenko wants to apprise you of his other income classifications, you will be notified."

According to Captain Forsythe, Kerchenko was involved in extortion, drug trafficking, and sex trafficking. I can't forget murder. But I needed to focus only on my immediate task at hand, which was to find out all I could during my probation period on the extortion end of illegal activities. IF, a big IF, I make it through that period, I'll worry about the other illegal operations at that time. Not knowing how long I had in 1993 or how long my probation period would be, I wasn't sure just how much information I'd be able to get. But, hell. What else did I have to do? Stalking Gina Mariani was not an option.

After the meeting with Makarov, it was time for dinner. I opted for the cafeteria. Not too many other guys were there. I ordered the special from the kitchen and ate in silence, thinking about all I had learned that day and realizing maybe I was getting myself in too deep. I was actually hoping somehow at that very moment I could get back to 2015. My nerves were getting to me, contemplating the enormity of the Kerchenko organization and the vast scope of its criminal activities. What had I gotten myself into? I needed to relax somehow. I went over to one of the servers and asked, "Hey, do you have any beer in this place?"

Thankfully, he gave me a six pack of Bud. I took it back to my room, turned on the TV, and watched some mindless movie until I felt sleepy enough to go to bed. It had been a very busy couple of days.

CHAPTER SIXTEEN
The Charade Begins

I had been sleeping in so many different places during the last several months that I was always confused when I awakened. Was I in Ma's apartment or Caruthers' condo? Was I at the Garden Motel or that small apartment the captain had placed me in temporarily? Was I in the jail cell with all those weird characters? It took me a few seconds to realize this morning I woke up in Kerchenko's mansion.

I hadn't gotten much sleep again. I woke up several times in a cold sweat, aware of the predicament I was in and not knowing how to alleviate the nerves and stress. I had to meet with Boris and Viktor at eight for a briefing, so at six I got up, showered, and dressed. I didn't feel like going to the cafeteria for breakfast, so I fixed myself some bacon and eggs in my small kitchenette. While sipping my coffee and tossing scenarios in my head, I heard a knock at the door. When I opened it, the same young guy from yesterday who had directed me to the dining room was standing there with a bundle of clothing in his arms.

"Mr. Gorelov, I deliver your clothing." He had spoken in that monotone voice as if I were supposed to know about this delivery.

"Uh, okay, thank you." I hadn't ordered any clothing, but I took the bundle from the guy and brought them into the room, laying them on the chair. I ripped the plastic wrapper from the bundle to find long sleeved black jerseys, black slacks, black socks, and black shoes, all in my correct sizes. Hmm. I guess these were my new uniforms. Nobody had mentioned anything about this. Apparently, I was in for many surprises.

I took the bundle into the bedroom and put all the clothing away. Keeping out one set, I then changed from the jeans I had just put on earlier into the black threads. Looking at myself in the mirror, I guess I looked the part of a Russian mobster. Ma always said I looked just like Grandpa Telek with those stern, rigid features. I really had never noticed before, but seeing myself in this dark gear, I agreed with her. Actually, donning this uniform gave me a little more confidence. Maybe I could pull this off after all.

I put my dirty dishes in the dishwasher and left in search of Petrov's office on the second floor. Both Petrov and Kozlov were already there when I arrived.

"Good morning, Mr. Gorelov, I hope you slept well," Petrov greeted.

I had to now show my tough guy image and act as if I were in complete control. "Yeah, yeah, let's get started here."

Petrov smiled wryly as he got up from behind his desk and walked over to a table under the window. "Here is a map of the territories under Mr. Kerchenko's jurisdiction."

Kozlov and I walked over to join him. I looked down at a map of Central Florida divided with red lines into sections. Kerchenko's Central Florida territory went north to Daytona Beach on the east coast, west to include Ocala, and over to the west coast to include Cedar Keys. To the south on the east coast it extended to Fort Pierce, then west to Sarasota on the west coast. That meant Orlando and Tampa were both under his domain. Hell! No wonder he had this extravagant headquarters. He must be a millionaire a hundred times over.

I played it cool while all this was going through my mind. Looking at the map, I asked general questions that wouldn't reveal the direction in which my mind was going. "So what do you have here? About thirty or thirty-five territories?"

Kozlov actually spoke then. He hadn't been much of a talker since I had met these two dudes. "There are forty territories. Some take in more miles while others take in more people. The city of Orlando is divided into four sections while Tampa is divided into six sections."

"Which is the most lucrative area?"

Kozlov responded, "The area around the attractions, of course."

I was getting interested and somewhat forgetting about my nerves. This was some operation! "How are the collectors paid? Does everybody get a set pay?"

Kozlov continued answering my questions. "Those working in

Protection Fee area of organization are paid by commission. So you see; it is very important we collect required fees due Mr. Kerchenko. If we do not, then it comes out of our own pockets. And nobody wants that to happen."

So if Kerchenko doesn't get paid, his cronies don't get paid either. Makes sense, in a criminal sort of way.

Petrov then went over the duties of the Protection Fee collectors. "Our duties not only entailed collecting fees, but also searching out new areas to 'protect.' This could involve established businesses not yet being levied fees, new businesses in area, or new types of businesses."

Petrov also went over some of the methods used to "persuade" the client to pay their required fees, such as threats against the person or his family, actual bodily harm to the person or family, robbery of business, and physical destruction of business or personal residence. Even though Petrov didn't mention death in his list of punishments, I knew it was the ultimate retaliation for unpaid fees. In other words, they would stop at absolutely nothing in order to collect their extortion money.

We broke for lunch at noon, but I was to return by three for a drive-along with Petrov and Kozlov. Since I now had my own ID to get on and off the estate, I was free to leave the property whenever I was not otherwise assigned. I hadn't been given permission to take one of the SUVs out on my own, so I took the Buick. My plan was to stop by Corky's to see if Dingo was available. First, I went to a fast food restaurant and grabbed a chicken salad for lunch. I also wanted to be sure no one was following me. It was too early in my employment for them to trust me completely, ergo my probation period. That probation might include them keeping their eyes on me when not in their presence. So I sat near the window at the restaurant, watching out for any black SUVs or any other suspicious looking vehicle. After about a half hour, it appeared I hadn't been followed. I grabbed my drink and went out to the Buick.

Just as I was about to pull out of the parking lot, what was pulling in but, yes, a black SUV. While I was at the curb, the SUVs window rolled down, and Kozlov's face appeared. "Where are you headed, Gorelov?"

I tried to act as calmly as I could. "I just had lunch. I'm on my way to Corky's for a couple of beers."

"Maybe we see you there." Kozlov rolled up his window and parked his vehicle.

I took off, my nerves about to snap. But then I thought, they knew I hung out at Corky's before, so my stopping there shouldn't look suspicious to them. I realized it was probably a good thing I didn't lie about where I was headed. Telling them the truth was a more natural statement. Here I made a smart move without even realizing it. At least I hoped so.

At Corky's I wasn't sure if I should approach Dingo or not, knowing the Russians might show up. But I could use a beer anyhow.

Donnie was behind the bar. "How you doing, Max? What'll it

be?"

"Just a Bud, Donnie." Looking around the bar, I didn't see Dingo anywhere. He could've been back in his office. I was debating with taking the chance to search him out when he came walking back from the stockroom carrying a case of beer. He saw me and nodded. "How's it going, Max?"

"Okay, Dom, how about with you?" Donnie sat my beer on the bar, and I took a long gulp.

I know I really didn't need to talk to Dingo, but I wanted to. Was it worth the risk? The Russians could be coming in the door at any minute to check on me. I can't blow this gig before it actually begins. So I just sipped my beer.

By two-thirty the Russians hadn't shown up. Maybe they trusted me. It was time to go back to Kerchenko's place. I missed my chance with Dingo. Hopefully, I'd get another when I really needed it.

So I went out to the Buick and drove back to Isleworth. As I pulled up to the guard station, a black SUV pulled behind me. I showed my ID and went on to Kerchenko's property, showing my red star emblem to the patrols at both gates. Inside the second gate, I drove around and parked the Buick in the same spot as it had been. Kozlov pulled up beside me. I'm not sure if they had been following me, but at least I didn't do anything suspicious.

Petrov stepped out of the car. "Are you ready to go, Mr. Gorelov?"

"Let me go take a leak. Be right back."

CHAPTER SEVENTEEN
Ride Along

When I was a kid, my friends and I used to play Hide and Seek. If I was It, I'd hide my eyes against the big tree in the backyard and count to one hundred. Sometimes I got bored counting and would skip a few numbers. My friends couldn't hear. They were in their hiding places far away. After I reached one hundred, honestly or dishonestly, I'd move away from the tree. I'd first look around the yard, scoping out where I would search first. Then I'd yell at the top of my voice, "Ready or not, here I come." I basically said the same thing when I came back out to start my tour. "Ready or not, here I *go*."

Petrov started our journey with his own territory. Kozlov drove to West Colonial and headed east toward Orlando. We didn't stop at any of their client's businesses, but Petrov would point them out as we passed by them. He had given me a note book and pen to write down the name and address of each business and how much they owed monthly on their Protection Fees. I guess having a hard copy of this information was not a problem to them. So I took the notes even though I'd remember all the information anyhow

When it got dark, we stopped at one of their customer's restaurants for dinner. Petrov explained we were then going to start on collecting fees. "You are only to observe. Either Kozlov or I will talk to the client. You will take notice of what we say and how we say it. We only collect cash. If there is to be any other arrangement, Mr. Kerchenko or Mr. Dudin will tell you in advance. Full payment is due each month or the client pays his debt some other way. Do not ask questions while on client's property. When we are back in car, we can discuss your concerns. Are we clear?"

"Oh yes, we are clear. Let's go." I acted excited. It helped to mask my heart beating a mile of minute from the nerves.

The first place we stopped was a nail salon in a small plaza along a heavy traffic area of West Colonial. The shop was run by a little Vietnamese woman about half my size. I felt sorry for her the minute I saw her. She was at the reception desk looking at some receipts when we walked in the glass doorway. The second she saw who we were, her eyes widened and her mouth opened, releasing a heavy sigh.

Petrov, who also towered over her, walked up to the reception desk. He leaned over the desk to the little lady's level and spoke to her in a low, harsh voice. "Mrs. Phan, do you have your payment ready for me?"

She practically jumped backwards and blurted in a heavy accent, "Yes sir, yes sir. One moment please." She dropped the receipts on the desk, some falling to the floor below, and scurried back through the store. She reminded me of a scared duck wobbling away from a predator as she waddled away from us. Two minutes later she was back with a tan envelope. "Here you are, sir. It is all there. You won't be back until next month, okay?"

Petrov took the envelope from her shaking hand. He removed the contents, and I watched as he counted out fifty one-hundred dollar bills. Five thousand dollars! Unbelievable! How could she afford to pay that much every month? This was just a little shop. I don't know what the cost of getting your nails polished was in 1993. Hell, I didn't know what it was in 2015 either. I just knew it couldn't be so much for her to afford giving this tyrant five thousand bucks every month. I really had a difficult time hiding the shame I felt being part of this robbery. How was I ever going to do this on my own?

"Hmm, Mrs. Phan. You have done well. Have nice evening." Petrov grinned sardonically as he replaced the bills and put the envelope in his pocket.

Back in the SUV, I didn't know what to say. I didn't want to hint at how I was really feeling. They'd shoot me on the spot. So I took a very deep breath, mustered up my courage and snickered, "Piece of cake!"

The next stop was a bar a few blocks from the nail salon. As we pulled into the parking lot, Petrov informed me of his concerns at this location. "This client was short last month. If he does not pay this month's payment and five thousand he owes from last month, we will have persuasive discussion with him."

What was I about to witness? The fear in Mrs. Phan's face when she saw us walk in her shop was enough to make me hope and pray this owner had the correct money ready.

The place was fairly crowded. Petrov led us to the bar and addressed the bartender, "Where is Mr. Dulakis?"

By the look on the bartender's face, he recognized Petrov. "Back in the office."

Petrov walked to the right passing a few booths and tables of customers. He stopped before a door at the end of a short hallway. He knocked twice but entered without waiting for a response from inside. "Mr. Dulakis, how are you this evening?"

Dulakis' expression was enough to inform me he was not happy to see us and was not doing very well at all. With an unsteady voice he blurted, "I… I thought you wouldn't be here until next week."

"No, Mr. Dulakis, this is the correct week. Do you have our money?"

"Uh, sure, uh," he stuttered. "Let me get it out of the safe."

Just as Dulakis got up from behind his desk, both Petrov and Kozlov pulled out their revolvers. Kozlov barked, "Don't try anything you will regret, Mr. Dulakis."

"No, no, I'm just getting your money. That's all."

Petrov demanded, "If you think you can pull out weapon, you will be dead before you have chance to turn. Unlock your safe, then step away. We will get money out."

Dulakis cautiously proceeded to the other side of the room with his hands slightly raised. At the safe, he trembled as he entered the combination to the lock, then quickly stood, and moved aside next to the safe with his hands out in front. "Okay, okay, please, take your money."

Petrov, still holding the weapon on Dulakis, quickly nodded toward me. "Get the money out of the safe."

Dulakis quivered, "It's in that top envelope, man."

I looked at Petrov, then Dulakis. The poor guy was shaking like a leaf. But I had to appear tough and unconcerned for him. I walked to the safe, opened the door, and pulled out the top envelope. Standing up I reached out to hand it to Petrov.

Without taking the envelope, he ordered, "Count it."

Since it was a bulky envelope, I took it over to the desk and removed the wad of money. After counting out the bills to myself, I announced, "There's thirteen thousand here."

I heard both Petrov and Kozlov let out deep breaths. Then Petrov chided, "Mr. Dulakis, Mr. Dulakis, what is this? You are short *again!*"

Dulakis, physically shaken, uttered, "It's just two thousand. I... I can have it for you next week. Please! Please! Give me until next week."

Kozlov didn't hesitate. He walked over to Dulakis and whacked him on the side of his face with his revolver. Dulakis fell to the floor with a loud thud.

Petrov yelled to me, "Go in safe. See what else is there."

I walked back to the safe, stooped down to look inside. "There are several stacks of bills in here, different denominations."

"Take it all," barked Petrov.

From the floor Dulakis cried, "No, no, please. Don't take that money. I need it to pay my rent."

"Mr. Dulakis, you know your Protection Fees come before any other obligation." Petrov turned back to me. "Take it all!"

So I gathered up the several stacks of various denominations and dropped them on the table. Kozlov asked, "Where are envelopes?"

Dulakis, knowing he was defeated, moaned, "In the bottom desk draw."

I went around the desk, retrieved a large envelope, and stuffed the stacks of bills inside.

Petrov and Kozlov put their revolvers away and started for the door. I followed with the envelopes. Petrov said to Dulakis as he went out the door, "We will be back next month. If you don't have required fees on day they are due, you will not just receive love tap to face. Do you understand?"

Dulakis was holding his bloody face while propped up on his elbow. "Yes, I understand."

Back in the SUV, Petrov looked in the envelope with the stack of bills. "Good job, Mr. Gorelov, good job." He put both envelopes in the large glove compartment with Mrs. Phan's envelope. Then he closed the compartment. "Next customer, Viktor."

The next stop was at a mom and pop convenience store. When

we entered, a young guy about my age was behind the counter. Petrov approached him. "Where is Mr. or Mrs. Patel?"

The clerk didn't look frightened. I assumed he didn't know who these Russian dudes were. "They ain't here." He pushed his greasy hair out of his eyes and chewed on his gum.

Petrov then asked, "Did Mr. or Mrs. Patel leave an envelope for me?"

"Who are you?"

"I am Mr. Smith. They should have left an envelope."

"Nope. They didn't tell me nothin' about no envelope."

"Are you positive about that, young man?" I noticed a bit of impatience in Petrov's voice.

"Yeah, man. I'm sure. They didn't leave nothin' for nobody."

Petrov did that deep breathing thing again. Then he leaned over the counter into the guy's face. "This is very important, young man. You tell Mr. and Mrs. Patel that Mr. Smith and Mr. Jones came by to get package, and it was not available. Tell them we are very disappointed about their negligence. You get message to them. You tell them we will be expecting two packages tomorrow night."

The clerk's blasé facial expression turned to one of fear. He finally realized we were not here merely to greet the Patel's. Petrov was breathing in the dude's face. "If for some reason Patel's don't get my message, you do know who I will hold responsible, don't you?"

The clerk's entire demeanor changed. He was terrified. "Yes, sir! Yes, sir! I'll make sure they get your message."

Petrov backed away, sent final daggers into the dude's eyes, and then we walked out the door.

Back in the vehicle, Petrov turned to face me. "Now, Mr. Gorelov, we did not like outcome of this collection. This client will pay dearly this month and every month from now on. We cannot allow this type of behavior."

We made four more stops that evening: another bar, a gas station, a restaurant, and a tattoo parlor. We had no issues with any of them. However, each of the owners was terrified when confronted by Petrov and Kozlov. I felt ashamed to be part of this injustice, but I had to think of the big picture. I was involved in all this to put an end to it. Since I was actually seeing firsthand how these poor business owners were treated by the Russians, it gave me more resolve to find a way to stop their unlawful and cruel torment. I had to be patient. The opportunity would come—I hoped.

CHAPTER EIGHTEEN
Just One Of The Gang

For the next several weeks, I rode around with Petrov and Kozlov throughout their area of Orange and Lake Counties. I made a list of all the businesses they contacted, their owners, and the amount of money they fraudulently extorted from them. Since Petrov and Kozlov were aware of my note taking, I had the freedom to write anything down. Little did they know, I didn't need the notes. I'd remember all of it. I'd remember especially the cruelty they inflicted on those who were short or late with their payments. Mr. Dulakis wasn't the only client physically hurt during my probation period. I saw fingers chopped off; I saw knees broken; I even saw them blind a guy in one eye. All the while I kept my mouth shut, pretending it didn't matter to me the way they were inflicting unjustified physical, mental, and financial pain on all these people. That was definitely the hardest part. But I remembered what they did. Oh, how well I remembered.

Thankfully, I was not told to assist in any of the violent persecutions, but I knew my time would come if I had to become one of these fee collectors. I did, however, have a hard time living with the knowledge of how this entire organization existed on the pain and agony of innocent people.

I also knew eventually Petrov and Kozlov would approach Dingo at Corky's to enlist him as a client. I had only witnessed one client solicitation and it wasn't pretty.

Kerchenko's men did research on a business before they'd approach it. A new Mexican restaurant had opened up in a plaza on West Colonial. Juan's Restaurante was run by Juan and Rosaria Jimenez, legal immigrants from Mexico. In downtown Orlando, they had previously had a restaurant in a rented shop. When it was vandalized, rather than use their insurance money to stay at that same location, they moved to Winter Garden. They remodeled a space previously occupied by a thrift store, and they had opened the month before our visit. Their lunch crowd was good, but they were still trying to promote the dinner clientele.

At three o'clock on a Wednesday afternoon, Petrov, Kozlov, and I entered the small but colorful restaurant. Only two other customers were already in the place. Petrov led us to a table far from those patrons. A slightly overweight woman dressed in a bright red skirt and a yellow peasant blouse approached our table. She handed us menus and said with a thick Mexican accent, "Good afternoon, senòrs. Can I get you something to drink?"

Petrov ordered three Coronas for us and put the menus aside.

When the waitress returned with our beers, Petrov said, "I wish to speak to the owners. Are they available?"

The woman looked startled, but her eyes had a knowing look to them. Maybe she also had to deal with the Russians in her prior location. "I am Rosaria Jimenez. My husband and I are the owners. What do you want?"

"We are here to offer you mandatory protection from thieves and vandals. It is my understanding you had problems with these in Orlando."

She now looked frightened. "Let me get Juan. He will talk to you." She hurried in the direction of the kitchen.

We sipped our Coronas while we waited about five minutes before Juan appeared. As he exited the kitchen, he stopped and looked around, wiping his hands on his white apron. Spotting us, he came over to our table. "What is this about? We don't need protection. We have insurance. Please, either order your food, or pay for your drinks and leave. Thank you."

He started to walk away, but Kozlov grabbed him by the arm and squeezed tightly. "Do not leave. Sit!"

The man was visibly terrified. He kept looking around the room, hoping for someone to save him. The two other patrons became aware of something they didn't want to be a part of or to witness. They dropped their money on the table and quickly exited the restaurant.

"What do you want from us?" Juan Jimenez's voice shook as he spoke.

Petrov leaned toward the man, knocking over one of the empty Corona bottles. "We want to help you protect your business. Police cannot help you, but we can. All you need to do is give us twenty thousand dollars at end of every month, and I guarantee you will have no problems keeping your business safe. We will be very generous. You do not have to pay us for this month, but we will be back end of next month for our money. Do you understand?"

"But I can't afford that kind of money. We just opened this month. We haven't built up our customers yet?"

"Well, Mr. Jimenez, that is reason we are being generous and not insisting you pay us for this month."

Jimenez looked defeated. I didn't know what was going through his mind, but I felt so sorry for him. The poor guy was just trying to make an honest living. He was still recovering from the issues he had at his other location. Now this.

"Okay, okay. I try."

"No, Mr. Jimenez, you don't try. You *do!*" warned Kozlov.

Petrov got out of his seat. Kozlov and I followed. Jimenez sat in his seat with his head lowered. As we were walking out the door, Kozlov yelled, "And do not call the police. You will regret it if you do."

After witnessing what poor Jimenez went through, I knew Dingo was in for the same kind of treatment when the Russians would visit him. The day I first met those guys, they had tried to approach Dingo. However, after my fake explosion at the bar that evening, apparently it was more important for them to follow me out the door to see if they could enlist me into their organization. As far as I knew, they had not yet been back to Corky's for another attempt at the extortion. I didn't know whether or not the captain had coached Dingo as to what he was to do when that occurred, but I somehow wanted to warn him to expect it soon.

Although my work schedule was grueling, I was getting days off. Nothing regular. I usually didn't know when my day off would be until the day before. Each free day I had, I'd visit Uncle Nick and Aunt Inga. I wanted it to appear like something I regularly did. I'd update them on the information I'd learned from my activities since my last visit with them. Therefore, the captain was gaining knowledge piece by piece.

I was beginning to truly appreciate this older couple. They made life seem a little more normal than being a member of the Russian mob. They were definitely authentic Russians. Uncle Nick told me they had come to United States in 1980 and never regretted their move.

Every time I drove to their house, I would be absolutely sure no one was following me. A few time, I noticed a black SUV following a car or two behind me. It could have been just a coincidence, but since I was still on probation, it probably was Kerchenko's men. Just to be safe, as the captain had suggested, at those times I'd park on the street instead of the driveway. None of the captain's men had been in Uncle Nick's house on those days, so there never was any imminent danger of Kerchenko's men discovering the real reason I visited Uncle Nick.

I also stopped by Corky's occasionally on my nights off. I was still very careful about keeping my new identity safe and continued to act the part of Max Gorelov. A few times I was able to talk to Dingo. In our last bathroom conversation, I asked him how Gina Mariani was doing.

Dingo started out with a concerned look. "She still refuses to go into a Witness Protection Program even after the captain told her the Russians were staking out her home. So the captain told me to move in with them to help with their protection. Mrs. Antonelli is a great cook, so it's good for me too. When I'm working at the bar, a policewoman stays inside the house. The captain has also stationed a patrol car outside the house twenty-four seven. He said it'll be money well spent once we catch Kerchenko and his scumbags. I'm still afraid for those ladies and that kid. Those Russians are vicious. I'm hoping they think if they have eluded any capture and prosecutions thus far, then Gina is not a good witness and therefore, not a threat or a target for them."

"Yeah," I agreed. "She worries me too."

"She plans to come back to work at the bar soon too."

"What! No way! Can't you guys discourage her? Those Russians are planning to come in the bar soon to harass you into buying their protection. She can't be here when that happens. It's way too dangerous!"

"Hey, Tank. Believe me. We tried to convince her. She is a very stubborn woman. She knows the police and I are working on some kind of sting. I guess since Donnie and I are both involved, it's pretty obvious. She doesn't know anything about you, though. But she says she has a right to see this to the end. Her dad and her husband deserve it. And since she and her mother own Corky's, what can we do?"

"Well, I guess I see where she is coming from. But she's in so much danger, sticking around here."

"Hey, you're preaching to the choir, man."

"Yeah, yeah. You're right. I just hope she isn't in the bar when the Russians decide to pop in on you. Have they been back since they were in here with me that last time?"

Dingo pushed his lower lip out and squinted his eyes, trying to remember. "If they did come in, I didn't see them or they didn't create any issues. You might ask Donnie. He'd know more. I'm back in the office a lot these days."

"Well, I guess there isn't much we can do about Gina Mariani other than what the captain is already doing. Has anybody talked to Mrs. Antonelli? Maybe she has some influence."

"Yeah, we've tried that route too with no luck. Both of them want to see this finished. They feel they really need to be around when Kerchenko goes down. I'd feel the same way if I were in their shoes."

"Just be sure you keep an eye on them, okay?"

****

Other than the stressful ride-alongs, my time in the Kerchenko organization became routine. I want to say mundane, but I never could think of people's livelihoods or lives like that.

The illegal shakedowns usually started about three or four in the afternoon, going to the businesses who closed around five or six. Then we'd stop at one of the client's restaurants for free dinners. Afterwards, we'd start our collections again by visiting other restaurants and bars in that order. We usually got back to the estate about two or three in the morning. On the property was a building they called the Bank, a windowless structure with dense cement walls and thick, steel doors, one in front and one in back. No keypad was available to enter a code. A buzzer was attached to the right side wall. Petrov would press the buzzer, and one of four guards equipped with heavy, automatic weapons would look out the peephole in the door before opening it. All three of us had to show our red star ID emblem before the guard would admit us. As we walked into the building, we entered a small hallway. The only furnishing in the room was a table to the side holding bottles of water, a coffee pot, Styrofoam cups, sugar, and cream. Sometimes donuts or cookies were also on a platter. Four guards were always in this room, night and day. Directly in line with the entrance door on the opposite wall was another steel door. One of the guards would press the keypad to open this door.

On the other side of the door was a gigantic, open room with constant activity involving about two dozen men and women. Long tables were set up in the middle of the room with several computers and calculators on each of them. Off to each side were two massive, steel safes, which I'm sure held millions of dollars. We turned in all our money directly to Kerchenko's chief accountant, Bogdan Makarov. Someone in his department counted the money in our presence, and someone else recorded it in a physical ledger as well as a DOS program on a computer. If the collections were short, then the sums given to the collectors were less. So it was to their advantage to collect the full amount on time. I'm sure if a collector repeatedly presented short cash, he'd not be in that line of work for long. He'd be "eliminated" from that position.

In the instructions given to me, I was told any physical infliction short of death was allowed to entice the client to keep current. If sufficient physical pain had been administered and they were still chronically late, it was time to discuss this client with Dudin and Kerchenko.

The collectors would get their percentage immediately, which was also recorded in the ledger and on the computer. I still got my money in my desk drawer. I wasn't ready for commissions yet. I didn't care. I wasn't interested in the money. I had my sites on bigger things.

Thus, everything was run like a legitimate and efficient business except everything was handled in cash, and of course, it was far from legitimate.

I'd usually get to bed around four in the morning. Since we got in so late from the collections, I'd sleep until noon. I'd grab a quick breakfast or lunch, work out for an hour or two, and then the routine would start all over again.

It was a Thursday night, my last night with Petrov and Kozlov before being transferred to another group of henchmen. We had made a few collections in south Orange County. All the clients were up to date, and we had no issues with any of them. On our way back from our last pickup Kozlov turned onto Nawinah Cortland Road. It was only midnight. I thought it was a little early to return to Kerchenko's property. We usually stopped at a couple of bar clients about that time, and the only one I knew of on Nawinah Cortland Road was Corky's. My heart skipped a beat. This was it. We were going to shake down Dingo.

Kozlov parked the car in Corky's parking lot. My nerves were getting the best of me as I exited the back seat. How was I going to handle this? Would I be able to stay in character while Petrov harassed Dingo? I had no choice. I had to keep it together.

Before we walked into the bar, Kozlov pulled out a cigarette. Great! Even though I hated those things, I needed one too. I reached in my pocket and pulled out my pack that was growing stale from nonuse. Never did a cigarette taste so good, stale or not. Never did I need one so badly. It really did calm me down somewhat.

After stamping out the cigarettes on the ground, the three of us walked into Corky's, proud and in control. Donnie was bartending. Then out of the corner of my eye, who should appear returning to the bar with a tray of dirty glasses but Gina Mariani! I had no gun on me, so I couldn't do much if things went sour. I knew Donnie had a gun behind the bar, but could he reach it in time if he needed it?

Then I quickly got hold of myself. We weren't here to collect any money. Corky's had paid dearly whatever debt they previously had with the Russians. They had paid with the lives of Carl Antonelli and all those poor suckers who were in the bar back in April. We were just here to talk and threaten Dingo. Nothing more. I hoped.

Gina noticed us as we walked in, but I immediately realized she didn't recognize any of us. She merely continued on her walk behind the bar to get rid of the dirty glasses.

Since it wasn't too busy, three adjacent stools were vacant at the bar. Petrov ordered Stoli for us. Donnie was acting very cool. He casually got our drinks and placed them on the bar. Gina Mariani had placed the dirty glasses in the sink with several others and started to fill another drink order.

Petrov was staring at Gina. What was going through his mind? I could tell she didn't recognize him. Was he aware of this?

Donnie was serving another customer at the end of the bar. When he looked up Petrov signaled him to come over.

"What can I do for you, man?"

"I wish to speak to Dominic Antonelli."

Donnie, still acting casual, asked Gina, "Hey, Gina, can you get Dom for these guys?"

Okay. I wasn't imagining it. Gina stiffened her entire body when Donnie asked her to get Dingo. I think Petrov caught it too. I sure hoped Dingo and Donnie had a plan regarding what to do with her when this time came.

Gina took the beers to the customers who ordered them, and then she slowly went to get Dingo. She looked like a robot as she passed by the bar, keeping her eyes straight ahead.

About ten minutes later, Dingo came down the short hall and over to us. Gina was not with him. "Good evening, gentlemen. You asked to see me?"

Petrov folded his hands on the bar. "I believe we have some unfinished business to discuss."

Dingo acted very cool and composed. "Ah, yes. You are the gentlemen who were trying to extort money from me for so-called 'protection fees'. Are you also the men who murdered my brother?"

I was stunned! What was Dingo doing?

"Oh, Mr. Antonelli, you are mistaken. We are simply here to help you keep your business safe. Your business could burn down tonight, or you could be robbed of all money in your safe. We can stop bad things from happening."

Dingo then inquired in a demanding voice I had never heard him use before. "Are you threatening me? You listen to me. I already have protection. I have round the clock police protection on this bar. If anything the least bit suspicious goes down, believe me, the police know where to find you. Now get out of my bar before I have you escorted out."

Petrov and Kozlov stood up. They were both seething! Their eyes narrowed and their jaws stiffened like vices. I took their lead and acted accordingly.

"Mr. Antonelli, you are a very brave but unwise man. And you are making a very stupid mistake." Petrov turned to go out of the bar.

In the car, Kozlov and Petrov were both silent. I wished I knew what they were thinking or planning. Why had Dingo acted like a tough guy? Hadn't he just put himself and Gina Mariani in real danger? Dingo even insinuated the Russians killed Carl Antonelli. Surely they would plan to retaliate.

After several minutes of silence, Petrov ordered, "Drive back to the property. We are finished for the evening."

No one spoke the entire way back to the Kerchenko estate. I had hoped they'd reveal what would happen next. At the same time, I was trying to think what was happening back at Corky's. Why was it I was supposedly in the loop with the police and with Kerchenko and yet I knew nothing?

After we pulled into the parking lot at the estate, Petrov took out his phone. Dialing an extension, he said into the phone, "Dudin, we must speak."

Nobody told me not to follow them to Oleg Dudin's office, so I did, in silence. Maybe I was at least going to hear what the Russians planned to do about this recent situation.

Seated in Dudin's office, black tea was brought in to us. Dudin took a sip of his tea, and then set it down in its saucer. "What is the problem, Mr. Petrov?"

Petrov explained what had transpired at Corky's. I listened attentively to his version. He told Dudin about Dingo's attitude and response, but he also talked about Gina Mariani. "I do not think she recognized us specifically. However, she definitely knew who we represented."

No one spoke for a while. Only the sounds of our tea being lifted on and off the saucers could be heard.

Finally, Dudin said, "The action of this Antonelli cannot go unpunished. Do you think he is serious about having police protection at all times?"

Kozlov responded, "Oh, yes. He was serious. Could you blame him after what happened back in April?"

"Yes, yes. Then we must get to them in some other way. I must talk to Ivan about this. I will get back to you soon. In the meantime, stay away from that establishment and the owners."

We finished our tea and left for our own suites. Since a decision on retaliation had not been made without Kerchenko's approval, I was hoping I would be made aware of what they decided when it was eventually made.

CHAPTER NINETEEN
Eyes Wide Open—Most Of The Time

Always in the back of my head was the *threat* or the *hope* I'd unexpectedly find myself back in my old life. I couldn't decide. I was fitting in with the organization, but I was terrified constantly. Yet no one actually gave the impression they suspected I was not who I claimed to be. In 2015, I had no worries. Of course, I didn't. Ma did all that. In fact, I was the reason for many of her worries. It shouldn't be that way. I was an adult. I needed to step up and act like one. My adult life in 1993 was giving me that opportunity. I needed to take advantage of it, quit bellyaching, and act like the man I should be.

Luckily, I was off on Friday, the next day after our visit to Corky's. It was my opportunity to go to Uncle Nick and Aunt Inga's house. Since we had not stayed out as late Thursday night, I was able to get my workout in early and arrive at their house in time for *oped*. They already knew about our visit to Corky's the night before. However, I told them of the Russians' plan to retaliate. "They haven't yet determined what they plan to do about

Corky's or Gina Mariani. I hope they clue me in when that decision is made.

"Oh, another thing. As of tomorrow, I'll be with two different collectors. I'm not sure which ones yet, but I'll get the information to you as soon as I can."

On Saturday I started my tour of duty with Smirnov and Ivashin, the dudes who handled the west side of Orlando south of West Colonial. Lucky me. My friend Luka also road with us. He never talked much to me, but I tried to be friendly with him. I didn't want to get on his bad side more than I already was. Any negativity he felt toward me might get back to his father, and I needed to be in good standing with everyone in the organization.

I was shocked at the difference in the territory these guys had compared to Petrov and Kozlov's area. For the most part, it was made up of poor business owners who were struggling to keep their businesses afloat in a very bleak and depressed part of town. To think they had to give such large percentages of their monthly intake to these Russian thugs was irrational. I witnessed several times when the owner was only a few dollars short and was severely physically penalized. I wasn't sure how much more of this I could take.

And these businesses were holding on by the skin of their teeth. I could tell by the equipment in their shops or the décor in their restaurants. They barely had enough money to pay for their products and employees. I felt so helpless being a witness but having my hands tied.

Smirnov and Ivashin were just as ruthless as Petrov and Kozlov. Luka was probably the most heartless. Brutality was part of their job, but that kid carried it to extremes. He seemed to thrive on it. All three of them were immune to the violence they inflicted; they were immune to the poverty surrounding them; their only concern was the money they collected at any cost. I was getting sick and tired of all the cruelty and callousness. If it wasn't ending soon, I didn't know how I could endure much more.

I maintained my note taking with these guys also. I needed as much evidence as possible to bring this organization down. With the evidence being both on paper and in my head, the police would have a double guarantee of the crimes of these villains.

The following Sunday morning was our breakfast meeting in the cafeteria. Both Dudin and Kerchenko attended. If anything, I'd call it a sort of pep rally. They both agreed protection fee collections were up, but so many new businesses had moved into the area who had not yet been approached. Dudin mentioned the prostitution trade on South OBT was doing well with all the tourists in town. Throughout these two men's discussions of the various phases of their criminal activities, I thought to myself how the meeting was ironically like some typical, legitimate corporation's board meeting; conversing about profit and losses; determining how to increase productivity; and giving "atta-boys" to exemplary employees. It was so sad and harsh, it made me sick. Somehow they had to be stopped.

****

We had a close call one night while I was riding with Smirnov, Ivashin, and Luka. We had stopped at a twenty-four hour convenience store in the Paramore area run by an Arab dude named Mahir Basara. It was about two in the morning when we arrived, and no customers were in the store. The dude didn't have all the money he owed to the organization. After Ivashin learned Basara was short on his payment, he told Luka and me to take him out the back door. We went around the counter, each of us grabbing the guy by one of his arms. He pleaded as we dragged him along, "Please! Please! I will have the money next week. Do not hurt me! Please!"

I had to block out the sound of his desperate pleading while I dragged him, not knowing what Smirnov and Ivashin planned to do. It was one of the hardest things I've ever done.

Smirnov and Ivashin followed us out the back door to the alley behind the store. Luka stood Basara up against the stucco building. He began to punch him, first in the face, then in the gut. It was evident Luka was enjoying the punishment he was inflicting. Each time the Arab would collapse, I had to prop him up again so more punches could be smashed into him. The poor guy was screaming in pain.

When we had gone out the back door, Smirnov had left it open. All of a sudden, two black guys appeared at the doorway. When they saw what was happening, they took off back through the store and ran out the front door. They must've taken the time to call the police because within a few minutes, we heard sirens in the distance. Ivashin said, "We get out of here now."

The Arab dude collapsed to the ground, hitting his head on a garbage can as he fell. We rushed around the store to the SUV and were gone before the police arrived.

I was thankful those two black guys showed up. If they hadn't, I think Luka would've killed the Arab. Unbelievably, we still did other collections that night, just not in the Paramore area. When we got back to Kerchenko's property, Ivashin, Smirnov, and Luka went to report the incident to Dudin. Ivashin told me to call it a night.

I thought that would be the end of it. However, later that morning when I was still sleeping, I got a call from Aunt Inga, telling me Uncle Nick was sick. That was the signal to alert me something was wrong, and the captain wanted me to get in touch with him immediately. Though I had only had a few hours' sleep, I knew I'd better find out why Aunt Inga gave the signal. I quickly got dressed and drove the Buick to Uncle Nick's house. Since this seemed to be an emergency, I parked on the street rather than the driveway and rushed into the house.

Once inside, Aunt Inga led me to an office in the back of the house. Heavy drapes were closed on the two windows and only a dim floor lamp lit up the room. Caruthers was seated on a small couch next to one of the windows.

"What's going on?" I asked, very concerned.

"Were you involved in that incident last night?"

"Uh, are you talking about the Arab at the convenience store in Paramore?"

"Yeah. That guy was beat up pretty badly. The police got an anonymous call. When they arrived, the Arab told them four Russian men attacked him. Then he confessed the men were extorting money from him."

I wasn't surprised with what Caruthers said. We had heard the sirens. What did surprise me was that poor Arab dude actually squealed on us. He had just put his life in grave danger.

"Yeah, I was there. I had to hold the guy while Kerchenko's son battered him. Is he going to be okay?"

"Well, it depends. Of course, when he mentioned the Russians, we knew exactly who he was talking about. At this very moment, Captain Forsythe is sending a couple of detectives to talk to Kerchenko. He doesn't think anything will come of it, but he wants Kerchenko to be aware the police are watching him. However, he didn't want you on the property when the police arrived, not knowing what might happen."

"Yeah, I was surprised when Aunt Inga called this morning. I figured I'd better get here as soon as possible. You know, that Arab has put his life in serious danger now."

"Well, he has a ruptured spleen, a broken nose, a couple of broken ribs, and several missing teeth. Lots of cuts and bruises too. But he has decided to go back to Saudi Arabia. He says it's too dangerous here. So he'll be okay. The captain was concerned for you."

I stayed at Uncle Nick's for a couple more hours just to be

sure whatever was going on back at Kerchenko's property was over and done with by the time I got back. Before Caruthers snuck out the back door, I gave him the notes I had been taking. His vehicle was parked on the street behind Uncle Nick's house.

When I did get back to the mansion, I went to bed for a couple more hours. I heard nothing of what happened when the police came on the property. Kerchenko's men were not the type to gossip. And I wasn't going to ask. I simply played dumb.

After three weeks with Smirnov, Ivashin, and Luka I was finally transferred to the Bank and worked under Bogdan Makarov, the chief accountant. I was still on probation, but I think Kerchenko wanted to try me out in a more mentally challenging position. What a relief! At least I didn't have to witness or participate in the cruel and unjust treatment of innocent people. Instead, I counted the collection money in the early morning hours. It really wasn't challenging. I knew how to count. But it was definitely a more pleasant job than beating down poor business owners. The cash going through the system involved all phases of the organization: money from the drug trade, prostitution, sex trafficking, and protection fees. A lot of cash. Kerchenko's territory was huge!

I did well at this job. I'm quick with math. Ma always chastised me about my abilities, saying she couldn't understand why I was so good at math and remembering things yet I was such a deadbeat wasting away my life. If she only knew what I was up to in 1993, she'd be proud of me now.

This new assignment meant I stayed up even later than when I was on the collection teams. I was warned I might not get off work until six or seven in the morning, which was no big deal to me. I adjusted my sleeping, eating, and workout habits. I stopped by Uncle Nick's house later in the day, so I was still able to get messages to Captain Forsythe. Even though this was a better job and I didn't have to witness or take part in any violence, I was worried about not being able to forewarn Dingo about what Kerchenko planned for them. It had been several weeks since I had been to Corky's with Petrov and Kozlov. Uncle Nick had told me nothing unusual had occurred yet. So Kerchenko was either planning something big, or he had something more important to think about.

I settled in to the new job very easily, handling bags or envelopes filled with cash from the various collectors. I'd quickly separate them into stacks by denominations; I'd count each denomination and mark the total on a chart; then using the calculator I'd add up the chart totals. It was not unusual to have a collector's total count go into the hundreds of thousands. And I wasn't the only counter, although I became the fastest. I didn't put the information into the computer or into the official ledger. Other guys had that job. However, the computer would verify the totals I had reached. I was never wrong; my chart total would always match the computer total.

At first I was completely in awe of all that cash. I thought of all the things I could do with it. Ma and I could buy a nice house and move out of our dingy apartment. She wouldn't have to work at Carneys anymore. I could get serious about college and pay my own way. I could buy both Ma and me new cars.

However, no way would I ever dream of taking any of it. I knew it came from innocent people who were hurting very badly because it was in Kerchenko's possession. Even if no one was harmed physically or mentally from the confiscation of the money, it still wasn't right. I'm just not a thief.

However, the biggest deterrent was the video cameras Kerchenko had throughout the building to catch every movement of every person in the entire Bank. You couldn't pick your nose without being seen by one of those cameras. So, with the guards standing around with AK 47's, I knew what would happen if I slipped a couple of hundred dollar bills into my pocket. My blood would be all over the money I was counting.

I was gaining more and more knowledge of Kerchenko's operations as well as gathering names of many of his henchmen. On my visits with Uncle Nick, I relayed what I had learned to him. I wrote nothing down while in the Bank. I had no reason to do so. Because of my ability to remember, it wasn't necessary. I recited what I had learned to Uncle Nick, and he'd somehow get the evidence to Captain Forsythe. I didn't know how that part of the plan worked, but I didn't care. I did my part. Let someone else worry about the other roles.

It was a good thing I had the memory I had because those video cameras were focused on us at all times. As with the money, if I would attempt to slip even a piece of paper into my pocket, someone was constantly looking through the data the cameras collected. An even stronger deterrent was the physical pat downs we got from top to bottom every time we'd entered or exited the Bank. But that guard with the AK47 was by far the strongest preventative of all.

Thus, life became a routine. I actually somewhat enjoyed this job except when I thought about where the money came from. Then I felt like a traitor.

Months passed, and my probation period ended. The accounting department became my permanent location. Makarov would give me different jobs to do. Sometimes I'd work in the Bank; sometimes I'd be stationed in an adjoining office near his, engrossed in various stages of the money handling and tracking areas of the organization. I'd willingly accept whatever challenge he gave me, and he was satisfied with my performances. I'm sure he relayed my conduct and abilities to Kerchenko.

It truly felt like working for some big corporation. I no longer witnessed the violence I saw when I was on the ride-alongs. I'd attend the Sunday morning meetings and hear the pep talks the various men in charge would give. I'd join in on the accolades given to men for special accomplishments. I even received recognition a couple of times from Makarov. But I knew, oh, how well I knew, this was not an ordinary business. This organization was built on the pain, the sweat, the blood, and the very lives of innocent people. Even though I acted as if my job with the

Kerchenko organization was the most important thing to me, my real job was to do everything within my power to put a stop to all of it.

****

Just short of a year had passed since I found myself in 1993 instead of 2015. On April 22, 1994, about noon, I was awakened by a knock on my door. Still groggy, I got up and looked through the small, eye level door to see who was disturbing my sleep. Boris Petrov stood there. I had not had any personal contact with him for several months. When I opened the door, he rushed into my suite. "Get dressed. We have job to do."

I was confused. "Uh, I'm not going to work for Makarov tonight?"

"No. We have other plans. Come to Mr. Dudin's office when you are dressed." Then he left.

I was apprehensive. Had they discovered I was a spy for the police? Why did I have to go to Dudin's office? I hadn't worked under him for a while. This didn't sound good at all

I had to calm down. Maybe it was something else. Maybe they were changing my job again. Maybe they needed another collector. After all, I had received extensive training in that area too.

I got dressed; trying to suppress my fears; trying to squelch the doomed feeling I might be walking to my execution that very day. Again, I had to put on my bravery persona. I couldn't allow them to know the terror I felt inside.

Reaching Dudin's office, I knocked on the door. It was opened by a huge Russian dude. Probably about a dozen guys and one woman were in the room. Most everyone was seated around a long conference table. Dudin was at the head of the table with Luka on one side and Petrov and Kozlov on the other. An empty chair was at the opposite end of the table.

Dudin commanded, "Sit, Mr. Gorelov."

I sat on the vacant chair, clasped my hands firmly together to avoid revealing how much they were shaking. I felt as if everyone in the room were staring at me. Silently, I actually started to pray, asking forgiveness for all the mean things I had done in the past. Somewhere in the middle of the pray while asking God to please give me a painless and humane death, I heard Dudin mention my name. "Mr. Gorelov, we are here to discuss a very important mission that will take place tonight."

Still praying I thought, *Oh, God, they're going to make me wait until tonight before they kill me. They're going to make me fret about it all day. I'll probably die of fright, and they won't need to kill me.*

Dudin interrupted my prayer again. "We will punish..."

No, God, it isn't going to be a quick death. They're planning to torture me! My thoughts were out of control.

Dudin continued, "...those at Corky's Bar for their rebellious attitude. Mr. Kerchenko is disgusted with the many problems they have caused us recently and in the past."

Thank you! Thank you, God! I prayed silently. *They don't plan to kill me tonight.* Then I realized I might be safe, but what about

Dingo and Gina Mariani? What did Kerchenko have planned for them? I became more alert. My hands stopped shaking, and I controlled my emotions to listen attentively.

Addressing everyone in the room, Dudin announced, "We will kidnap Mrs. Antonelli and the child of Gina Mariani."

CHAPTER TWENTY
Covert Operation

When I was a kid, sometimes Dad would let me worry about a punishment for a day or two before he'd actually execute it. Now, most young boys are not like most young girls. Girls get punished for things like lying, tattling, maybe even stealing small things like candy or gum. But boys can be really nasty. They fight. They might drink or smoke. They might steal major stuff.

One time this buddy of mine, Skip, and I got in serious trouble. Rightly so. At the time, we both lived on this hill, and we made a dummy out of old clothes stuffed with newspaper. Then we put the dummy in the middle of the street, making it look like a dead body. In order to see the reaction of the drivers when they ran over it, we planned to hide in the bushes when a car came down the hill.

Well, what we thought of as a practical joke, Dad thought of as a cruel and dangerous prank. This car drove down the street unaware of our dummy until its front tire thumped over the fake body. An old lady had been driving the car. She screeched to a stop, jumped out of her car, and started screaming and crying hysterically. Skip and I were in the bushes laughing so much we cried too.

Dad wasn't laughing. He'd been in the living room reading the paper when he heard the lady's screams. He knew who put the dummy in the street as soon as he saw it lying there. It was dressed in one of his old sweatshirts. First, he tried to console the lady. It took him several minutes to calm her down. Ma brought out a glass of water for her. Dad was able to convince the lady not to press charges against us, so the police were never called. But that didn't mean we weren't in serious trouble. Dad sent Skip home immediately. Then in a calm but stern voice he told me to go to my room; he would deal with me later. I figured I was in store for a big lecture, which that alone was a grueling punishment, sitting for two hours while Dad made me recap the incident and tell him why it wasn't just a practical joke.

But there was more. I wasn't allowed to associate with Skip for an entire month. By that time Skip found another best friend. During Dad's lecture he told me I had a week to think about what I had done. So I stewed for a week, worrying what he had in store for me. When the week was up, he made me go house to house on our entire block and explain to the people what I had done. He followed me so I was unable to skip houses or lie about my actions.

So why am I telling this childhood calamity? Because it is similar to what the Russians planned. They had been belittled by

Dingo, representing Corky's Bar, and wanted him to know there were serious consequences. They had let him stew about it for several months. Dingo and Gina Mariani needed to realize their mistake and be punished. I'm not saying the Russians were correct. I'm just saying that's the way they thought.

But I never expected them to kidnap the grandmother and the baby. How were they going to achieve this? Uncle Nick had told me police officers were constantly stationed one inside and one outside the Antonelli house twenty-four seven. I don't know if Mrs. Antonelli ever took the baby to Corky's. However, if she did, police were constantly guarding that location also. After I thought about it, though, I realized this was the Russian mob. They were capable of just about anything with the manpower, the artillery, and the technology they had. And they could get away with it unscathed.

Somehow, I had to make sure this was *not* one of those times. It may sound absurd, but I think I finally realized why I was sent back to 1993. Early Sunday morning will be exactly a year since I first got out of my truck to find myself literally transported back to the year I was born. That has to mean something. Or maybe not. I found myself trying to justify the time spend in 1993. Why? What was I here for? There had to be a reason. All this Russian mob stuff had to be part of it.

Dudin explained how the kidnapping would go down.

"We will use two vehicles. Kozlov, you will drive first car with these passengers: Petrov, Luka, Volkova, Gurin, and

Gorelov."

Oksana Volkova was the woman at the table, and Artur Gurin was a big Russian muscleman sitting next to her. That Oksana was as huge as the Gurin guy. Her name was appropriate. She looked like an ox.

Dudin said the second vehicle will have six Russians dudes in it. The largest part of the task would be performed by those in the first vehicle. Those in the second will be parked at a nearby plaza to be available if needed.

He continued with his instructions. "Kozlov, you will drive first vehicle to Millbrook development and turn up Millrun, which is first street before Millstone, Antonelli's street. You will drop off Gorelov at house on Millrun adjacent to Antonelli house, and Gorelov will creep back through their yard to backyard of Antonelli house. Kozlov, you will park SUV on Maple Drive, which is street running perpendicular to Millstone and Millrun. You will keep motor running.

"Gorelov, you will take duffel bag containing EMP Pulse thermo-nuclear device and drop it in garbage can in Antonelli's back yard. When you have duffel bag secured in garbage can, you will contact Petrov on two way radio we give you.

"Petrov, you will set off remote charge on thermos-nuclear device to cause anything electronic or battery operated in and near Antonelli house within hundred yards to be shut off or destroyed."

This charge, resulting from the remote activation of the EMP Pulse thermo-nuclear device that I will be carrying in the duffle bag, will even affect electronics not plugged into outlets. So not only will the Antonelli house be completely dark and without phone service, but so will at least all the immediately surrounding houses, street lights, and vehicles. Therefore, that police officer in the driveway of the Antonelli property will not have the use of his car radio or his vehicle.

Dudin continued his instructions. "Kozlov, your vehicle will be safe enough distance away and not effected by EMP outage. You will drive back to Millrun and drop off all other passengers. They will creep through adjacent property to join Gorelov for kidnapping."

We sat in Dudin's office for about three hours going through the plans over and over until everyone was sure of their specific tasks. We were not to kill the police officers, but we were to disarm and neutralize them with an injection of Etomidate. We had to work fast because the drug will only keep them out for about fifteen minutes. Each of us was given a small, maroon, plastic container with a syringe filled with the drug.

After our extensive briefing, we returned to our own quarters to prepare for the operation.

****

All those taking part in the maneuver met in the parking lot at midnight. Corky's remained open, and verification was made regarding Gina Mariani and Dingo still working at the bar. Our two vehicles travelled into Nawinah toward the Millbrook development. The second car pulled into the parking lot of the nearby plaza amongst a few other cars also parked there. As planned, Kozlov turned up Millrun Drive, dropped me off, then drove up the street and parked on Maple Drive.

With the EMP pulse duffel bag strapped over my shoulder, I cautiously made my way in the dark to the Antonelli house. In the backyard, I put the bag inside one of the two garbage cans, then took out the two-way radio and called Petrov. "The bag is secure."

Petrov responded, "Affirmative. In two minutes I will activate EMP. Your radio will no longer work. Get in position to take out officer in police vehicle. When lights go out, he will rush out of his vehicle to enter house to check on old woman and child. Disable him immediately."

I went to the backyard next door and crept in the shadows of the side of that house so when all the power went out, I could approach the police vehicle from the rear passenger side and sneak up on the officer from behind.

I was in position behind a large oak tree in the neighbor's front yard when the lights went out. Quickly, I ran behind the police car while holding the Etomidate syringe in my hand and waited for the officer to exit. Within a few seconds, he opened his door. Immediately, I pounced on him, twisted my arm around him, and injected the Etomidate into his neck. He was squirming and kicking with his arms and legs flailing in the air, but I overpowered him and held tight for a couple minutes until the drug took effect. Then I gently released his unconscious body to the front seat of his car.

At that moment, Kozlov's vehicle pulled up and the others swarmed toward the house. Kozlov parked the vehicle in front of the house, remaining in the vehicle with the motor running. I followed the others. Gurin, the Russian dude, kicked at the front door. It splintered and cracked but didn't open. He gave it another swift kick, and the hinges broke loose. As we stormed through the door, the shadowy figure of a female police officer was coming toward us. Flashlights were flicked on as Luka grabbed the officer and injected her with the Etomidate. As she dropped to the floor, we rushed toward the stairway. Mrs. Antonelli was descending the stairs with a look on her face that I will never forget. Her eyes looked like huge marbles protruding from their sockets. Her mouth was opened in a silent scream. Gurin grabbed her and pulled her the rest of the way down the steps. The ox woman continued up the stairs followed by Petrov and me, searching out the sound of a baby crying frantically. In the baby's room the ox woman picked up the child, wrapped her in a blanket from her crib, and swaddled her next to her bosom.

By the time we got to the bottom of the stairs, Luka and Gurin had Mrs. Antonelli in the front yard. All of us rushed into the waiting vehicle, and Kozlov took off. Petrov got on his radio to tell the second SUV we were headed back to Kerchenko's estate, and the operation was a complete success. We were in and out of there in record time.

In the far back seat, Mrs. Antonelli was seated between Luka and Gurin. She was sobbing softly and praying in Italian. The ox woman and the crying baby were seated next to me. I had never felt more like an asshole than I did at that moment with both the old woman and the tiny baby miserably weeping.

Kozlov drove the speed limit but took a back way to the property, which I didn't even know existed. It must not have been part of Isleworth's development because we entered only the two gates, which Kerchenko's men were guarding. Kozlov entered the first gate, and then proceeded down the winding drive through the second back entrance gate to the mansion.

When Kozlov parked the SUV, everyone exited the vehicle, Luka and Gurin roughly forced Mrs. Antonelli out of the SUV as she continued to sob and resist them. I was waiting for them to exit the back seat so I could close the door when I noticed a plastic maroon container on the seat. It must've fallen out of Gurin's pocket. Luka had used his on the policewoman in the Antonelli house. I discreetly grabbed it and pushed it into my pocket before closing the car door.

As I watched them firmly grasping poor Mrs. Antonelli, I wished I had been able to comfort her and tell her everything would be alright. But even if I could, I'd be lying. How the hell did I know if I could turn this disastrous event into something positive? At least no one had been seriously hurt. The two police officers we had injected would be okay. They'd probably be groggy and disoriented for a while, but they'd have no lasting effects. I'm not sure why Dudin didn't order us to shoot them, but I was very thankful he hadn't. Maybe Kerchenko and he figured they didn't want police homicides on their hands. Regular people, okay; just not police.

When we got into the mansion, Petrov and Luka escorted Mrs. Antonelli into the private wing. Oksana followed with the still crying baby in her arms.

What a mess I'd made! Things were worse now than when I first started this undercover task. Now the Russians had the grandmother and the child. Poor Gina Mariani. How much more could she take? Why couldn't I stop it somehow? No. Instead I was actually part of the kidnapping, a key operative. How could I ever make this tragic event into something positive? There had to be a way. Otherwise, what was I doing here? I vowed somehow, some way, I would make this right.

CHAPTER TWENTY-ONE
Another Change Of Duty

I had the next day off and took the opportunity to go see Uncle Nick and apprise him of the kidnapping. While we were seated at the kitchen table, I rested my elbows on the table and covered my face with my hands. Finally, I said to him, "I felt horrible being a part of that reprehensible operation, but I had no choice. If I didn't participate, they'd know something was wrong. There would be serious consequences for me and also to Captain Forsythe's plot to finally connect Kerchenko to all his corruption. I had no choice..."

Uncle Nick knew I regretted having to be part of the kidnapping. "Max, your hands were tied. You had no choice." He told me what transpired after the kidnapping. "When the two police officers on duty at Antonelli house became conscious and functional, they rushed to nearest neighbor who had power and called Captain Forsythe. Then bedlam erupted in Millbrook subdivision. Police set up spotlights so forensic crew could search for clues. Entire area was cordoned off with crime tape. Police officers were stationed throughout development. Anyone entering and leaving development was required to show ID. I think crews are still at crime scene today."

Apparently, the captain had informed Gina and Dingo of the incident as soon as he was aware of the kidnapping. Gina was hysterical when she found out about it.

Uncle Nick continued, "Dingo, he promptly closed bar, and he and baby's mother rushed to police station. Restoring electricity and electronics at Antonelli house and surrounding houses will take some time to replace and repair. Baby's mother and Dingo were placed at undisclosed location."

I also wanted to see if Uncle Nick had any ideas regarding how to now rescue the grandmother and the baby. I knew they were in Kerchenko's wing of the mansion, but I had no idea how I could gain access to it. If I happened to find my way into that wing, what could I do about Oksana Volkova? She was a *big* woman! I knew I couldn't overpower her.

Uncle Nick was as clueless as I was. "I will get word to Captain Forsythe to see if he has any suggestions. I'm sorry. I wish I could help you more."

The next day I went back to work in the Bank counting more and more money. Since I worked into the late morning hours, on the guise of keeping in shape, I'd jog around the property in the afternoon. While on those runs, I never saw Mrs. Antonelli or the baby. I had hoped the ox woman would take them outside for some fresh air and a change of scenery. On the nice days, I even took my meals out on the small picnic area fairly near the mansion. I thought perhaps they might be brought out there, but no, they were never around.

On my next visit to see Uncle Nick, he informed me a ransom of three million dollars had been demanded from Gina Mariani. Ironically, I had to snicker and shake my head when I heard that ultimatum. I spouted off to Uncle Nick. "What does Kerchenko think he's doing? No way could she afford even one percent of three million. He knows she doesn't have tons of money. It's just a scam for whatever reason, just like everything the monster does. He's playing games. He's going to kill Mrs. Antonelli and the baby. I have no doubt."

I had to somehow find a way to save them. And it had to be soon.

Almost a week after the kidnapping I got a break and came up with a plan. It would be very risky, but I had no choice. Time was running out. Kerchenko was not a patient man. Whatever he was planning to do would be done soon.

On April 28 around noon, I again heard a knock on my door. This was beginning to be a regular occurrence. Staggering to the door while wiping the sleep from my eyes, I looked through the small door to see who had disturbed my precious sleep. It was Petrov again. I opened the door and grumbled, "This is becoming a habit with you, Boris."

Petrov was not one for small talk. "Get dressed. We have new job for you. Meet in Mr. Dudin's office."

Of course, I was very curious. Petrov had acted in the same

manner the last time he had awakened me for the kidnapping caper. That time I was scared shitless they were planning to kill me. What could this be? Could this actually be another job, or was he such a good actor, and this visit to Dudin's office was really going to end my life?

I pushed that lame idea out of my head. Nothing had happened to make them suspicious of me. I'd been doing a good job at the Bank and in other the areas of accounting assigned to me. I'd been able to think of all the money I handled daily as just pieces of green paper. So they couldn't have faulted me with anything on the job. I had also carried out my part of the kidnapping without a hitch.

Could it be Uncle Nick and Aunt Inga were exposed? That was a possibility. However, they had no reason to suspect them for anything either. If they hadn't connected them with Captain Forsythe when I first started working for Kerchenko, they would have no reason to do so now. My probation period had ended months ago. What reason would they now have for searching into my background and ultimately connect them to the captain?

So I put all my fears out of my paranoid head and got dressed. Before going out the door, I slipped the Etomidate into my pocket, just in case.

In Dudin's office, only Petrov, Kozlov, and Oksana were seated in front of Dudin. Oksana? Why wasn't the ox woman with Mrs. Antonelli and the child? Who was watching them now? I camouflaged the confused look on my face and took the empty seat. Whatever they were discussing when I entered the room came to a pause. My heart skipped a beat! Maybe they *were* discussing my fate.

Dudin addressed me directly. "Mr. Gorelov, you have fit well into our organization, and Mr. Kerchenko has found your performance very satisfactory."

Hey! Praises for me! I guess I had been a good actor. This wasn't my death sentence.

Dudin continued, "Because Mr. Kerchenko needs a man who is both astute and dedicated, he has another special job for you. We currently have a situation where these three will be called away for an unexpected assignment." He motioned toward Petrov, Kozlov, and Oksana.

"Tonight we will be confiscating a truckload of lovely, young Mexican girls on its way to Florida. Oksana Volkova especially will be needed to help make these young females feel comfortable when truck is intercepted. She will not be able to assume her regular duties tonight, and we will need someone to guard the woman and child."

Hallelujah!

"Currently, they are being guarded by Mrs. Kerchenko, but she is not as well equipped for that responsibility as you or Volkova. She will remain with you to care for any female needs that may arise, but you will be there to keep the three of them safe. You will start your task immediately. The suite is equipped with all your needs. Do not leave it. I know you have not eaten yet this afternoon. As soon as you are settled, *oped* will be served."

Dudin reached in his desk drawer and pulled out a Makarov 9x18 mm. "Here is your weapon in case of emergency."

Dudin handed me the pistol, an extra magazine, and a box of ammo. I stood up and took the extra magazine and ammo, putting them in my pockets. Then I took the pistol, turning it and testing it in my hand.

I was so excited. At last! Somehow I knew this would be my opportunity. I didn't know exactly how, but by tomorrow Mrs. Antonelli and baby Carla would be safe.

"Because of this new development with the Mexican girls, if you should need assistance, many of your associates will be unavailable. Mr. Kerchenko has also been called away for a crucial meeting. Thus, this is a very important assignment entrusted to you, Mr. Gorelov. You will be on your own. Do you have any questions?"

I wanted to determine how much time I'd have to come up with a plan and to execute that plan while being confined on the estate. "Do you know how long the assignment will last?"

"We should be back on the property by daylight. Do not fall asleep. You must be alert at all times."

"Oh, no, I won't. I definitely had enough sleep to last me for at least twenty-four hours." I was positive I wouldn't be the least bit sleepy. Planning an escape like I had to do would keep anybody awake.

Dudin stood up from behind his desk. "Then that will be all.

Mr. Kozlov will take you to the captives."

I pocketed the gun at my waist and followed Kozlov through the maze of hallways to Kerchenko's private wing. To enter the elevator leading to his wing, Kozlov pressed a code. I memorized the four digit number. Neither of us spoke while the elevator climbed to the second floor. He never was much of a talker. Upon exiting the elevator, we walked down a long hallway covered with rich, gray carpeting. The walls were painted a creamy, light pewter and lined with original oil paintings of various landscape scenes with an unmarked door thrown in now and then. At the end of the hall, Kozlov pressed the code to open the wide steel door. Again, I memorized this code.

The gray carpet continued on the other side of the door into a large sitting room furnished with various maroon and dark gray upholstered chairs and couches with shiny ebony end tables adjacent to most of them. Off to one side, I saw an archway leading into a dining room. Off to the other side were various doors, which I assumed led into the bedrooms. Seated on one of the chairs was a beautiful woman, perhaps in her forties, with gorgeous red hair and a flawless complexion. She was slowly leafing through a magazine.

On the opposite side of the room sat Mrs. Antonelli. Her face was very sad, and her eyes were bloodshot. She was cradling the sleeping baby in her arms. As I entered, her facial expression changed. I sensed a pleading, desperate look on her face. Did she think I was there to do harm to her? Oh, no, Mrs. Antonelli, just the opposite. I'm here to get you out of here. I saw her glance at the Makarov pistol at my waistband. Yes, she thought I planned to inflict more pain on her.

I looked away from Mrs. Antonelli and turned toward the beautiful Ludmilla Kerchenko. She had gotten out of her seat and walked toward me. When she spoke, her English was almost void of any Russian accent. "Good afternoon, I'm Ludmilla Kerchenko. Please call me Milla. I assume you are Maxim Gorelov?" She extended her hand to me.

I took her soft, velvety hand and gently shook it. I answered her in English. "Yes, ma'am. You can call me Max. You will be safe with me until Oksana returns."

When Kozlov saw that our introductions were taken care of, he departed. Before leaving he revealed, "I saw you watching as I entered the code to the suite. I do not have to give you those numbers. You are very observant, Mr. Gorelov."

I wasn't sure if that was a compliment or a threat.

After Kozlov left, Milla showed me around the suite. A small kitchenette with white marble floors and sparkling, black appliances was off the dining area. On the opposite side of the main room were three bedrooms, each with a different décor and each having its own bathroom. Security cameras were scattered about in all the rooms near the ceiling out of anyone's reach. I assumed sound devises were also hidden in various locations to detect any conversations taking place in the room. A pink crib was set up next to the double bed in the room Mrs. Antonelli used. The entire suite was very chic.

When we returned from my mini tour, Mrs. Antonelli was still in the same position with the same miserable expression on her face. She looked up at me but quickly looked away. I would need to gain her trust somehow.

There was a knock at the door. Milla entered the same code Kozlov had used and opened the door for our *oped* food. The server laid the food out on the dining room table. We had noodle soup in a mushroom broth and a huge hunk of black bread. We also had *blini*, a Russian crepe made from buckwheat flour. Ours were served with savory smoked salmon and creamy mushrooms. Honey cake with black tea was our dessert. The food was delicious. However, I don't think Mrs. Antonelli agreed. She had placed sleeping Carla in a small bassinet in the sitting room when Milla begged her to come to the table to eat. She took only a couple of spoonful's of the soup and just a few bites of the *blini* and salmon. Russian cuisine is very different from Italian food, but I doubt it that variance was the reason she was not eating. She had other things on her mind. I was hoping I could eventually help put her mind at ease.

After *oped*, Mrs. Antonelli wheeled the baby in her bassinet into the bedroom. She said she was going to take a nap also. Milla sat back down and picked up the magazine she had previously been perusing. I went over to the large picture window to see if I could get my bearings on the direction we were facing. I had to somehow plan our escape. I noticed this part of the mansion overlooked the parking area. Only one SUV was on the blacktop. The others must have left already. Kerchenko was also probably gone. So if I was able to get Mrs. Antonelli and Baby Carla out of here, how could we get away? Since my current job kept me on the property, I had no need to have access to the SUVs. Therefore, I had not yet been given the authority to use any of them. I knew the keys would probably be on the keyboard near the cafeteria. However, if that one vehicle on the parking lot was already being used by someone, he may have the keys in his possession. My Buick was now parked in the organization members' personal vehicle garage where I had parked it after my last trip to Uncle Nick's house.

With thoughts of escape swarming my head, it took me a few seconds to realize Milla was asking me a question. "Max, tell me about yourself. Are you from Florida?"

I turned around and walked over to a chair somewhat facing her. "No, I'm from Illinois." I then told her of my alias identity and my fake upbringing in Highland Park.

She asked me next, "What brought you to Florida?"

"Well, truthfully, I was getting in trouble in Illinois. You know, hanging around with the wrong crowd after graduating high school. My dad knew I could do better and wanted me to have a fresh start."

"That's good. So why Florida?"

"My dad's brother, Nick Gorelov, lives in Nawinah with my Aunt Inga. Dad figured Uncle Nick could help me get a good start down here."

I was looking at Milla while I was recapping my bogus situation. With the mention of Uncle Nick and Aunt Inga, the look on beautiful Milla's face changed. Her mouth opened, her eyes widened, and the magazine in her hands fell to the floor.

Not knowing what her reaction meant, I too was apprehensive. "Is something wrong? What did I say?"

She picked up the magazine and put it in the rack at the side of her chair. Her face went blank as she stared at me. She was confusing me more and more, and I was getting very concerned. Her friendly attitude had instantly morphed into suspicion.

She sat rigidly in her chair and spoke in an unusually quiet voice. "Did your Aunt Inga used to be Inga Salova?"

Did my heart skip a beat? How did she know this? I calmly put my right hand on the gun at my waist. "Yes. That was her maiden name."

She leaned back in her chair and looked away. We were both silent. I wanted to ask her how she knew Inga's maiden name, but I was afraid of her answer. I gripped the gun waiting for her to decide what to say or do next. What I didn't expect is what she actually did. She burst into tears! This I didn't know how to handle. I just sat in the chair like a stone hoping she'd give me some explanation for her unexpected behavior.

Suddenly, she reached over and opened the drawer in the table beside her chair. I thought she was going to pull out a gun. I gripped my pistol, pulled it out, and pointed it at her.

Instead of a gun, she took out a box of tissues. When she saw me pointing the pistol at her, she screamed and stood up shaking her hands, the tissues falling to the floor. "No! No! Don't shot!"

"I... I thought you were grabbing for a gun. Okay, okay, I'm going to put this pistol away. Please sit back down. I'm not going to shoot you."

She backed up to her chair. Sat down, and began to cry again.

Hell, what was I to do? I got out of my chair, picked up the tissues, and at arms' length, handed the box to her. "Here are your tissues. I'll sit back down now." In slow motion I returned to my chair, walking backwards. "Please. You owe me an explanation. What did I say to upset you?"

She hadn't stopped crying, so I waited patiently. Finally, between sobs and tissue dabs to the eyes, she said, "Inga Salova is my aunt."

CHAPTER TWENTY-TWO
Confessions

I don't think I would have been as shocked if she had said Hillary Clinton, was her aunt. How could my phony Aunt Inga be her real aunt?

"You're shitting me, aren't you? She can't be your aunt."

"She is my aunt."

"Okay, how is that possible? You're the wife of probably the most powerful man in Florida, maybe the entire country. How can we both be related to Inga Salova?" I had to have answers, no matter what the consequences.

She was quiet. I sensed she wanted to say something, but for whatever reason wasn't saying it. I definitely couldn't give my identity away to the wife of Ivan Kerchenko. I don't know why, but I was feeling sorry for this woman. Is that ironic or what? One of the richest women in the world and I was feeling sorry for her. "Please, please explain this to me."

She blew her nose, dabbed at her eyes again, and then went back to staring at me. I waited. Then in a more authoritative voice than I expected, she demanded, "Max Gorelov, who are you for real?"

I didn't expect that question. "Uh, I'm really Max Gorelov. Why would you think otherwise?" What was happening here? What a quandary! Out of everyone in Kerchenko's organization, no one ever suspected a hint of my real identity. Yet this woman was suspicious of me within an hour of our meeting.

"No, you are not Max Gorelov. I don't know who Max Gorelov is, but I know that is not your name. You look and act like all the other Russians here. You do the despicable deeds they do, but I know you are not Max Gorelov."

Despicable deeds? Why did she use those words? Is she not the wife of Ivan Kerchenko? Does she not condone all the cruel, murderous acts he and his henchmen perform on a daily basis? This woman was really mystifying me, but more than that, she was rubbing me the wrong way. I overstepped my boundaries. "Let me ask *you* a question. You are the wife of one of the most powerful and richest men in this country. Surely, you know how he has achieved that status. Here you sit in this mansion, a home more luxurious than any other I have ever seen, and you ask me why *I* do the things I do? If you feel your husband and his entourage are performing 'despicable deeds', why don't you put a stop to them or get out of Dodge? Or are you so selfish you are more concerned about your precious, extravagant lifestyle that you turn a blind eye to all the carnage done by your husband and his men? And here you personally sit in this room knowing the woman and child you are guarding have been kidnapped and held for ransom, most likely to be murdered soon. Yet you callously sit here and read a magazine."

Oh, no! What have I done? After I spoke, I knew I should've kept my mouth shut. But I guess the stress of being part of Kerchenko's organization had finally gotten to me. Truthfully, I think I knew I was going to end it tonight. What did it matter what I said to this woman? But how I would handle this woman just added to all the other issues of escaping and saving Mrs. Antonelli and Baby Carla.

Ludmilla started to cry again, not deep sobs, but the tears started trickling from the corners of her eyes. She was holding a tear soaked tissue in her small hands, and she began to pull and straighten the tissue. She whispered, "Because I'm a prisoner just like that poor woman and baby."

I almost fell out of the chair! What did she mean?

I was about to ask her when she began to explain. "I 'm telling you this because I know you are not really Max Gorelov. After that outburst, it is very apparent you are not telling *me* the truth. Perhaps you will tell me who you really are after I confess to you."

She cleared her throat, dabbed her eyes one more time. "Seven years ago I met Ivan while I was waitressing at a Russian restaurant in Orlando. I had been in the USA on a green card for a year. Aunt Inga is my mother's sister. She had her citizenship by then and was my sponsor. Ivan took a liking to me. I also liked him. He was handsome, friendly, and considerate. We began to date. He would take me to places I didn't know existed. You see, I'm originally from Moscow. My family is poor, and I came to USA to earn money to send back to them. I thought I was in love with Ivan. I didn't know how he got his money. I'm ashamed to say at that time I guess I didn't care or think to find out. I was so happy to be able to partake of the finer things I never even knew existed in all the world. He bought me beautiful clothes and jewelry; he set me up in a lovely apartment; and he gave me money to send home to my family. When he asked me to marry him a year after I met him, I was overjoyed. How could this rich, handsome man want me? Yes, he was several years older than me, but my father is twenty years older than my mother. So that meant little to me.

"Before we were married, I had never been to his home. He would always come to my apartment. When he first brought me to his estate after our honeymoon, I couldn't believe how beautiful it was. But I was terrified. I saw armed guards everywhere. I asked Ivan why there were so many on the property. He simply told me he had many enemies, and he needed the guards to protect him and his home. At first, I believed everything he told me. I was very naïve, but I am not a stupid woman. I overheard and I saw some of the appalling things he and his men have done. By then, it was too late. Ivan knew I had learned too much about his life. He says he still loves me, but I am kept on a very tight leash. Wherever I go, I am either accompanied by Oksana Volkova or one of her strong women. You've seen Oksana. Her women are as tough as she is.

No one has ever hurt me, probably because I have never given them any reason, but my life here is hell. In an instant, I would give up all my beautiful, designer clothes and this extravagant lifestyle to be free. I no longer have any contact with Aunt Inga. Ivan still sends money to my family in Moscow, but he monitors my letters and phone calls to them. About a year after our marriage, I approached the subject of a divorce with him. He slapped me in the face and threatened me never to mention the subject again."

She took another tissue and wiped her nose, sitting back in her chair. "So you see, Max, or whoever you are, I need to know why you are here."

This was the wife of Ivan Kerchenko. She just confessed to me she was held on his property unwillingly. Her story was almost as outrageous as mine. If I hadn't heard it directly from her, I wouldn't have believed it. I was in a very awkward position. She was expecting me to tell her something. If I told her the truth, would I be asking for a death sentence before my mission was accomplished? She could be baiting me, just waiting for me to slip up. Maybe Dudin or Mr. Kerchenko put her up to this. Those men are capable of anything. However, if she was telling me the truth about her situation, she could be very helpful with getting us off the property. If she was lying... well, I had both the gun and the Etomidate. I could overpower her very easily.

After careful consideration, I decided to tell her exactly why I was in her home. I cleared my throat and sat back in my chair. I prefaced my dissertation by saying, "Milla, although your admission greatly shocked me, I can top it tenfold."

She had stopped crying and tilted her head to the side with a bewildered expression.

I started from the beginning: my truck accident; my eye-witnessing of the murders at Corky's; my cell time and why Captain Forsythe inducted me into service; my change from Tank Telek to Max Gorelov; and my second induction—into the Kerchenko regime.

"Nick and Inga Gorelov aren't actually my uncle and aunt but my contacts with Captain Forsythe. They never mentioned you in all my conversations with them. So naturally, your admission of being Inga's niece was definitely a shock to me."

When I had completed my speech the only word to describe the look on her face was complete amazement. Her eyes were now dry, and there was no sign of sadness left on her face.

"Mary, mother of God!" she blurted. She surprised me again. I guess she was Catholic.

"So your name is Tank," she uttered while tossing it in her brain.

"Well, actually it's Talbott. That's a horrible name my mother decided to give me. She's the only one I allow to call me that."

"Talbott... Tank... Telek." Again, she was working it through her brain.

"Well, the Telek comes from Telekhov. My grandfather changed it."

"Telekhov…. So you are Russian?"

"No. I'm an American of Russian descent, actually only half Russian. My mom is Scottish and English. I only know about Russia from what my grandfather had told me or what I read in books."

"But you speak the language well."

"Yeah, well, Grandpa was a good teacher, and we spoke it around the house while he was still alive, sometimes even when my dad was alive. Then I had a tutor to help me brush up when I took on this assignment with the police. It came back to me rather quickly."

"Tank, you were right. You definitely surpassed my story." She hesitated and stared at me. "But, the amazing thing is I actually believe you. How could that be?"

"Milla, it took me days until I believed it myself. I'll be here a year early tomorrow morning. I have no idea why I've been here this long. Most of all, I don't know if *or* when I'll go back to 2015. I'm just working it one day at a time."

"Why do you think this happened to you?"

I wanted to form my answer as best I could. I leaned back on the chair and looked up at the ceiling, scanning and trying to find the words to say. Instead of finding an answer, my eyes found one of the cameras focused on Milla and me. Suddenly, I remembered these cameras were recording our every action. What about the listening devises? I jerked upright and pointed to the camera as I looked at Milla.

She looked up at the camera, then back at me. "Oh, they are not working now. I told Ivan, I did not want his men snooping on me. The cameras are even over the toilets. Disgusting! He said he would have them turned off. See? There is no light on that camera you are looking at. Even though he doesn't trust me, he trusts Oksana, my constant guardian. And apparently he trusts you also. So no one is videotaping or listening to us. Have no fear.

"So tell me why you think you are in this predicament."

I was still a little edgy. Would an army of whoever was left on the property burst through the door and drag both of us to our deaths? Well, if no one came after she admitted her circumstances to me, I was fairly sure she was correct about the cameras and listening devises being turned off.

I told her my speculation about my being in 1993. "I think I'm here to bring your husband down."

The look of shock and surprise was very evident on her face. "You what?"

"I'm here to put a stop to your husband's illegal, cruel, and deadly activities. Why else would I have witnessed those murders at Corky's Bar? I don't think it's at all a coincidence that I am part Russian and I had the means to convince the police of my story. I was also able to trick your husband, a very wise man even though very treacherous, into believing my bogus identity. I think tonight is the reason and the culmination of all that has happened this year. Maybe I'm here to help you escape your husband also. Why else would you have told me your story?"

By the expression on her face, I thought she was agreeing with me. She leaned forward toward me, resting her forearms on her thighs. "What are we going to do about it?"

CHAPTER TWENTY-THREE
Persuasion

Yes, what was *I* going to do about it? I thought I only had Mrs. Antonelli and Baby Carla to worry about. Now I had another person to consider. After hearing Milla's story, I couldn't let her stay in this place. She had to be included in the escape plan. I needed first to determine if she was willing to take the risk. If she wasn't, then I was faced with a bigger dilemma: did I trust her not to give my true identity away before I had a chance to get Mrs. Antonelli and the Baby Carla to safety?

Slightly nodding my head, I said to her, "Tonight I'm taking Mrs. Antonelli and the baby to a safe house where they can be protected by the police. At that point the Nawinah police and other law enforcement agencies will be either invading this property or planning the invasion. Of course, for my own safety, I'm also not returning to this estate after I get my hostages free. Are you willing to come with us?"

She looked shocked. "Tonight? Why tonight?"

"Because this is my opportunity. And, like I said before, I feel this *is* the time. I've been given this chance, and I don't want to pass it by. Another break may never come along. How often are most of the guards gone at the same time your husband is also away? It has to be tonight. You need to make up your mind now."

She hesitated, but I could tell she was thinking seriously about my proposal. "I'll do it… tonight!"

****

It was nine o'clock and completely dark outside. Milla knocked softly on Mrs. Antonelli's door. She called out quietly so as not to awaken the baby. "Lucia, are you awake? Lucia? Please come out here. We'd like to talk to you."

Milla stood at the door for several minutes. Then she turned to me and shook her head. She waited another minute, then came back to her chair and sat down. "Shall I go in to awaken her?" She had a worried look on her face.

Just then the bedroom door opened, and Mrs. Antonelli stepped out, leaving the door slightly ajar presumably to hear the baby in case she woke up. Mrs. Antonelli walked over to Milla. "What do you want?"

"Please, sit down. We need to talk to you. I will prepare us some tea."

Mrs. Antonelli first looked at Milla, then at me, but she sat down in a chair to the right of Milla's chair. Milla went to the kitchen to fix us tea. We had a lot to discuss.

I began, trying to explain our situation to her. "Mrs. Antonelli, I'm not who you think I am."

She immediately argued, "What do you mean, you are not who I think you are? You are one of the monsters who came into my house and took me and my grandchild. I know exactly who you are. You are an evil and heartless man." She snapped her head away so she no longer had to look at me.

"Please, Mrs. Antonelli, just listen. Let me explain. From what you have seen, I know you've no reason to trust me, but after you hear me out, I hope you change your mind." I waited for her to face me.

Milla brought in the tea and sat it on the table within the reach of the three of us. I took mine while Milla handed Mrs. Antonelli's to her, knowing the woman was in no mood for tea or any sort of refreshment. She did accept it and took a sip. Milla grabbed her cup and sat in her chair.

"I don't really work for Ivan Kerchenko. Well, I guess I really do. However, he also doesn't know who I am. I have just had a talk with Mrs. Kerchenko. Apparently, she is also being held against her will by Mr. Kerchenko the same as you and your granddaughter."

I saw a look of surprise on Mrs. Antonelli's face, then disbelief. "Do you think I am stupid? A rich lady and a monster holds me against my will, and I am supposed to believe the two of you are not who I think you are? As well as a monster, you are a crazy man."

She was very upset. Rightly so. Maybe if I started my explanation, she might believe me.

"My name is Tank Telek. I'm actually working undercover for Captain Forsythe of the Nawinah Police Department. I know you know the captain."

She was listening. I had her attention but not her trust yet. I needed to convince her. I had to bring up something I knew she wanted to forget ever happened. I tried to make my voice sound as sympathetic as possible.

"Ma'am, I have something to tell you. Last year, I actually witnessed the death of your husband and all those patrons in Corky's Bar."

She actually dropped her cup of tea, spilling it on her lap and the carpet. Milla quickly put her tea on the table to rush over to her. "Oh, let me help!" She picked up the teacup, then hurried to the kitchenette, bringing back some towels to sop up the hot liquid. Mrs. Antonelli simply stood there staring at me.

"I'm so sorry, ma'am, but I had to tell you this. That's the reason I'm working with Captain Forsythe."

After Milla dried as much of the liquid as possible, Mrs. Antonelli sat back down, still staring at me.

"Let me explain. I was actually in the restroom when two Russians came into the bar. I was about to leave when I heard shots. Of course, I froze. I opened the door just a crack and saw the Russian dudes who I later identified to the police. They were talking to your husband when all of a sudden they just shot him and your daughter. Coward that I was, I stayed hidden in the bathroom. You must believe me. If I thought I could've done anything to help them, I would have, but it happened so fast. Then I knew if they were aware I was in the bathroom, they would've killed me too. So I hope you understand. That's why I agreed to help Captain Forsythe bring down the man who ordered your husband's murder, the same man holding you hostage here.

"For the last few months, I've been working undercover as one of his employees. I've been supplying the captain with all the evidence I gathered against Mr. Kerchenko from drug trafficking, extortion, prostitution, and sex trafficking. None of us ever expected him to kidnap you and your grandchild. But that's what happened, and tonight I'm taking the three of you to safety."

I waited for her to say something, anything. When she didn't, I continued, "I went to see your daughter a couple of times while she was in the hospital. I felt so bad for her, losing her father and her husband. Now I'm working with those police who are working undercover at your bar, Dingo, who is pretending to be your brother-in-law, and Donnie, the bartender."

Still no response from her. Maybe if I mentioned the night I was stalking Gina. "Remember the night several months ago when the police actually pulled in your drive and came to your door? I had also been on your street, making sure you were okay. The police had been driving by, checking up on you. When I saw some of Kerchenko's men parked across the street, I stopped the police and made them actually go to your door. When the Russians saw the policeman go up to your house, they drove away. Afterwards, the captain placed an officer inside your home.

"Mrs. Antonelli, I really want to help you. I want to take the three of you to a safe house. I'm going to call my outside contact so he can warn Captain Forsythe to get his men at the safe house."

I waited for Mrs. Antonelli's reply. When she said nothing, I tried again.

"So will you come with me? You're not safe here. I don't think I'll get another chance like this. As soon as Mr. Kerchenko's men and Oksana come back, you'll be in grave danger. What do you say?"

She didn't speak immediately. Then she asked, "How can I believe you? I don't know you. You look like every one of the other thugs. In fact, you were one of them who took me and my granddaughter. How can I trust you now?"

"Mrs. Antonelli, I had to be part of the kidnapping. I had no choice. If I hadn't gone along with it, I would've blown my cover and ruined our chances of putting Kerchenko away for good. You have to believe me. I know you want that man put away so he can never hurt anyone again."

Milla tried to help convince her. "Lucia, I too need to escape from this place. I did not know Tank before tonight, but he convinced me he truly wants to save us. Please. Agree to come with us."

I took out my bulky 1993 cellphone. "I'm going to call Nikolay Gorelov. He's my contact with the captain. He has been posing as my Uncle Nick and keeping me in touch with the police. Maybe you'll believe him."

I dialed Uncle Nick's number. "Hello, Uncle Nick. Listen carefully. Tonight is the night I'm getting Mrs. Antonelli and Baby Carla out of here. Also, Ludmilla Kerchenko is escaping too. She told me Aunt Inga is her actual aunt."

I told him of my plan to get the three of them off the property and to the safe house, and I listened to his response. He told me Aunt Inga would be overjoyed with the prospect of getting Milla out of her situation. Her aunt had been so concerned for her safety since she began dating Ivan Kerchenko. He'd inform the captain of my plan, and he'd send a swat team to the safe house.

Milla wanted to talk to her aunt. I gave the phone to her as I assumed Uncle Nick gave his to Aunt Inga. Milla spoke to her aunt in Russian in a happy and tearful voice, saying she would see her soon and was so thankful for her pending release. Then she handed the phone back to me.

"Uncle Nick, we'll be leaving in about an hour. I'll be driving the Buick the captain had loaned me." He wished us luck and said he'd be waiting at the safe house.

After I hung up I turned to Mrs. Antonelli. "Well, will you come with us? You know you aren't safe here."

She still looked at me skeptically. "How do I know you don't plan to take us somewhere to kill us tonight?"

I was getting frustrated. What could I say to convince this woman I wanted to save her, not put her in greater danger?

Milla tried again. "Please, Lucia, you need to go with us. We need to leave as soon as possible. You must believe us. This is our only chance. I know my husband. He will not let you go even if he would get the money from your daughter. Tank is not the evil one; my husband is."

Mrs. Antonelli put her hands together as if she were praying. She even closed her eyes and swayed her body back and forth. I waited.

Soon she opened her eyes, took a deep breath, and uttered, "We will come with you. Please don't kill us."

Milla quickly went over to her and hugged her.

CHAPTER TWENTY-FOUR
Culminating Showdown

Everything I had gone through this past year was leading up to this very moment. I could feel it in my bones. This was what I'd been waiting for, hoping for since I landed back in 1993. This was it.

We had to get ready as swiftly as possible. Mrs. Antonelli went into the bedroom to prepare the baby, changing her and wrapping her in a snug blanket. Milla got the baby's formula and bottles out of the refrigerator and packed them in an insulated bag. I give her credit. Milla didn't want to take the time nor the risk to pack a bag of clothes for herself for fear she might be accosted by one of the guards. If necessary, I had my pistol and one dose of Etomidate to use. I also asked Milla if she could find a dark blanket to take with us.

When Milla went back into the bedroom to retrieve the blanket, I heard someone accessing the code at the door. I froze. Who could that be? We had not ordered any food. Milla was coming out of the bedroom and stopped when she heard the noise.

Mrs. Antonelli was still in with the baby. Milla threw the blanket into the bedroom, rushed to sit down, and picked up the magazine, pretending to read it. I also quickly sat in one of the chairs. I put my hand on my gun in case I needed to test my ability to shoot another human being.

The door flew open and in walked Luka. Immediately, I could tell he was either drunk, high on drugs, or both. Without saying a word, he staggered to an empty chair and plopped into it.

Milla asked, "Luka, what are you doing here?"

I decided I'd wait to see what would transpire before taking any type of action. I hoped Mrs. Antonelli would stay in the bedroom until I figured out what to do.

Luka's eyes were bloodshot, and he slurred his words when he answered Milla. "He didn't want me to go get the girls. He told me, 'Luka, you are too immature'. He didn't trust me with them. What did he think I would do? Rape them right then and there?"

Before he continued, he took a bottle of vodka out of his pocket and took a long swig.

"I'm his son. I should be given some responsibility. No, instead he gives the good jobs to everyone else. Look at you, Max Gorelov. Why are you here? Why did he not pick me to guard these important hostages? He treats me like a boy, not a man."

Milla tried to reason with him. "I'm sure he wanted you to be in charge of the property, to keep everything safe for him when he returns. That's a big job, you know."

"Ha! Important job! What could happen here? This place is

secure. No one gets in or out without his knowledge, even when he isn't here. And do you think he would invite me to his important meeting with the Columbian drug lord? No, I'm not worthy. He tells me I have to gain his trust. What does he want me to do? He doesn't trust his own son!"

He stopped talking and began to stare at me. He slowly lifted his hand and began to point his finger and shake it at me. "And you, Max Gorelov, all you have to do is tell him how beautiful his painting is, and he wants to make you his right hand man. I know what you are trying to do. You can't fool me. You think you can take my place."

He stood up and started to walk toward me. I also stood. "Luka, I'm not trying to do anything of the kind. I just want to do a good job so I can make a little money. That's all. I don't want to take over what is rightfully yours. You deserve it, not me. I've seen how you work. I'll tell your dad what a great job you did when we kidnapped that baby and that old lady."

He stood there about a foot away from me, staring with his red eyes. I could smell the liquor on his breath. "No, no. You want to get rid of me so you can take my place."

He made a fist with his hand and was about to punch me. I grabbed his arm and pushed him backwards. He was so drunk it threw him off balance. He fell to the floor as did the vodka bottle, the remaining liquid seeping into the carpet.

Milla ran over to him. "Let's get him into the bedroom. He is so drunk he can barely stand up."

I grabbed one arm under his shoulder while Milla grabbed the other. Luka mumbled something neither of us could understand. We dragged him into the bedroom.

"We're going to lay you on the bed, Luka, so you can sleep this off," said Milla. "You don't want to be like this when your father gets home."

Again, Luka said something inaudible, but he didn't give us any resistance. We struggled to lift him onto the bed then walked out of the room, closing the door behind us.

Mrs. Antonelli came out of her bedroom. "Does this mean we are not leaving?"

I answered, "Oh, no. We're still leaving. We just have to change our plans slightly."

Milla asked, "Do you think he will be out for the rest of the night?"

"I'm not going to take that chance." I reached into my pocket for the Etomidate. "Now that he is relaxed, it'll be easier to administer this. With this plus the booze and drugs in his system, he'll be out at least until morning. Then he might be very confused as to what actually happened."

I got the syringe ready for the injection and went into the bedroom. Luka was fast asleep, or passed out, whichever. He flinched slightly when the needle penetrated his skin, but he didn't awaken.

At ten-thirty we were ready to leave. Baby Carla was sleeping in Mrs. Antonelli's arms when we started our escape. Milla had picked up the dark blanket, and I grabbed the bag filled with the baby's things. Milla pressed the code to open the door. The four of us creeped down the long hallway as silently as possible. When we came to the door at the end of the hall, Milla opened it to see if any guards were nearby. The hall was deserted. We walked through the doorway and exited the private wing of the mansion.

Thankfully, Milla knew her way around the house better than I did. She led us to an exit door on the south side of the building closer to the garage where my Buick was located. As we went out this door, overhead lights shone brightly around the property. However, the property on this side was also deserted. I wasn't sure if any cameras were pointed at us, but at that point it was too late to worry about it. We hurried to the garage.

When we reached the side of the garage, the entrance door was locked. The door had a glass panel at the top of it. Nearby were some landscape stones decorating the edge of a grassy area. I forced one about six inches in diameter out of its place in the row. Slamming it into the glass panel, the noise caused us to stop and look around for anyone who might have also heard the glass shattering. No one appeared.

I took my jacket off, wrapped it around my fist and arm, and punched out enough glass so I could reach the lock. Releasing the lock and opening the door, the two women entered the garage. I followed while I took my keys to the Buick out of my pocket. I unlocked the doors; Milla got in the front passenger seat; Mrs. Antonelli and the baby got in the back. I then went over and opened up the wide garage door.

As I pulled out of the garage, I warned Mrs. Antonelli, "Just as a precaution when we get out of the parking lot and near the guard area, you should probably squeeze down on the floor and cover yourself and the baby with the dark blanket Milla brought. I think we can get by the guards with Mrs. Kerchenko in the car without suspicion, but if any of them see you, it will alert them and send up a red flag. We don't need any red flags."

I planned to go out the back way of the property. Less gates and guards to go through. Mrs. Antonelli put the baby on the floor on one side of the back seat and scrunched herself on the other side while pulling the blanket over both of them. Milla helped to cover them completely. Our luck was holding out. The baby was still sleeping.

I drove down the dark road leading to the exit. "Milla, the guards will probably question me about where and why I'm taking you somewhere this late at night. What should I tell them?"

Milla looked over at me and then into the back seat. "Tell them the baby is sick. We are going to pick up her prescription at the twenty-four hour pharmacy."

"Do you think they'll believe that?"

"I think so," she replied. Babies get sick sometimes, and with what that little child is going through, it is very logical."

"Have you ever left the property under any similar circumstances before?"

"Well, no…," she confessed.

"Oh, boy! We may be in for some opposition."

"Normally, I would send one of the women to get anything for me. However, since most of them are on this new assignment, that is not possible. The rest of the staff is aware we are shorthanded. Maybe they will believe us. We will have to convince them."

I was then approaching the guards stationed at the first gate. The baby was still quiet. I pulled out my ID emblem.

As I stopped at the station, the guard came over to the vehicle. In Russian I said, "Max Gorelov here. We are in hurry. I am taking Mrs. Kerchenko to get prescription for Mariani baby. She is ill and doctor prescribed medicine."

The guard looked over at Milla, I got to hand it to her. She had a concerned look on her face, not fear, but as if we were really on the mission I described. She knew the guard and used his name when she spoke. "Dmitry, the baby is very ill. The doctor said we need to get her medicine immediately. He called it into the pharmacy. We need to pick it up."

Dmitry looked at me and asked, "Who is guarding the hostages?"

I hadn't expected this. Luckily, I thought of Luka. "Luka Kerchenko is sitting with them until we return."

It worked! He believed me. He signaled for the other guard to open the gate. We were on our way!

At the second gate, the guard only wanted to see my gold circle ID before he signaled for the gate to be opened. Then we drove off the Kerchenko property.

I couldn't believe it! My hands were trembling as they grasped the steering wheel. I drove slightly above the speed limit but very carefully. Mrs. Antonelli brought herself and the baby off the floor. Baby Carla was stirring and starting to fuss. Mrs. Antonelli took out a bottle and began to feed the baby. Soon the only sound in the car was the baby sucking on the bottle. However, we were all apprehensive. Something could still go wrong.

As I was driving, I thought about Luka back at the mansion. If Milla had only been married for about six years, then Luka was not her son. I was curious. "What happened to your husband's first wife?"

I could feel Milla's eyes on me for a few seconds. "I am not sure. Luka was a teenager when I met Ivan. At first, I thought Ivan was still married and was just treating me like his mistress. That still may have been the case before we were married. I don't know. He didn't tell me he had a son until after he had asked me to marry him. Then I asked about his first wife. The only answer he gave me was that she was not with them anymore. Of course, I thought they were divorced. That would have been anyone's assumption. However, after we were married and I saw how he earned his living, I had my doubts. He does not talk about her. Neither does Luka. Actually, I am afraid to ask him any more about her. I don't want to know the answer. I am afraid because I fear I would eventually meet the same fate as she has if I stay with him much longer."

I understood how she felt. However, I wondered about Luka.

If he was only a teenager, wouldn't he be suspicious. Or maybe he already knew what happened to her—and didn't care.

We dropped the conversation, and I drove to Nawinah Cortland Road. It was almost eleven o'clock as I passed Corky's Bar, still lit up with patrons' cars in the parking lot. Driving south, I kept an eye out for the abandoned shack and *For Sale* sign that Dingo had told me would mark the dirt road. A couple of times, I slowed down to look closer out my window, knowing I definitely did not want to miss the turnoff.

Suddenly, I saw the large sign and slowed down to make my turn. No one was following us. A car had been behind us, but it went straight as I made the turn. The road was rutted and bumpy. I slowed down so as not to upset the baby too much, still glancing out my rearview mirror for any other vehicle headlights. The night was very dark, and I saw no structures of any kind along the way. I checked the odometer when I turned onto the road. When I drove for about two and a half miles, I slowed down even more so I wouldn't miss the house.

"There should be a house on your side. Keep an eye out for it. It'll be back a ways from the road but should have an outside light on."

Just as I was explaining to her, we both saw lights off to the right about fifty yards back. "That's got to be it!"

I slowed, made the right turn, and drove down the long drive. At the back of the house several police cars were parked haphazardly on the property. As I pulled between two of them, the back door of the small house opened and numerous people came flooding toward us. Mrs. Antonelli, still holding the baby, rapidly exited the car. Coming toward her was Gina Mariani. The three of them embraced, kissing, crying, and whispering to one another.

Milla hesitated when she exited the passenger side. She appeared to be lost and confused. I empathized with her. The life she had known for years had suddenly come to a halt. She was in for a very rugged adjustment and a very different lifestyle. But it had been her choice. I think she made the right decision. Her life was constantly in danger living with Ivan Kerchenko. She needed to get away from him.

Also coming toward us was Nikolay and Inga Gorelov. Milla recognized her Aunt Inga. They rushed to embrace each other. I knew with the help of this couple, she would have a good life. They would be crucial in helping her to adjust.

We were escorted into the small safe house. With people everywhere, there was barely room for everyone. The captain, Dingo, and Caruthers were there as well as several other policemen. So much activity was happening. The noise and commotion were overwhelming. As for me, I felt the most wonderful feeling of relief. I found the first open chair and immediately plopped down in it. I couldn't believe we had escaped without a single incident. It seemed so easy, yet I knew how dangerous it really was. I thought about all the things that could've gone wrong. What if we hadn't left in time and Kerchenko had returned before we got off the property? Or what if Petrov and

Kozlov had returned with Oksana? What if a camera caught us exiting the mansion or breaking into the garage and guards rushed out to confront us? Or what if the guards at the gates didn't believe our story about going for a prescription with Luka watching the hostages? If only one of those things had happened, this outcome would've been completely different. We were so lucky. I had to thank both Milla and Mrs. Antonelli for that. And the sleeping Baby Carla. I couldn't have pulled it off if not for them.

I saw Dingo coming toward me with a couple of bottles of beer. "How about a beer, young man? I think you deserve it."

I took the beer, but got up and gave him a big bear hug. "Can you believe it? We pulled it off! The captain has more than enough on Kerchenko to take him down. He won't see daylight for the rest of his life. And who knows how much life he'll have left? Once he is incarcerated, he becomes a target for all those who he conned over the years. Don't think they won't want their revenge. I'm so glad it's over. Maybe I can get on with my life now."

Puzzled, Dingo asked, "What do you plan to do now?"

"Well, I've been thinking about it a lot. What I've done the last few months and culminating with saving both Mrs. Kerchenko and Mrs. Antonelli, oh, the baby too, I think those things are why I was brought back to 1993. I'm not sure exactly why I was the one who was chosen. It could be because of my Russian heritage. Maybe it was because my life was going nowhere, and I needed to have a purpose. If I get to go forward to 2015, I'm changing my life. I'm going back to college. Maybe I'll major in history, take some Russian, or maybe I'll teach. Or I could go into criminal justice. That was sort of what I've been doing this past year."

Dingo was the devil's advocate. "What if you don't get back to 2015? What will you do then?

"I don't know.... I don't know...."

As I was contemplating that situation, I saw Captain Forsythe coming my way. "Tank, fine job, fine job, young man." He vigorously shook my hand. "I can't thank you enough. We couldn't have done it without you. We have our task force gathered, including several federal agencies, the FBI, the DEA, even the CIA. We're breaking onto Kerchenko's property in a few hours taking him and his organization down once and for all. We're going in through both entrances, plus a few helicopters in the air."

I thought I'd better warn him. "Captain, you know most of his troops are off capturing a truckload of girls from Mexico, and Kerchenko himself is also not on the property."

"We know all this. As we speak, a separate group of officers is taking care of those apprehending the truck of young women. And we know Kerchenko is currently in a hotel room with several Russian diplomats and a half dozen young hookers. So we're focusing our operations on three separate locations. Don't worry, Tank. We got this covered."

He placed his hand on my shoulder. "Thanks again, Tank. You were truly a man of your word. Your mother would be very proud of you—if she ever finds out what kind of man you have become."

"Captain, I intend to show her. This whole experience has also been good for me. I learned what I'm capable of, and I'll carry it with me wherever my life takes me now."

As he was about to walk away, the captain said, "Well, Tank, if there is anything, anything at all, I can do for you, please let me know."

"Thanks, Captain, I'm good."

While sitting in the chair, sipping my beer, Gina Mariani approached me. As with each time I had seen her, I couldn't help but notice how beautiful this woman was. Remembering how pale and fragile she had looked, when I had seen her in the hospital so many months ago, I was amazed at how she now looked radiant and strong. Was it possible I had actually fallen in love with this woman I didn't really know? Or was it simply the weird circumstances surrounding our acquaintanceship? No way was love even conceivable with her. I had to get that stupid idea out of my head.

I stood up when she was in front of me.

"Mr. Telek... Tank? How can I ever thank you for what you've done? The captain explained everything to me. I... I... guess we even met before... at the bar. That night. I don't remember much at all about it, but the captain said you were there and witnessed my dad's murder. He told me how you have been working undercover to bring his murderers to justice. If that isn't enough, now I find you have saved my mother and my daughter. Thank you so, so much."

She came closer and gave me a deep hug. I could smell the sweet fragrance of her flowery perfume as her body snuggled against mine. I could feel the tender softness of her skin, the pressure of her breasts against my chest. The musky aroma of her fresh, clean hair made me dizzy with pleasure. I closed my eyes and drank in the scent and the feel of her tantalizing body clinging to me. I wanted it to last forever, but she shyly broke away.

I stuttered for words. "Uh, it was nothing, really." What a stupid thing to say!

"Well, it has meant everything to me. Thank you again," She shook my hand.

The touch of that small, fragile hand sent shivers down my back. *Stop it! You fool!*

"Maybe I'll see you again sometime," she said as she dropped my hand and walked away.

I wish, Gina Mariani, I wish....

I then met with Captain Forsythe, Ben Caruthers, and a few of the captain's key men in a private room. I clued them in on any details they needed about the property. Milla joined us for this part of the session to verify any questions they might have. I also updated them on any other activities of Kerchenko's organization I hadn't already told them. Then I thanked the Gorelov's for their assistance in this operation. Aunt Inga said she would be sure Milla was safe in her new life.

I then said good-bye to Milla. "Thanks for your help in this escape plan. I don't know if I could've pulled it off without you."

"Tank Telek, I'm sure you could have done it on your own. You are an amazing and resourceful man. It is I who must thank you. I am so much happier already, and I've only been away from that man for a couple of hours. Thank you, and good luck." She gave me a hug and a kiss on the cheek before going back to Aunt Inga.

I said my good-byes to Captain Forsythe and Caruthers also. They asked me what I planned to do next. I told them I wasn't sure. Tonight I was going to rent a hotel room and relax. I would decide my next step after a good night's rest.

Then I said good-bye to Dingo. "Hey, man. Thanks for everything. Thanks for believing in me from the very beginning. I wish I could say, 'see you later', but as you are aware, I don't know what 'later' has in store for me."

I could see a tear escaping from Dingo's eye as I gave him a final, big hug.

****

It was starting to rain as I left the safe house. I knew what I planned to do. Whether or not it would work remained to be seen. I drove to the end of the dirt road and turned north on Nawinah Cortland Road. It was approximately the same time, same day exactly one year ago I had traveled the same road under similar circumstances. The road was deserted and slippery because of the rain, and that steady, light rain unexpectedly began to pour down like I was driving through a car wash. I had the windshield wipers on full blast, but I still had extreme difficulty seeing where I was driving. The road curved and wound through the deserted, unpopulated area between Nawinah and Fantasy Empire. The Buick's tires were hydroplaning on the puddles in the road, and as I was trying to steer the car around this big curve called Demon's Bend, I lost control of the Buick. It swerved and skidded off the road, bumped around for several yards at about forty miles an hour through small brush and tall weeds, and ended up crashing head on into a large oak tree. Since I had neglected to fasten my seatbelt with all else going on in my mind, my body jerked and joggled with every movement of the truck as it vaulted off the road. When the Buick struck the oak tree, my head was hurdled into the front windshield with such force that I blacked out.

CHAPTER TWENTY-FIVE
Celebration

A couple of months after the takedown of the Kerchenko organization, Captain Forsythe called a meeting with all those involved in the covert activity they called "Tank." Only those who knew Maxim Gorelov's true identity and the mechanics of the Tank sting were present: Captain Ernie Forsythe (Nawinah Police Captain); Dingo (Darrell Crockett, former attorney, alias Dominic Antonelli); Sergeant Ben Caruthers (trainer and liaison to Tank Telek), Officer Donnie Davisson (undercover bartender at Corky's), Officer Evan Wilson and Officer Burt Nordstrom (undercover security guards at Corky's); and Nick and Inga Gorelov (undercover uncle and aunt to Maxim Gorelov).

After all were seated, the captain took a large bottle of champagne and some plastic wine glasses out of the box he had carried into the room. He poured the champagne into enough glasses for each of those at the meeting. Dingo passed them out.

Captain Forsythe cleared his throat. "I want to thank each and every one of you. You did a damn good job! Kerchenko has been put away for life with no chance of parole. He may even get the death penalty. His men are either dead or imprisoned. All remnants and factions of his organization have been disbanded and eliminated from Central Florida. You should all be very proud of yourselves."

Dingo began a slow clap. Everyone joined in with their own claps, hoots, and hollers. It took several minutes before the group calmed down to listen to what else the captain had to say.

"My only regret is that Tank Telek is not here to help us celebrate. He was one of a kind. Now, I don't mean to speak of him as if he were dead. Fact is, this has been the most bizarre operation in which any of us have ever participated. If any of you would ever try to explain it to someone outside this group, they would commit you to the looney bin. And that's where you would belong. Even after all that has happened, I still can't believe it. But as strange as this past year has been, you and I know we have Tank to thank for our victory. Without his brave and diligent undercover work, we would not have been successful. We can only hope and pray he has made it back, or should I say, *forward*, to his real life in 2015. We also hope what happened to him will have a positive effect on his life because it sure did on ours. Let's raise our glasses to a toast to Tank."

Glasses were raised high in the air. Everyone in the room shouted, loud and clear, "To Tank, wherever you are!"

CHAPTER TWENTY-SIX
Rude Awakening

I'm not sure how much time had passed before I finally woke up dazed and confused. Every bone in my body ached like hell. My head felt like it would explode off my neck. As I reached up to my forehead, I felt a deep, open gash with blood dripping into my eye and down my cheek. My arms were cut, scratched, and bloody from the oak tree branches that had torpedoed through Stacey's side window. I tried to move, but my body refused to obey my brain waves. I sat there for several minutes, resting my head on the broken head rest while I regained my senses and strength enough to try to exit the truck. With piercing pain throughout my body, I finally was able to open the driver side door and extract myself from the truck, grabbing tightly to the door handle before falling to the ground.

Disoriented and holding onto Stacey's door, I looked around the area to see where I had ended up and what my situation was. Stacey was a mess. Her front end was completely squashed and embedded into the oak tree, which also had a huge chunk taken out of its trunk. Smoke, steam, or both were spewing from under Stacey's broken hood and pluming into the drizzling night air. She would probably have to be totaled. Great! I had no money to get another vehicle. I had insurance, but who knows if it would be enough to get something decent and reliable. Besides, they would probably raise my rates now. Ma will have a fit. It was already high because of my age.

I retrieved my cellphone out of my pocket to call my mom. Just my luck! It was smashed and refused to turn on. I threw it back onto Stacey's front seat.

Okay. What was I going to do? I was several yards from the road, and at that late hour, I doubted if any vehicles would be traveling on it, anyhow. Hell, I used this road because of the light traffic. Since it was a back road, I didn't have to deal with traffic lights and tourists. Definitely, I would've been better off taking the main roads. Look at the predicament I was in because of that decision.

After surveying Stacey and my circumstances, the rain had somewhat slowed down. Testing my equilibrium, I limped toward the road, hoping perhaps at least one car would be driving by that late at night. As I was dragging my body onward with pain shooting through my head, my back, and my arm, I also felt a sharp pain in my leg. Looking down, I noticed my pants were ripped, and blood was oozing from a deep gouge on my thigh. I was a complete mess. I needed to get help as soon as possible.

When I got to the road, as I suspected, no cars were in sight in either direction. I waited for about fifteen or twenty minutes, hoping one would come along. The rain started to come down harder again, and I was feeling both light headed and nauseous. I needed to find someplace to call my mom. Looking into the distance I saw a lit sign on a building up ahead. I decided to attempt to walk to the building, hoping as late as it was someone would still be there. Maybe somebody could loan me their cellphone to call Ma. Maybe I could use their bathroom to clean up a little.

As I trudged through the puddles and slippery, uneven grass along the roadway and getting closer to the building, I realized it was a small restaurant or bar. Strange, I hadn't remembered seeing it on that road on my other trips back and forth to work. On the way to work, I was always busy listening to my iTunes, singing along in my magnificent baritone voice. Then on the way home at one or two o'clock in the morning, I never did any sightseeing. I was simply anxious to get home and into bed.

When I got closer to the building, the sign above the door read "Corky's Bar & Grill". I noticed about four or five cars in the black top parking lot. So I figured it was still open, and I grabbed the doorknob and slowly opened the wooden door.

It was dimly lit inside. My eyes had to adjust after the bright sign right above the doorway. A few patrons were sitting at the shiny bar. Other guys sat at round tables or booths scattered about the room. On the sound system some male country singer was singing about his truck. Behind the bar was an elderly, gray haired, bearded man probably in his seventies and a pretty young chick. The man had on a black tee shirt and a white apron around his waist and was washing glasses in a small sink. The pretty girl, who had long, black hair, was serving the patrons at the bar. She was dressed in jeans and a black tee shirt with "Corky's" stenciled across the front of it. I walked up to the girl and asked if I could use the restroom and borrow her phone. She looked at me and put her hands quickly over her mouth, "Oh my God! What happened to you?"

"My truck skidded off the road and hit a tree. Can I wash up in your restroom, then use your phone to call my mom?" I was feeling very light headed and dizzy.

"Sure, sure. Go ahead. The restroom is down the hall. God! You look awful! Are you okay? Do you want me to call an ambulance?"

"Oh, no. I'll be okay. I just need to clean up a bit and call my mom to pick me up."

"Uhh… Okay," she hesitantly said as she watched me walk back to the restroom.

I staggered down the short hallway where she had pointed. I was feeling more nauseated with each step. Suddenly, I felt myself drifting away. I felt like I was underwater. Sounds were slowly fading away. Then everything went black!

****

Where am I? I can hear soft voices, but I can't make out what they're saying. I can't even open my eyes. They seem to be glued shut. Can I wiggle my fingers? With every ounce of strength I could shoot down my right arm, I try to get that little finger to move. Something is heavy on my arm. What is it? Did my finger move? The voices are getting louder. I still can't get the glue off my eyes. Why did somebody glue them shut? I hear a different voice now. It's deeper than the others. I can't make out what they are saying? Are they talking to me? Is someone calling my name?

Let me try again to move my fingers. What's wrong with me? Why am I so weak? Okay, I can do this. I struggle with my brain to send a message for my muscles and tendons to move the hand. I think I did it! I think so! The voices got loud again. Yes. Someone is calling my name, but I can't answer them. My mouth is also glued shut and filled with gravel. I hear many voices calling my name. If only I could open my eyes. Let me try again. If I can move my fingers, maybe I can open my eyes. I strain against my eyelids, but the heavy glue is keeping them tightly shut. I feel them fluttering. Then a tiny streak of light seeps through the bottom of each eyelid. I hear someone clearly say, "He is trying to open his eyes."

Finally, I am able to open my eyes wider, but everything is blurry and so very bright. I close them again because the brightness is painful. I hear a deep voice saying, "Tank, take your time. Open them slowly. Someone turn out the lights. It's too bright for him."

I slowly try to open my eyes again. It's still blurry, but the brightness is gone, and it doesn't hurt so badly this time. Gradually, the haziness is starting to clear up. I see a man standing over me. I don't know this man. I've never seen him before. He must be the source of the deep voice. I see my mother. Why does she look so old? And I see an angel! Am I in heaven? The angel has long, flowing black hair and skin that looks like cotton candy. No... She must not be an angel. I don't see any wings. Don't angels have wings?

My mom grabs my hand. "Oh, Tank, at last! At last you're awake."

Ma called me Tank. She never calls me Tank. She always calls me Talbott. What is going on?

I try to speak, but my mouth is so dry and filled with crud. I hear myself making croaking sounds. The angel moistens my lips with an ice cube held in her delicate fingers. The way she keeps moistening them with her fingers is so sensual. I stare at her. She is a beautiful angel.

She walks away with the glass of ice and I go back to wondering where I am. I look at Ma, the only familiar face I see. Finally, I am able to make rasping sounds. "Where am I?"

"You're in a hospital, dear. Nawinah General. You were in an accident."

"An accident?" I whisper, more to myself than these people. What kind of an accident?"

"You were in a car accident,"

I feel my eyes darting back and forth. Something is happening! I hear the deep voice say, "I'm going to give him a sedative to calm him. He's a little too agitated. Let's not give him any more details just now."

I feel myself gradually sinking again. My eyes are heavy. I need to close them.

****

I wake up again. My eyes open more easily, and I'm able to focus more clearly. I can move my head a little more. I see Ma and that angel seated to my left. There's an old man standing next to the angel. He has very white hair and a beard. I don't think he is that man who had the deep voice. Maybe. I don't know. I can see a window behind them. It's dark outside. The lights in the room are not hurting my eyes this time. Ma comes over beside me and takes my hand. "How are you feeling, Tank?" She has a worried look on her face.

I remember what she had said the first time I woke up in this strange place. She said I had an accident. I can't remember anything about an accident. I remember going to work at Fantasy Empire. My mind was hurting trying to remember what happened next. I remember on the way home the roads were slippery and wet. Stacey was having trouble staying on the road. The wet roads. Oh! Demon's Bend. Stacey went off the road, and we hit a tree. That must be the accident Ma is talking about. "I'm sorry, Ma. I didn't mean to wreck Stacey. Is she fixable?"

Ma looks away from me and at the angel and the old man. When she turns back to me, she grabs my hand. "No, dear. She was pretty well totaled."

"Oh, no. How will I get back and forth to work?" I could feel myself getting very agitated.

Ma quickly said, "Don't worry, son. We'll think of something. You just get better. That's all."

****

I was in the hospital for three more days before the doctor would allow Ma to tell me what had happened after the accident. Eventually, I remembered walking up to the road and to a nearby bar. I remembered asking this pretty girl to use her phone and the restroom. That's it as far as my memory goes. Apparently, I had passed out in that bar. The girl called 911. They rushed me to Nawinah General. They got my ID from my wallet in Stacey's glove compartment, and someone contacted Ma. The girl at the bar, Carla Mariani, actually is the angel who I saw when I first woke up from the coma I'd been in for a year. An entire year! Can you believe it? I lost an entire year of my life. No wonder Ma wasn't worried about Stacey. I had a very severe skull fracture and damage to my brain. I also had received some serious cuts and injuries to my legs and arms. I guess for a while they didn't expect me to live. Ma told me Carla Mariani was by my side for weeks. She and Ma never lost hope I'd come out of the coma.

Of course, since I was in a coma so long, I was replaced at Fantasy Empire. I'm sure it wasn't too difficult for them to find another garbage collector.

It is now about five months since I was released from the hospital. I recently enrolled at the University of Central Florida, majoring in history. I might change it to criminal justice eventually. I don't know. I'd like to see if I could find out who killed my dad.

I actually got a grant to help with the college expenses. Strange... it had been anonymously set up for me in 1994 when I was only a year old. Ma said she knows nothing about it. She and Dad didn't set it up.

I'm also tutoring some high school kids in history and geography. I'm so fascinated with time and how it progresses that I have this constant need to look back into history.

What is the most unbelievable thing to me is Carla Mariani. She and I are dating. Yes, that beautiful angel whose face I saw when I came out of the coma. The same girl who called 911 to save my life. What she sees in me, I'll never know. I lost a lot of weight while wasting away in that hospital bed. I'm gaining my strength back and working out as often as I can. But still... she's so beautiful.

And that old man who was in the hospital the second time I woke up? He works at Corky's Bar too. He has the strangest name.... Dingo, like the wild dog of Australia.

ABOUT THE AUTHOR

Most sane people move from the north to the south in the cold weather. Not June. She is a mature lady who, after fifty years at the beginning of the cold weather, moved from Florida to her home town in Ohio to be near aging family members. Graduating Summa Cum Laude from Youngstown State University (when it was still Youngstown University), June was an art teacher for several years and then a staff accountant for a CPA firm before retiring at the end of 2016.

She is the co-author of a suspense/kidnapping novel, *Let Freedom Ring*, published in June, 2016, by The Wild Rose Press. It received a five star rating by both Amazon.com readers and The Long and Short Review. You can find June on her Facebook page, facebook.com/june.summers.940, or her website, junesummersauthor.weebly.com.